"Carlie, why are you here? What do you expect me to do?"

Kane's deep voice stroked her nerve endings and Carleen realized he was sexier than she'd allowed herself to recall. She swallowed when he laid his hand over the top of hers. Heat spread from her fingertips, up her arm and into her heart.

"I need to prove this impostor isn't me. I need to rescue my son. He needs me. He needs his mother."

Kane's bronzed and handsome face winced and Carleen knew she'd hit him where it hurt. He leaned toward her, his eyes narrowing, and all the hurt she knew he had suffered as a child, and longer, shone from deep within. "A boy needs his father, too."

"Yes, he does." Carleen braced herself and placed her hand firmly on the one covering hers. "That's why Jamie needs *you*."

Dear Harlequin Intrigue Reader,

Harlequin Intrigue serves up its romance with a generous dash of suspense, so sit back and feast on this month's selections!

Joanna Wayne continues her RANDOLPH FAMILY TIES miniseries with an exciting flourish in *A Mother's Secrets* (#577). Gayle Wilson brings another of her sexy, mysterious heroes to life in *Renegade Heart* (#578), the second title in her MORE MEN OF MYSTERY series. Look for the final installment in November.

We're delighted to introduce debut author Ann Voss Peterson and her book, *Inadmissible Passion* (#579). After someone tried to kill her, Brittany Gerritsen turned to the one man she vowed to stay away from—the man who called off their engagement. And our SECRET IDENTITY program heats up with *Little Boy Lost* (#580) by Adrianne Lee. When a look-alike impostor stole Carleen Ellison's identity and her sweet little boy, she had no choice but to turn to Kane Kincaid—her baby's secret father.

As always, Harlequin Intrigue is committed to giving readers the best in romantic suspense and that is a promise you can count on!

Sincerely,

Denise O'Sullivan
Associate Senior Editor
Harlequin Intrigue

LITTLE BOY LOST

ADRIANNE LEE

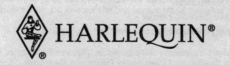

HARLEQUIN®

TORONTO • NEW YORK • LONDON
AMSTERDAM • PARIS • SYDNEY • HAMBURG
STOCKHOLM • ATHENS • TOKYO • MILAN • MADRID
PRAGUE • WARSAW • BUDAPEST • AUCKLAND

To Carl Adrian Pozzi. You were one of the good guys, Dad, and I am going to miss you… Always.

Ross Bennett of the READ list, Karen Solem, a great agent and, always, Anne Martin, Kelly McKillip and Gayle Webster.

ISBN 0-373-22580-6

LITTLE BOY LOST

ABOUT THE AUTHOR

When asked why she wanted to write romantic fiction, Adrianne Lee replied: "I wanted to be Doris Day when I grew up. You know, singing my way through one wonderful romance after another. And I did. I fell in love with and married my high school sweetheart and became the mother of three beautiful daughters. Family and love are very important to me and I hope you enjoy the way I weave them through my stories."

Books by Adrianne Lee

HARLEQUIN INTRIGUE

Don't miss any of our special offers. Write to us at the following address for information on our newest releases.

Harlequin Reader Service
U.S.: 3010 Walden Ave., P.O. Box 1325, Buffalo, NY 14269
Canadian: P.O. Box 609, Fort Erie, Ont. L2A 5X3

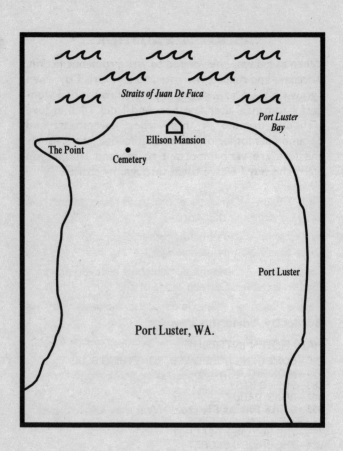

CAST OF CHARACTERS

Carleen Ellison—An impostor has stolen her identity—and her son.

Kane Kincaid—He'll face the demons of the past to save the boy he didn't know he had.

Jamie Ellison—Carleen's son knows who his real mother is.

Frances Ellison—Why does Skip's mother hate Kane so much? ·

Skip Ellison—Carleen's ex-husband has replaced her in every sense of the word.

Wil Ellison—Skip's healthy father died at a suspiciously opportune moment.

Lola Banks—Carleen's aunt blames everyone else for her troubles, Carleen most of all.

Starla Harding—Only Jamie stands between her and the fortune that should have been hers.

Vaughn Harding—Is Starla's husband concerned for her happiness, or his own?

Dr. Wade Newton—Does his practice extend to more than orthopedics?

Hugh and Phyllis Proctor—Will they know the real Carleen from the fake?

Dear Reader,

Hi, all. As far back as I can remember my mother was an avid reader of mystery and her tastes in books helped shape my own. So, I think it is only fitting that I now have her reading and enjoying the Harlequin Intrigue line. Thanks, Mom.

I love hearing from readers. Reach me at: P.O. Box 3835, Sequim, WA 98382. Please enclose an SASE for response.

Adrianne Lee

Chapter One

"Jamie?" Nameless terror reached inside her, a cruel, empty cold as though her heart were packed in ice, her belly frozen in the middle of a winter lake. Her head throbbed a jackhammer beat. She called louder, "Jamie?"

But she knew he wasn't there. An awful foreboding washed her veins, imbued her every pore, yanked open her gritty eyes and confirmed her worst fear. She was alone, somewhere far from her little boy.

On a sob, she dragged herself up onto her elbows and peered at her surroundings, not recognizing the shabby room. She muttered, groggily, "Where am I?"

Sunbeams knifed between the dilapidated window blinds, and dust motes skittered like fretful moths in the beams of morning light. The room held a single vinyl-covered kitchen chair, a metal TV tray for a nightstand, a nineteen-inch television set bolted to the wall, and the double bed supporting her body.

She sat up straighter, the sudden motion slicing pain across her scalp. Her mouth tasted as nasty as the bottom of a garbage pail smells. But she had to get up, had to do something about the chill, even though she knew a blanket or extra layers of clothing wouldn't touch the iciness gripping her insides. Relief would come only when she found Jamie.

Where was she? How had she come to be in this room? And how did she know the TV had no remote?

Her head swam, the room starting a slow spin, her stomach, a slow roll. She slammed her eyes shut, swallowed hard against the nausea and drew in two deep breaths. The sick feeling subsided. She opened her eyes again. But the confusion remained.

She edged out of bed, dragging bedspread and blanket with her, a makeshift cape. The linoleum felt frigid against her stocking feet. She stood, easing up with the effort of someone fifty years older and in poor health. One step at a time, she crept to the window, jabbed the blinds apart and peered out.

Her room connected with others, running *U*-shaped around a small parking lot. *A motel,* she realized, searching among the motley selection of automobiles angled before the other units for one that looked familiar. For her Lexus. The cruel cold deepened, and she called out again. "Jamie!"

The last time she'd seen him, she'd been buckling him into the back seat of the Lexus. But the Lexus wasn't in the parking lot. Nor was any other car she recognized. Where *was* she?

Somewhere near Port Luster? No— A noise in the bathroom brought her spinning around. The blinds clattered as she released them, then all was quiet. But she had heard something. Hadn't she? Maybe she was wrong. Maybe her son *was* here. "Jamie?"

She stumbled toward the bathroom, crying out his name, knowing she was fooling herself, yet helpless to abandon the sprig of hope flowering within her. "Jamie?"

She banged the door open on the tiny, empty cubicle. "Jamie!" His name wailed from her, the pain of it pulling her down by the knees while yanking her stomach into her mouth. Gulping bile, she slouched against the wall and rode out the wave of nausea. She didn't know how, but she knew *who* had her son, and she knew she had to get to the boy before it was too late.

For them both.

But how—when she had no idea where she was? She staggered to the bed, landing half on and half off the sagging mattress, losing several more minutes in gathering her strength. Maybe she should call the front desk and ask the clerk the name and location of the motel. She'd probably sound like an idiot. But better that than go insane with worry for Jamie.

But there was no phone. She hugged the blankets tighter to her chest, fighting desolation and a fresh spurt of illness. She wasn't sure she could make the hike across the parking lot to the motel office. She glanced at the TV. Maybe that would offer some insight. She shoved herself up from the bed again and stepped gingerly to the set.

Lifting a shaky hand, she poked the power button. The TV crackled and the screen filled with light, then glaring sound pierced her ears. She shuddered, lurched back, her socks slipping on the linoleum floor. Regaining her balance, she reached for the set again, fumbled, found the volume knob and nudged the noise level to slightly above a whisper.

The nausea swelled anew. She swallowed, bile burning her throat, and dropped back onto the bed. Why did she feel hungover? Her mouth was cottony, a foul taste lingering at the recesses of her tongue and in her nostrils, but nothing reminiscent of liquor. Then what—?

She sat straighter as an alternative idea popped into her less than lucid mind. Drugs? Had she been drugged? The possibility stunned her, but only for the span of time it took to consider her adversary. Why should the idea that he'd drugged her surprise her? The man had threatened her. Beaten her. Stolen her son. Using drugs to reach his ends was not beneath him.

And it would explain how he'd managed to wrench the boy from her—for she'd never have relinquished Jamie without a battle.

Anger seared through her brain, spreading lances of heat from the roots of her hair to the tips of her toes. The awful chill sped away, quickly replaced by a clammy warmth. Damn the man. He wouldn't get away with this. He wouldn't keep her from reclaiming her son.

The problem of her whereabouts rushed back at her. How far from her boy? How would she get to him? Dammit, she couldn't think. She glanced up at the television. A news program was on. At the bottom of the screen beneath the commentator, the date displayed was November sixteenth.

Her eyes widened and a shiver racked her. She'd put Jamie into the Lexus on the ninth. She remembered that distinctly because she'd had his hair cut the day before, on the eighth. How could she have lost a whole week? She hugged the blanket closer, clutching it to her chest with quavering hands. Her heart thumped beneath her knuckles like an off-balance washing machine.

She stared at her lap, trying to make sense of this, trying to recall anything of the past seven days. But all she remembered was clamping the seat belt across Jamie's tiny lap, then nothing. Blank.

She uncurled her fists and looked at both her hands. Her usually trimmed fingernails were broken, ragged. A testament to the hardships of the past seven days? She couldn't recall. One nail was broken to the quick. Had she struggled against her attacker? Why did she assume there had been only one attacker? Surely one person couldn't have subdued her *and* carried her off *and* dealt with Jamie.

Her mind filled with an image she wasn't sure she'd actually seen: Jamie screaming in terror, while she sank helplessly into a black abyss. Tears burned her eyes and a lump clogged her throat. Had Skip tried to comfort him, calm him down? No. She shook her head, knowing better. If he'd been there, Skip would have demanded Jamie be silent.

But Skip wouldn't have participated in anything as vile as drugging her, or kidnapping her son. He'd have hired someone to do it. Then, if she got away—as she had—and showed up to accuse him—as she intended doing—he'd call her delusional, and everyone would believe him because, of course, he'd have an unbreakable alibi. And he would sound rational. Credible.

Whereas an hysterical and frightened mother could well be denounced as a PMS victim, dismissed with a pat on the hand and meaningless bromides like "I hear you, dear." Or "Yes, dear, I understand your concerns." It was a world she'd come to know too well, a velvet prison built by a cunning master of control. Her flesh crawled with icy shivers at how sane Skip seemed. But she knew how truly mad he was.

Staring at her hands, she decided something else looked different. It took a minute before she realized her three-carat diamond-and-emerald ring was missing from her right hand. A gift from Wil to celebrate the birth of her son, it had been the only jewelry she'd retained from her marriage. She'd been on her way to sell it that morning. Had been wearing it, so as not to lose it. Where was it?

In fact, where were her clothes? She had on some sort of ragged jeans and an electric-blue and neon-orange plaid shirt. She'd left the house in an ecru cashmere sweater and slacks and high-heel pumps. Odd to recall such details so vividly while other details, events, remained fragmented. Or completely forgotten. The realization made her more certain that she'd been drugged. Repeatedly.

But that didn't explain the clothing. She only owned one pair of jeans. New Levis. She didn't recognize this brand. And she never wore anything orange; the color clashed with her auburn hair and her green eyes.

Both shirt and pants seemed to have been rescued from a rag bin, the denim torn in several places, the shirt sporting some crusty, dried stains. She cringed, not wanting to guess the origin of the stains. Flecks of something dark brown, like rust. Blood, maybe? And other, more gruesome spots. She shivered. Where had these clothes come from?

Maybe she could find out by checking the pockets or labels. She squirmed free of the blankets, struggled to her feet and dug her right hand into the front hip pocket of the jeans. Empty. She repeated the search with the left side. This time her fingertips struck something thin and plastic. The room key? She pulled it out. No. It was a credit card. VISA. She frowned. The name—Coral J. Clayton—was not her own.

She sank to the bed again, her gaze riveted on the card, her mind racing for some explanation. But there was none to be found. She knew no one named Coral Clayton. How had she come by this stranger's card? Had she stolen it in desperation?

She wasn't sure. But something about the VISA made her skin crawl. Her headache thump. She stuffed it back into her pocket, out of sight, banishing it like the secret it held.

Seeking an aspirin, and some cold water for her over-heated cheeks, she went to the bathroom. Above a stained sink hung a medicine cabinet with a cracked and tarnished mirror attached. She squinted at herself. As she'd guessed, she had a yellowed bruise on her left temple. Her eye was slightly puffy and her shoulder-length hair stuck to her scalp like the fur of a mangy dog in need of a long, soapy bath.

At the thought of a soak in a hot tub, she drew in a deep breath, realizing for the first time that it wasn't the motel room that stank. It was she. Sometime after getting into these clothes she'd been ill. On herself. *The source of the stains on her shirt.*

Even the rust-colored stains?

She winced, then plucked open the wall cabinet. It was empty. She smacked the mirror closed and splashed cold water on her face, longing for the strength to get into the shower and scrub herself until all the stink and drugs and pains were gone.

But the ache in her heart could be vanquished by only one thing: holding Jamie again.

At the moment, however, she hadn't the strength to help herself, much less her son. Frustration and desperation tangled inside her. She had to regain her stamina. To clear the remaining fog from her brain. Maybe more sleep would help.

No. Jamie needed her. She reached for the bath faucet. The room swam. She started to fall. Throwing her hands out to stop herself, she managed to catch the side of the tub. Bile layered her tongue and she swallowed hard, gripping the cold porcelain until the dizziness subsided.

Abandoning the idea of a bath, she slunk to the bed and eased down onto the mattress. The television droned on. She hadn't the energy to get up and turn it off, doubted it would even keep her awake. A tear slipped from the corner of one eye. "I'm sorry, Jamie. I'll be there as soon as I can."

She glanced dully at the TV screen. The newscaster, a striking Latino man with thick black hair and dark eyes, was definitely not any local anchorman she had ever seen, not from the Washington State Olympic Peninsula or anywhere in the Puget Sound area. He was talking, she noted, about the "Bay area." San Francisco? Could she be in California?

"Dear God, no." She blinked, striving to calm her rising pulse. The thought of being two states from Jamie, of trying to get to him from such a long distance away as California, started her stomach churning again.

What would she be doing in California?

Kane Kincaid!

The name screamed through her mind with such force, she knew she'd been looking for him. Knew he was her one hope. She recalled the last postcard she'd had from him. He'd written to tell her he was starting a business in California. In San Diego somewhere.

San Diego had a bay, didn't it? Was that where she was? If only the damn anchorman would clear up the question. But he didn't. She pressed her head back against the pillow and squeezed her eyes shut. If she *was* in San Diego, why wasn't she with Kane now? Had she spoken to him sometime during her missing week? Was he the one responsible for the bruise on her temple? The clothes she didn't recognize?

No. Her brains might be scrambled at the moment, but she felt certain Kane would never be brutal. Or mean. Not like Skip.

The anchorman said something that cut through her dark musings. A name. She wrenched up onto her elbows and gaped at the television. The images on the screen had turned from vivid Technicolor to an overall sickish green tint. Not her eyes, she realized, but some weakness in the TV. It suited her mood.

The anchorman was talking about Wilcox Ellison, her former father-in-law. Then a reporter on location filled the screen. He was standing, she realized with a jolt, in the parking area outside *EL,* the Ellison family's internationally famous sportswear company in Port Luster, Washington.

Camera crews milled before the main entrance of the four-story glass and red-brick structure that had been completed three years ago, right before Jamie was born. Competing news people jostled the reporter as they vied for a spot closer to the podium set up near the front door of *EL.* Every two seconds, the reporter gave an anticipatory glance over his shoulder. The word *Live* kept flashing in the bottom corner of the screen.

Frowning, she rose as though lifted by unseen hands and glided to the TV with the ability of someone not suffering the aftereffects of a debilitating drug. She turned the volume louder. Some force she couldn't name held her erect, adding braces to her wobbly knees as she listened to the reporter talking about her former father-in-law. He said, *"Wilcox J. Ellison was struck down by a heart attack around midnight last night, an unexpected and shocking death for a man in his supposed good health."*

"Heart attack?" she muttered, incredulity shifting through her tense body. "Wil Ellison? Impossible."

The reporter continued, "This news conference was called by Wilcox's son, Skip Ellison, and we expect it is to announce the change in leadership at *EL*. According to the terms of his father's will, Skip Ellison will be taking the reins as the new CEO and major shareholder of the company. Ah, here he is now."

The camera flashed onto Skip's face, and her pulse leaped, then leveled out. She watched her ex-husband's lips move without hearing a word he said, certain it was all platitudes about how sad he was at the loss of his father, while offering assurances to the world at large that losing its founder and chief would in no way impair service or product.

Her attention riveted on the man. Skip looked more handsome and dapper than usual—his white-blond hair stylishly wind-tousled, his wide mouth, like his mother's, proverbially lifted slightly at the corners, making it seem he was constantly amused, at some private joke, perhaps. He wore, she noted, the newest running suit for the *EL* line. The television chose that moment to correct the color on the screen, and she saw his outfit matched the piercingly cold blue of his eyes.

The camera scanned to Skip's right, and she froze. *Jamie*. Her heart raced into her throat. He was dressed like Skip in a running suit, but he resembled a miniature version of her, his hair slightly redder, his green eyes round and wide, the same cowlick at the right temple defying taming.

Even through the TV she could tell Jamie had been crying. "Oh, baby." She ached to hold him, to comfort him. He looked so desolate and lost. Viewers might assume his sadness was grief for his grandfather. She knew that might be part of it; Wilcox had adored the boy, lavishing him with attention and affection. But grief wasn't the only thing hurting her son.

She stepped closer to the set, reached up and touched the screen as though Jamie could feel her fingertips on his face, as though she could wipe away the tears from this distance. "Oh, my sweet baby."

As if he'd heard her, Jamie's right hand went to the tender skin beneath his chin. He tugged it with his finger and thumb, making their secret signal. *He was looking for her in the crowd.* The pain in her chest felt deadly. "I'm here, baby." She copied the signal, silently sending him comfort.

His other hand, she realized, was clasped in another's. An adult's. A woman's. A woman wearing an ecru cashmere sweater. His aunt Starla's or grandmother Frances's, maybe? But, no, that couldn't be. The wrist was too thin for either of them. Then who…?

The camera panned upward, then back for a wide-angle shot. Her heart stopped. The woman holding her son's hand was— Shudders rattled through her. "It's me."

But that couldn't be. The broadcast was *live.* Happening right this minute as she stood there watching.

"No!" she howled at the television. "You're not Carleen Ellison! I am!"

Carleen had barely uttered the protest when the monstrosity of Skip's betrayal hit her full force, buckling her knees, dropping her like a wounded doe. She lay there, desolate, her body limp, numb, her mind clear, for the first time in days, with the horror of it all. He'd replaced her—with an exact look-alike.

She hugged herself, the embrace of her own arms the only thing holding her together. He must think she was dead. That she wouldn't be returning to debunk this fraud. She shuddered hard as a colder reality sank in. Skip had her driver's license. By now he could also have stolen or changed her dental records, and her fingerprints were not on file anywhere.

"Even if I can get back to Port Luster, how will I prove I'm the real Carleen Ellison?" Fear tightened her throat. "How will I reclaim Jamie, if I can't prove who I am?"

She had to get Kane. Had to get to him now.

THE RESTLESSNESS was on him again, like a sickness in his blood—the need to pull up anchor and set out for a new port. Kane Kincaid laid his money on the counter of the marina office and bit down his impatience. What was his hurry? San Diego Bay had been good to him. Earlier this year, he'd actually upgraded his rust bucket, steel-hulled starter boat for the sixty-foot, fiberglass beauty now moored in slip 21 of this mom-and-pop operation.

Granted, the play was going out of this port, but so far that hadn't affected his business in any negative way. If anything, it was growing. Word of mouth. But money didn't drive him. What did was a nameless feeling that, like a shark, if he stopped moving he'd die.

He wished he could hurry Maude, the marina's manager, but she was an elderly woman and moved at the pace of a sea snail. To make matters worse, she had a portable, wall-mounted TV with the station turned so loud that he suspected she was deaf and too vain to get a hearing aid. Meanwhile, everyone who came into this office went out with their own hearing loss.

Kane glanced at the TV in annoyance. He'd had to shout to be heard above the news broadcast. An anchorman was talking about a woman whose body had been found in a seaside cabin room in Oregon. The woman was a suspected killer-for-hire who'd made the FBI's Most Wanted list for the past three years, and had a string of aliases to her credit.

He glanced back at Maude, who was scribbling on his bill with a pencil. She licked the tip of the dulled lead with her tongue. She'd told him once that if God had meant folks to figure on machines, He wouldn't have given them fingers and brains.

A self-declared Bolt Head—the nickname for devout fans of the San Diego Chargers—Maude wore a dark blue jersey with a gold lightning bolt emblazoned across her scrawny chest, and a matching cap with wisps of her wiry gray hair poking from beneath the brim. As if in explanation of the blaring TV, she'd said, "Don't want to miss 'Sports.' Gotta hear the latest on my Chargers."

Kane fidgeted, his impatience mounting. He had still to stow his groceries and fuel up. As he opened his mouth to hurry Maude along, the newscaster spoke a name that grabbed his attention. *Port Luster.* His home town. He frowned and glanced seriously at the TV for the first time since entering the office.

The anchorman was talking about Wilcox Ellison. Resentment tripped through him. Why couldn't the woman turn off the set? "What the hell's he doing in the news?"

"Huh?" Maude glanced over her bony shoulder at the TV. "Oh, him. He's dead."

Kane flinched hard, as though the old woman had whacked him with her cap. She didn't seem to notice, just kept rambling. "He was the one made those tennis shoes with the eels on the sides. Never owned a pair myself. A hundred bucks for one pair of shoes. Hah! They ain't no better than my Smart-Mart specials, just more spendy.'' She pointed her pencil toward her raised foot. ''Now, with these babies I've got me enough money left over for a week of bingo. Hundred bucks, humph, just for an eel on the side of your shoes.''

The logo on *EL* sportswear was the word *EL,* not an eel. But today, Kane found no humor in the old woman's mistake. ''How did he die?''

She glanced at the set again. ''Heart attack, they said earlier. Unexpected. During the night. Had some big whoop-de-do this morning about his son taking over the company.''

Kane reeled, stunned. He'd have bet nothing could fell someone with Wilcox Ellison's lust for life. Certainly not his heart. It was unbelievable. Wil had been the best advertisement *EL* had. He'd lived the image of his sportswear, jogged, lifted weights, watched his fat intake and bragged about having the cholesterol of a man half his age. Kane blew out a tight breath, lifted his hat and ran his hand across his sandy, sun-bleached hair. How could Wil have had a heart attack?

Not that Kane cared. As far as he was concerned Wil Ellison could rot in hell. Along with everyone else in Port Luster. Except…maybe…Carleen. *His Carlie.* But he wouldn't let himself dwell on her. He'd had his chance with her and he'd thrown it away. Just as well, since she'd shown how damn little he'd meant to her.

''I'm sorry you're leavin' us, Captain K, that I am. You've been a good tenant. But I understand a man without ties gets antsy. Too bad that nice Italian gal and you didn't work out.''

''Yeah, well…'' Kane's voice trailed off. What could he say? He hadn't been able to make the commitment Gina wanted. *Unable,* he'd said. *Unwilling,* she'd said. The disagreement had ended the relationship.

So, now there was nothing keeping him here—nothing and no one, here or anywhere else in this world. No family. No ties. No place he'd really call home, except his new boat. "Phone's disconnected. Shouldn't be any other mail you need worry about."

"That's good." She pressed her lips together and then sighed. "Our loss is Florida's gain, huh?"

"I suppose." Why not The Keys? Sure, there were hurricanes, but hell, California had earthquakes. Besides, he liked the distance it would put between him and the West Coast. At the moment that distance seemed somehow vital.

The old woman sniffed. "Can't believe you're nuts enough to brave the open seas this time of year, though."

He smiled at her. She meant well enough. Besides, he'd been called worse than nuts. "I know the dangers. I'll keep a close eye on the weather."

She clucked her tongue. "I swear you handsome sea rats all got saltwater in yer veins 'stead of blood."

What that had to do with anything, Kane couldn't guess. She handed him his bill, and he paid in cash, then he caught her gnarled hand in his big tanned one and kissed it. "Take care of Pop while I'm gone, Maude."

She blushed. "Mind you say goodbye to him."

"I'll do that at the fuel dock." He strode outside, glad to be away from the blaring TV.

Overhead, gulls cried and swooped. With regret, he took a last long glance at the beauty of San Diego Bay, at all the boat masts poking toward the skies, at the great naval warships anchored near Coronado Island across the harbor. He drew a deep breath. The air stank of diesel and seawater, an overall fishy, briny scent that was pure ambrosia to Kane.

The dock creaked beneath his feet as he hurried to the

Footloose and climbed aboard. This boat was his dream come true, the one thing in his life that had worked out as expected.

For fishing and cruising, it had two Detroit diesel propulsion engines with speeds up to eleven knots, an auxiliary engine with generator, full complement of electronic navigational equipment, full stern dive platform and a circulating live game tank. For human comfort, there was 110-volt household electrical current throughout, a head with shower, a clothes dryer, a spacious galley, dining and living areas, and air-conditioning.

What more could a man want?

Carlie's face flashed into his mind, a haunting image, the passion in her fiery green eyes able to taunt him still these four years later. Why her? Why now? He forced the vision away.

He ducked into the cabin. Grocery sacks littered the galley floor and countertops. He began stowing his supplies in the cabinets and refrigerator. He had enough food for a month. He planned on taking his time getting to Florida. He wanted to enjoy the coast, see some of the ports along the way—and, God willing, he would not encounter any hurricanes.

Now that he was near leaving, his nerves twitched, the restless, anxious feeling hounding him anew. He moved more quickly, recklessly transferring cans from sack to cupboard shelf. The need to hurry badgered him. He couldn't get out of San Diego Bay fast enough. For the past week, he'd sensed something bad coming for him, something that would stop him in his tracks if he waited around for it.

With luck, he'd be long gone before it found him.

Chapter Two

Carleen stood in the tub. Icy shower spray beat on her face and body until she shivered violently, but she resisted the instinct to shut off the freezing downpour. Her head was clearing, the wooziness subsiding. The frigid water didn't bother her; it was the awful voice she'd started hearing in her mind that did, her son's sobbing voice crying, "Mommy, Mommy, Mommy."

Imagination? Or memory? Had she actually heard Jamie? The cries rang so clear and hard inside her throbbing head. She strove to recollect anything, or any time when she might have heard him wailing like that. A hazy image floated above the fog shrouding her recall, the image of herself reaching out to Jamie, of their fingertips colliding—just before a black curtain rendered her unconscious. Her chest ached with fury and frustration and worry.

But mostly, she was terrified. Jamie's stricken face, his tear-filled green eyes, haunted her. How would she reclaim her son? Her life? Who was the woman who'd been holding Jamie's hand during the newscast? How had Skip managed to replace her with this imposter? How long had he been planning to replace her? From the day she'd asked for a divorce? Or longer ago than that?

She shut off the faucet and stood stock-still, water beads and goose bumps dotted her skin. Who was the woman? Carleen had no siblings, no long-lost twin sister. A clone? Like that sheep Dolly, who'd been born a full-grown ewe? No. That was ludicrous, crazy thinking…drugged thinking.

More likely the woman was an actress.

But was that really logical? What actor would take on such a role? And for how long a run? A lifetime? Or until a decree could be obtained giving Skip full custody of her son?

"Jamie." Revulsion churned her tender stomach, and weariness blasted through her. She knew if she let it, the worry and fear would reduce her to a helpless, quivering mass, and her son would be lost to her forever. She couldn't allow that to happen.

With an effort, she forced Jamie's pitiful sobs from her mind. She reached for the towel. The fabric, an over-bleached frail piece of cloth that absorbed little, felt like sandpaper on her chilled body, but with every scrape of it against her skin her determination to find Kane Kincaid grew. Maybe he was listed in the phone book.

She thought again of the trek she'd need to make across the parking lot. The small task seemed over-whelming. It was too far removed from standing naked in an ugly motel bathroom. She decided to concentrate on first things first. Like getting dressed. Tiny steps would see her through.

Steeling herself against the awful realization that the dirty clothes she'd discarded before bathing were all she had, she turned the panties inside out and drew them on, followed by the filthy ragged jeans, then the god-awful shirt. She'd scrubbed off the worst of the stains, but just knowing what they were again roused her gorge.

These stranger's clothes punctuated her lost identity.

She tried not to dwell on that. Once dressed, she studied her reflection in the mirror. She couldn't say she saw much improvement. But without makeup to cover the bruise, or a comb to untangle her curly red tresses, this would have to do.

She tugged on the socks, and after an energy-sapping search of the room found a pair of tennis shoes beneath the bed. They were a cheap knockoff brand. And a half-size too large. At last, tangible proof that this wasn't a bad dream, that she hadn't bought these clothes. Then who had? Coral Clayton? Or someone else?

Carleen's head swam as she bent over to lace the shoes. She rested on the bed for a few minutes. Then, fearing she'd lose her momentum, she struggled up, made certain the VISA card was secure in her pocket and stepped outside.

She heard the steady rumble of traffic nearby, spotted a plane in the vivid, cloudless blue sky. The sun caused her to squint. The air was warmer here than in her room, warmer than Port Luster this time of year, but rife with the same scent of seawater. The possibility that she was actually near the Pacific Ocean, perhaps in California, maybe even San Diego, offered Carleen her first ragged ray of hope.

The motel parking lot was even emptier than when she'd peeked out the window. Only two cars remained, one near her own door. But she'd found no car key in the room and hadn't a clue if she'd driven here in this car. Feeling her energy waning again, she searched for a phone. She spotted one directly across from her, in front of the motel office, wedged between two lofty palm trees. There were no palm trees in Port Luster—or Washington State, for that matter.

"Definitely California," she whispered.

Dizziness attacked her as she moved cautiously toward the phone. Steadying herself against the booth, she lifted the phone book. A San Diego phone book. Her reedy hope pumped stronger. She pulled the weighty reference onto the tiny shelf of the phone booth. It fell open to the *Yellow Pages.* Carleen flipped through until she found Charter Boats. Someone had torn out the page. "No."

Her confidence faltered. What was the name of Kane's company? She frowned, trying to dredge the answer from her clogged memory, but drew a blank.

Panic filled her chest. She had to remember. Think back. It was catchy. It had reminded her of something. But what? *What?* The answer wouldn't come. The marina. What was the name of the marina where he moored his boat? What was the name of his boat?

Her mind was a wind tunnel with everything blown away. Like her life. She could recall nothing from his postcard. If only she'd written back to him. Kept in contact. But she knew why she hadn't. Guilt sifted through her—guilt and another older worry. Her hope withered.

But she wouldn't give up. She began thumbing the *White Pages,* found the *K* section, all the while praying Kane was listed. Her shaky index finger touched the name Adam Kincaid and moved downward.

There it was.

She stared at his name, the lettering seeming to leap at her, but the number wavered before her eyes and she could hear the roar of her pulse. She swallowed and drew in a wobbly breath. "Calm down, Carleen. Calm down."

Change. For the phone. A quarter and a dime. She reached automatically for her clutch, remembering belatedly that she had no purse. Had no money. Nothing but the stranger's credit card. She tore the page from the phone book and started in to the motel office. Maybe they'd let her use their phone—if the call was local.

"Señora!" The shout came from behind Carleen.

She pivoted toward the voice, uncertain who the caller wanted. A middle-aged Latino woman with a laundry-laden maid's cart stood before the room Carleen had just left. She was staring at Carleen. They were alone in the parking lot.

"What?" Carleen asked.

"Excuse. You mean to leave key in door?"

Key? Had she left it there all night? She frowned, trying to recall. The ramifications of the crimes that could have been perpetrated against her if the wrong person or persons had discovered the key slowly penetrated her numbed mind. But the fear she would have felt under normal circumstances eluded her. Nothing felt normal anymore. "I..."

The maid stared with tired eyes. "You checkin' out now, or no?"

"Yes."

The maid turned away and smacked open the door, Carleen already forgotten, just another passer-through in the life of a service worker. Already forgotten. Would Jamie soon feel that way, too?

Her breath hitched, and she forced her energies back to the task at hand. Calling Kane. Clutching the torn page, she entered the motel office.

It smelled of stale cigar smoke, discarded fast-food wrappers and body odor. A husky man with greasy black hair and a swarthy complexion sat behind the counter playing solitaire on a Mac computer. He didn't glance up as Carleen entered, despite the jangle of the bell over the door. She approached the counter.

The man muttered something in Spanish that sounded

like an expletive. Without taking his eyes off the monitor, he said, "Rooms are thirty a night, no hourly, no pets, no remote for the TV. We accept all the major cards."

No remote for the TV. So that was how she'd known; she'd been told when she checked in. She had a hazy recollection of a night clerk, a leathery-faced woman with black hair and a widow's peak. Carleen shook herself. "I don't want a room. I'm checking out."

He glanced at her then, frowning as he spied her bruise, but his gaze was disinterested, as though a battered woman was nothing unusual in his daily routine.

"Which room?" he asked. She told him. He searched his paperwork, then nodded. "Just leave your key in the room, *Señorita* Clayton. You've already signed the charge."

She had? Using Coral Clayton's name? She shouldn't be surprised, but she was. What else had she done in her "lost" week that might surprise her? She thought again about the odd sensation she'd felt just holding the card. She shivered. "I wonder if I might use your phone? I mean, if this isn't a local call, then I can charge it to my VISA."

She held up the page she'd torn from the phone book. The man frowned with disapproval. "What's the area code?"

She read it to him. He nodded. "That's local. Help yourself." He plunked the phone onto the counter, then dropped back into his chair and started another round of solitaire.

Carleen lifted the receiver and punched in Kane's number. After a moment, the phone began to ring. Her heart leaped. What would she say to him? But instead of Kane's voice, a recorded female voice said, "The number you dialed is no longer in service. If you think you've gotten this message by mistake, hang up and place your call again.''

She did as directed, praying she'd misdialed. That the connection had gone askew. But when the message came on again, her stomach dipped. Dear God, had Kane moved? Left the area? No. Don't panic. There had to be something else she could try.

The marina. She dropped the phone on its cradle and asked the clerk, ''Do you have another telephone book?''

''Nope.'' He didn't look at her, but there was no mistaking the annoyance in the sudden set of his shoulders. ''Just the one outside.''

She'd bet he was lying. ''Sir, I have a friend who runs a charter boat service out of one of the local marinas. But I can't recall which one. And the page listing Charters in the phone book is missing.''

He glanced at the torn page she held, flashing white teeth in a nasty grin. ''*Sí*, people rip out those pages all the time. It's a regular crime wave.''

She ignored his sarcasm. ''Could you tell me some of the names of the marinas around here? Maybe something will sound familiar.''

He heaved himself up and leaned his elbows on the counter. She'd bet he hadn't bathed in a week. ''Close or far?''

''What?''

''The marina—near here, or not?''

''I don't know.''

''*Gringas.*'' He swore under his breath. ''There's Sports Fishing, Admiral Marina, Sea Tide—''

''That's it!'' she cried, cutting him off as she recognized the name of the marina from Kane's postcard. ''Sea Tide.'' She remembered it because it reminded her of seaside, and because it stabbed at her headache for some inexplicable reason.

"How far is it from here?" she asked, rubbing at the base of her neck.

"Three blocks." He lifted his arm, sending off a waft of stench, and pointed out the dirty window above his computer monitor. "We're on Rosecrans. It's off Scott Street, on North Harbor Drive. You can walk, or drive."

She frowned. "Drive?"

"Your car." His pointing finger shifted toward the blue Ford angled crookedly in front of the room she'd vacated.

Her car? If she'd rented it, where were the keys? In it? She thanked the clerk and left, eager to shed his company. Eager to find Kane.

The keys *were* in the ignition. She doubted this was a low-crime area, and thought again that she'd been lucky to have awakened this morning at all. She needed to curb her recklessness, for Jamie's sake.

She climbed into the car. On the passenger seat, she found a rental agreement in the name of Coral Clayton. She hadn't even a vague memory of renting the car, just some images of driving like a drunk, weaving in and out of traffic, searching for an address on the waterfront.

She was lucky she hadn't crashed. Lucky she hadn't killed anyone. The thought sent a new unnamed fear through Carleen. Why? What awful thing couldn't she remember?

She swallowed hard. Her energy was waning. She had to hang on. For Jamie. *Jamie, Jamie, Jamie.* The mantra helped. She started the car. The gas tank tripped a notch above the *E* and stopped. The clerk had said Sea Tide Marina was three blocks or so down the road. She ought to have enough gas for that.

Five minutes later, she'd found the marina at Point Loma, nestled between Sports Fishing and Admiral Marina on North Harbor Drive. Sea Tide Marina seemed to consist of little more than three or four docks. Carleen started up a ramp toward a small cubicle marked Moorage Office that looked like an oversize cabin of a tugboat.

The sun bounced off the water alongside the worn wood docking beneath her feet and burned her tender eyes. She scanned the marina, jam-packed with sailboats and pleasure boats and fishing boats of every make and shape and size, their masts poking the blue sky. Huge warships were anchored in the bay beyond. And beyond that, the Pacific Ocean, as far as the eye could see.

Movement closer in caught her attention. At the end of one of the three connected docks, a large boat was easing from its slip. Squinting, her hand cupped above her eyes, Carleen couldn't see the name, just a large royal-blue *F* on the stern.

The day was growing warmer by the minute. Gulls cawed overhead, their shrieks like pinpricks against her nerves. She hastened into the tiny office, wondering how much longer she'd be able to keep going without collapsing. She'd never felt so weak. So out of control. She clutched the counter for support.

Her knees were wobbly; the effort to come this short distance had zapped too much energy. She was running now on pure will. An elderly woman dressed in a football jersey and baseball cap was flipping through channels on a TV with her remote control. Her back was to Carleen.

Carleen said, "Kane Kincaid. Is he here?"

The woman didn't move.

Carleen asked louder, "Is Kane Kincaid here?"

This time the woman jerked as though she'd been

prodded between the shoulder blades. She dropped the remote onto a desk and spun around.

"Oh, my," she said, taking in Carleen. "That's a nasty-looking eye you've got there, girl."

"Is Kane Kincaid here?" Carleen asked again, ignoring the woman's question.

The woman's bloodshot eyes narrowed. "What you want with Captain K?"

"Captain K?"

The woman nodded, causing her cap to bob on her head. "Kane Kincaid."

This woman knows Kane. Carleen felt her hope returning. "I'm an old friend."

The woman didn't look convinced.

Carleen was losing patience. "Is Ka—er, 'Captain K' here?"

"Nope." The woman clicked her tongue. "Not anymore. He's heading off to Florida. To The Keys. Left a few minutes ago. Ya just missed him."

"Missed him?" Carleen's heart plummeted. She started to drop, too, catching herself at the last minute. Tears sprang to her eyes, and she swallowed against the knot in her throat. "Minutes ago?"

"Yep." The woman stepped from behind the counter. "He was moored in slip 21 these last couple years. Had himself a growing concern with that charter business of his, but he's restless. Footloose, just like his boat."

Carleen followed the woman to one of the four windows looking out over the harbor. She perused the docks, her gaze going to the spot pointed out by the woman, the end slot where she'd seen the big boat easing away moments ago. Her throat tightened.

The woman said, "Had the *Footloose* parked right there. Brand-new. Pretty boat."

Footloose. Named for the Kevin Bacon movie, or after the way Kane felt about himself? Although he was a huge Kevin Bacon fan, she suspected the latter, and figured he would not appreciate her showing up on his dock to jerk him into the real world. He'd been lucky, he'd escaped her reach. "Oh, Jamie."

"Pardon?" The woman frowned at Carleen.

"Nothing." *Only everything.* Carleen leaned her face against the glass, her gaze wandering the boats as though the *Footloose* might materialize by her wishing it. *Footloose? F!* Had that been the boat she'd seen pulling out? Wasn't that the boat over there? "Isn't that the *Footloose* at that end dock?"

The old woman glanced to where Carleen gestured. "Why, yes, it is. Oh, that's right. I forgot Captain K told me he'd say goodbye to Pop when he gassed up."

"Isn't there some way to stop him? Make him wait until I can get there?"

"Well, sure. I can call the gas dock." The woman shuffled back to the counter. *Hurry!* Carleen screamed silently, her gaze shifting frantically between the woman and the boat. *Wait, Kane! Wait. I need you. Jamie needs you.*

The woman dialed, then cursed softly. "Darn Pop, he's got the phone off the hook again. He talks to someone, then don't hang it up proper."

Carleen's heart felt ready to explode. "Can I walk to that dock?"

"Sure. Just go to the end of this one, turn right, then all the way to the end of that one, and you'll see the bridge." The woman picked up a set of binoculars and glanced to where Kane's boat sat. "I don't think you'll make it in time, though. They're all done gassing up the *Footloose.*"

But Carleen didn't hear. She was out the door, running.

Chapter Three

"Kane!"

Kane's hand froze on the ignition key. The foreboding he'd sensed coming at him all week, all month, rushed over him like a chilling breeze blown in on a single word.

"Kane!"

He wheeled around, squinting against the glaring sun. A woman was running down the dock, her dark red hair flying around her head and glinting like a fiery halo. The blinding light at her back gave her an ethereal appearance.

His breath caught. If he didn't know better, he'd swear it was Carlie. The Carlie who'd made him feel loved, then shown what a liar she was by marrying his cousin eight weeks later.

"Kane!" she called again, the cry weaker, her steps shorter, less frantic.

And yet, a sudden, inexplicable urgency propelled him from the fly bridge, down the ladder and over the side of the boat. He landed ten feet from her with a soft *thud*.

She jerked to a stop, her breath heaving from her. He cupped his hand over his eyes and blinked as his focus adjusted. She was panting, trying to smile, a baffling combination of relief and fear flashing through her green eyes. The same green eyes that too often stalked his lonely nights. Carlie's eyes.

Confusion knifed him. It *was* Carlie, but not as he'd ever seen her. My God, what had happened to her? "Carleen...?"

Carleen's heart caught at the uncertainty in Kane's voice. He wasn't sure it was *her*. He doubted he was seeing *her*. Oh, God, no. If he didn't believe she was the real Carleen Ellison, no one would. Realizing she sounded pathetic, but unable to conjure anything more intelligent, she said, "Kane, it's me. Carlie."

He was the only one who called her Carlie. She had loved that name once, but would never use it again. It was a name that evoked a time of passion, a time she would never forget, a time she would forever regret. Now, however, it was all-important to get through to him any way she could. "It's me, Carlie."

"What are you doing here?" He took a step toward her. His hand, so tanned and large, so roughened from his life labors, so tender with a woman, reached hesitantly for her face.

She flinched as though he'd meant to slap her.

He scowled. "My God, Carlie, what happened to you?"

Carlie. He'd called her Carlie. She closed her eyes, moaning on an exhaled breath. *He recognized her. Didn't doubt her.* Relief broke over her like a wave hitting a surfer, snatching the remainder of her energy. She stumbled toward him, and the forward momentum carried her face-first toward the dock. She hadn't the strength to throw her hands out, to catch herself or impede her fall.

She barely heard his startled cry, only felt those strong hands clasp her upper arms, rescuing her inches from impact with the wet creosote planking. He lifted her, folded her against his chest as though she were feather-light, and a sense of security she hadn't known in years embraced her.

But consciousness was slipping away. For the first time in a week, she met the darkness without fear.

AWARENESS RETURNED SLOWLY. Carleen felt a gentle swaying as though she were nestled in a cradle. She heard a soft lapping from somewhere beneath her, a peaceful sound, a peaceful feeling completely unlike the last time she'd awakened on this endless day. But she knew the feeling of peace was a lie. She inhaled, pulling in a vaguely familiar, clean, masculine scent that stirred long-denied memories of happy times, passionate times.

But passion was for dreamers. For the losers in this world. She'd learned and relearned that the hard way when Kane walked out on her four years ago. From then on, she'd banned passion from her life. Her heart would never rule her head again. But it was amazing how memories of loving moments with Kane could still blindside her on occasion, teasing her, luring her, much as sirens of old had lured unwary seamen to dangerous shores. The difference was, Carleen recognized the call of passion for what it was. Knew the dangers of being swept in by Kane Kincaid. She couldn't, wouldn't be tempted.

She opened her eyes, identifying the swaying and the soft tapping. She was on a boat. Kane's boat. In Kane's bed. The thought swirled heat about the cold spot in the center of her heart. No. It mustn't thaw. It had to stay cold. Iced over.

She shoved up on her elbows. She was in a king-size bunk, in a cabin whose decor was in shades of blue as warm as Kane Kincaid's eyes, with accents of white and yellow as bright as the sun-bleached streaks in his thick, dark blond hair.

When had she noticed his hair in the brief time before she'd collapsed? Disgusted with herself, she pushed her unmanageable mane from her cheek and sat up. The dizziness was subsiding, and her stomach was demanding food, even though she didn't feel hungry. What time was it? How long had she been out? Had Kane hauled her aboard and taken off for Florida, carrying her with him as a captive?

No. Other than the easy rocking, the boat, she realized, wasn't moving. She climbed out of bed and stood. Her legs no longer seemed two pieces of wobbly licorice sticks. She crossed the small cabin and peered out a porthole. She was looking dockside at slip 21. She'd thwarted Kane's departure. Good. But precious time had been lost.

She used the head, then washed her hands and glanced at herself in the small mirror. As it had earlier today, the image startled her. The paleness of her cheeks made her eyes look enormous; the ugly, obscene bruising around her left eye was yellow and purple with a tinge of green. The spray of freckles on her nose seemed more vivid than normal. She wished for some way to improve her appearance before facing Kane again.

Like makeup.

But there was none in the bathroom cabinet, and it occurred to her that she'd been expecting some. Expecting Kane to have some special woman in his life. Did he? If so, the woman wasn't going to Florida with him aboard the boat. Not that Carleen cared. Except, of course, how the presence of yet another woman in his life would affect Jamie. And it *would* affect him. She filled a paper cup with water and tossed down a couple of aspirins.

It was time she and Kane talked. With her stomach knotting, all notion of eating gone, she started out into a hallway, passed three other bedrooms, then climbed a short stairwell into a galley with a living room area beyond. The cool tones of bleached oak on the floor and cabinets were balanced by the warm teal, cream and flecks of yellow on the cushions and wall hangings and blinds. The area lacked feminine touches, yet exuded a homey feel.

Something like Kane himself.

She thought of Skip's yacht, of its pristine furnishings that all looked as though he'd wrapped them in plastic covering, as sterile as a lab, as cold as his heart—the black-and-blue decor as mean as his abusive soul.

Kane sat propped in a teal-and-white striped chair, his feet on an ottoman, his back to her.

Her heart leaped at the sight of him. Despite the years apart, despite the way he'd left her, she'd never been more glad to see him. Or more frightened. She gripped the galley counter, her gaze locked on the back of his head, the set of his shoulders. There was a sweet thrumming through her veins, a reaction to years of affection toward this man.

She'd fallen in love with him in junior high school. She'd never told him that. Never had the chance. He hadn't even noticed her until they were in college at the University of Washington, her junior year.

Funny thing was, that was when Skip had noticed her, too, as though whatever interested Kane, interested him. She hadn't given Skip a thought. She'd been too swept away by Kane. Too blinded by her passion for him.

Passion. The very word sent shards of resentment through her. It had been the bane of her family. Her father's passion for gambling had infused her childhood

and teenage years with poverty and humiliation and secrets that had continued on into her early twenties. Her
mother's passion for her father, a bone-deep loser, had
led her to cruelly turn her back on her widowed sister
and her niece and nephew. And Carleen, well, her passion
for Kane had led to the horror that now afflicted her and
her son.

Despite her aversion for passion, she discovered to her
dismay that embers of it still stirred inside her at the idea
of sharing this small space with Kane. But she wouldn't
let that deter her from her purposes in coming to him.
Jamie. Unshed tears tightened her throat. Her son had
spent another day in the hands of a strange woman, an
imposter calling herself "Mommy."

His frightened, confused expression flashed into her
mind, and freed the panic she'd held at bay. No. She had
to stay cool, logical. Totally rational. Jamie's well-being
depended on that. On her. She pushed down the anxious
sensation, but couldn't stop the nervous tremors in her
limbs. She shifted her hand on the counter and bumped
a spoon, sending it airborne. It clattered to the floor. *So
much for cool and composed.*

Kane lurched up and around. "Carlie?"

"Sorry. I didn't mean to startle you." *Sorry, I didn't
mean to land on your boat and upend your entire life.*
But that was exactly what she was about to do—upend
his life in ways he might not forgive her for. But she
needed him. Jamie needed him. Needed them both.
"Sorry."

"Quit apologizing and tell me what happened to your
face." He seemed a giant in this spacious cabin, his head
nearly touching the ceiling. But she supposed it was her
fear making him seem so massive. He stepped toward
her, and, unbidden, her gaze swept over his body. He

wore faded jeans that hugged his lean hips, his muscled thighs; a T-shirt that cleaved his broad chest, his large arms, his flat stomach.

Her mouth watered, and her ability to think straight seemed to desert her. *The way Kane had deserted her?* She shook herself at the comparison. She mustn't forget that he'd run out on her once. He might do it again. Especially when he learned the truth. The whole truth.

He asked, "Were you in a car wreck or something?"

Of course, she realized, he'd likely spent the past hour or more considering dozens of different scenarios, seeking some sort of answer about her condition. A car wreck was as good a guess as any. Reflexively, she touched the tender area around her eye and winced, wishing she'd stopped herself before making contact. "I don't know how I got the bruise."

He frowned. "You don't know?"

"I can't remember."

Concern slipped into the grooved smile lines around his eyes and mouth. He motioned her to sit on the sofa and joined her there, facing her. He wasn't wearing shoes. There was something intimate about his stocking feet, some memory she refused to meet. He stretched his arm along the sofa, the action shortening the distance between them. "Why don't you remember?"

She twisted her hands in her lap. How did she tell him all she had to? She supposed she should start with this past week—or as much as she remembered of it.

"I was abducted from my home on the ninth. A week ago, now."

"Abducted?" He swore. His gaze swept her from top to toe, and he scowled. "Have you called the police?"

"No. I came straight to you."

"What? Then I'll call them now." He jumped up and

headed for the phone. "Then Skip. He must be worried sick about you."

"No!" Carleen scrambled off the sofa. "No! You can't call Skip."

Kane slammed down the phone and swore again. "I've had it disconnected. I'll have to use the phone in the marina office."

She caught his arm as he passed. "No, Kane! Listen to me."

The terror in her voice seemed finally to reach him. He stared down at her, his warm blue eyes going dark, looking deep, his expression alluring. Warning buzzers sounded inside her head. His voice was almost a whisper. "Why not?"

"Skip is the one who had me abducted."

"Skip?" Kane's eyebrows shot up. "That's ludicrous. Why would Skip have his own wife abducted?"

She could barely swallow over the knot in her throat. "Jamie."

He straightened. "Your little boy."

Carleen's stomach clenched. He knew about Jamie? How? To her knowledge, he hadn't kept in touch with any one of the Ellisons. Or anyone else in Port Luster. "Yes. *My* son."

Kane flinched and stepped back as though she'd repelled him in some way. "You're claiming your husband had you abducted in order to, what—?" He flapped his hands wildly. "Kidnap his own child?"

"Apparently, you haven't heard that Skip and I were divorced three months ago."

He went still, then blew out a breath as though she'd punched him in the gut. "Why?"

Why? The question threw her. It sounded as though the idea of Skip and her divorcing had never occurred to him. Why? she wanted to ask him in return. Where had he gathered his knowledge of her marriage? From television? Newspapers? Had he assumed she and Skip were a perfect match because they smiled for photographers?

If so, the truth would shock him. Though she could give him a blow-by-blow account of reasons, she knew the overall one would do. "It was an abusive marriage. I'd taken enough."

He looked stunned and furious all at once. His hands curled into fists at his sides, and his voice was volumes higher. "Did Skip do that to your eye? Or your kidnappers?"

"I told you I don't remember, but you can bet Skip was behind it."

Kane heaved a noisy breath and sank onto the sofa with the weight of a man who had more to process than his brain could handle. She supposed he did.

She drew a bracing breath, and as much to wipe out the static silence as anything else, she went on. "The divorce was kept quiet. Skip let me go without fuss. I figured he didn't want me testifying about the abuse in court. That he wanted it kept out of the papers. If anything, I was grateful. But I should have known he was up to something. He doesn't let go of anything that belongs to him."

Kane pressed his lips together, the way she'd seen him do hundreds of times over the years. It was what he always did when he pondered something. "I know my cousin, and you're right. I can't imagine him giving you up." His eyes had a hard edge. "Or being abusive, or having you abducted."

Her bottom lip trembled. She caught it between her upper teeth. She had to convince him. "Did you see the newscast today?"

"You mean do I know my 'uncle' Wil is dead? Yes."

She saw the mix of emotions on his face and winced inwardly at her thoughtlessness. At the need for it. "Then you didn't see the broadcast?"

"What broadcast do you mean?"

"Skip called a news conference and announced to the world that *EL* would continue on as it has, despite his father's death."

Kane wiped his jaw with his palm. "Now, *that* sounds like Skip."

She stared at the chipped polish on her fingernails. "He had his family with him. Including Jamie." She paused for effect, then added, *"And me."*

"You?"

"That's right. But I wasn't in Port Luster this morning. I was here, in San Diego, in a motel room three blocks from Sea Tide Marina."

"But how…?" His gaze swept her face again, and then he shook his head. "That doesn't make any sense. None of this makes sense. I think that bump on your head scrambled your brains."

"No. I swear it's true." She felt all hope of gaining Kane's help slipping away, felt the old sense of not being able to count on him well up inside. Desperation swelled beneath it. "Skip thinks I'm dead and he's hired some imposter to take my place. Probably until he can convince the court that I'm giving him full custody of Jamie. Then I suspect the woman will embark on an around-the-world cruise and never come back."

"Carlie, this is crazy. You come waltzing back into my life after four years and tell me this insane story—"

"I didn't walk out on *you,* Kane Kincaid. I would never have left you a note and disappeared."

He blanched. "Okay, I deserved that. But given our

history, why me? Why am I the one you've come to with this?''

She hugged herself against a sudden chill. Why *had* she come to Kane? Given her drugged and confused state, why had his name occurred to her? Because he was the only one she could trust? No. That wasn't true. There was Hugh Proctor, the lawyer who'd acted as her guardian after her parents' deaths. Then why Kane? Because he deserved a chance to help with Jamie. And... ''Because...I thought you'd believe me.''

He blew out a hard breath and ran his hands over the sides of his head, mussing his hair. ''Honest to God, Carlie, I don't know what to believe.''

She drew a wobbly breath. Tears stung her eyes. She bit back the urge to rail at him like the frantic mother she was, recognizing that this kind of passion was purely negative. The more she raved, the more she would impair her credibility. She had to stay calm. Rein in the hysteria. But she couldn't hold back the feeling of defeat. It verged on drowning her.

''I guess I can't blame you. But if you don't believe me, no one will.'' The desperation in her voice pinged against her own ears. She hated it, hated the look of confusion darkening his eyes. A taut band circled her chest, cut off her breath. If she didn't get control she'd hyperventilate. She had to calm down. Convince him that this had all happened to her.

''I came to you, hoping you'd help me.''

''Help you?'' He was struggling to keep his voice even. But she could see his growing anger. ''Help you do what? Get even with Skip by taking his son away from him? I don't get in the middle of custody fights.''

Carleen flinched. Words lodged in her throat. The words that would get him to help. She lurched off the sofa and strode toward the sliding glass door that led onto the deck. The sun still pounded the earth, and a breeze whipped the flag hanging from the mast, the steady snap of steel and flap of cloth like an urgent call from Jamie. *Hurry, Mommy, hurry.*

But Carleen knew instinctively that rushing wasn't an option at the moment. She wasn't sure Kane could take another shock. Or whether she could stand the rejection of another of her truths. Even in her panic, she knew today had handed him about all the devils a person could deal with in any given twenty-four-hour period. Wil's sudden, unexpected death. Her showing up looking like the victim of a car wreck. Her accusations about his cousin Skip. She needed to let him process those things before laying the rest on him.

She spun away from the window. "I haven't eaten in…" She couldn't say how long. "Would you have any saltines? Or toast? And tea?"

"Of course." He seemed glad for the distraction. He went into the galley, started the water for the tea and made her some toast.

Neither spoke as he prepared the food. Then, while she ate, he sat across from her in the banquette. She concentrated on the toast, chewing slowly; on the tea, sipping. She didn't look at him, but felt his gaze on her. Felt the scrutiny. What would his decision be?

She was draining the last of the tea when he laid his hand over hers. Heat spread from her fingertips, up her arm and into her heart. Dare she hope?

Her throat thickened. She set aside the teacup and lifted her gaze to his. The years of fishing in bright sunlight had bronzed his skin, roughened it in a pleasing, healthy way. He was more sexy than she'd allowed herself to recall. To her distress, she wasn't as immune to him as she insisted she was.

"Carlie, why are you here?" His deep voice stroked her nerve endings. "What do you expect me to do?"

She swallowed. "I need to prove this imposter isn't me. I need to rescue my son. He needs me. He needs his mother."

He winced, and she knew she'd hit him where it hurt.

Kane leaned toward her, his eyes narrowing, and all the hurt she knew he had suffered as a child, and longer, shone from deep within. "A boy needs his father, too."

"Yes, he does." She braced herself and placed her hand firmly on the one he had covering hers. "That's why Jamie needs you."

Chapter Four

Kane gaped at Carlie, her meaning stabbing through his mind like a searing poker, sharp and stinging and shocking. Had he understood her? He needed to ask, but his tongue seemed too large—as though it had swollen, as if speaking would gag him.

She blew out a breath. "I just told you Jamie is your son. Aren't you going to say something?"

"*My* son?" The words came out strangled.

She looked hurt and defensive. "Is that so hard to believe?"

"No. Yes. God, Carlie, I—" Kane felt as though he'd been asked to accept one thing too many in the past few hours. His brain was on fire, his body was icy and numb as though every nerve ending had frozen. In short order, this day had gone from great to bad to something incomprehensible. Scabs had been ripped from old vulnerabilities. Old resentments. Old pains. Rousing all the old questions. His lifetime of confusion. But this—this was the most unexpected, startling—

His body gave a hard shudder. He lurched from the banquette, stalked to the sliding glass door and shoved out onto the deck. He drew a deep breath, filling his lungs as though he'd been drowning and only just resurfaced at the last second.

He closed his eyes, shutting out the colorful boat masts, the brilliant sky, the scenic harbor. With the sun beating on him, he dredged the memories of that last night in Port Luster. It had been four years ago, yet it came to him as fresh as the air filling his lungs, as vivid as the spray of freckles on Carlie's nose.

He'd have lost his sanity that night, if not for her. But as the night stretched into morning with the weight of her head nestled in the crook of his arm, the ripe curves of her naked body warm against his, he feared she was falling in love with him. The way he'd felt, *that* was the worst thing that could happen to her. Carlie deserved a man who was whole. Kane hadn't anything to offer her that night, except his misery and his passion.

So he'd decided to get out of her life for a while. He'd needed time to think. Time and space to vent his rage and frustration. To come to terms with the fact that he might never know who had fathered him. He hadn't awakened her. She'd have argued him out of leaving. But staying would have been the wrong thing for him. For her. For them. He'd been so sure of that, that long-ago morning.

He opened his eyes, his gaze falling on a pair of sea-gulls wheeling overhead without a care in the world. *My God, had he left Carlie pregnant?* Something wintry and hard coated the lining of his stomach. It couldn't be. They'd used protection. No. He frowned. That wasn't exactly true. He'd been inconsolable. Insatiable. Their lovemaking the only thing keeping him in touch with reality.

That last time, near dawn, the condoms were gone.

He rubbed his face with his hands. He should have

stopped. He shouldn't have put her at risk. Twin barbs of regret and shame dug at him. But, did he have a son? Had he fathered Carlie's little boy?

He glanced toward the cabin. She was fixing another cup of tea. Her attention was on the task, as though she hadn't a concern about what he was doing, that he was taking an eternity to consider what she'd laid on him. He'd been a cad four years ago; he was being one now.

But he didn't totally trust all that she'd told him. Partly because she hadn't tried to find him and tell him she was pregnant. Partly because she'd led him to believe she loved him, then married Skip eight weeks later.

How many times had he asked himself over the past four years if he had ever really known her?

Kane could see she verged on hysteria, like a mother bear frantic to reach her cub and rescue him from harm's way. Such a mother would employ desperate measures. Was Carlie frenzied enough to use any tactic to gain his help? Even elaborate lies?

Or was she telling him the truth? Had she been abducted? Had Skip beaten her? Hired someone to pose as her? Did Skip believe she was dead?

He scowled against the rush of his agitated thoughts, against the doubt and confusion, against the toughest question of them all: Was he Jamie Ellison's biological father?

A deep longing awakened inside him at the very possibility. But he feared embracing that possibility, feared buying into it, feared wrapping his heart around it even for a single second—without irrefutable proof.

He watched her stir the tea. She glanced up and at him as though sensing his gaze on her. If she was telling him the truth, then he had not only walked out on Carlie, he'd walked out on a son—his son. But Carlie wasn't blameless. She'd wasted no time securing a wedding proposal from his wealthy cousin.

All the anger he'd felt the day he'd discovered that Carlie had married Skip descended on Kane. He stormed back into the cabin. "Why didn't you tell me?"

"Tell you?" That look of hurt glinted anew from her eyes. Her shoulders were squared, her chin jutted. Despite her devastated condition, her garish clothing, she retained that pride he'd always admired. "That you'd made me pregnant, you mean?"

"Yes, damn it. If Jamie is my son, I had the right to know."

"Maybe you did, but by the time I found out I had…married Skip." Ire flared in her eyes as though her marrying his cousin was somehow Kane's fault.

But that was the rub. That was what he didn't understand. If she had loved *him,* why had she married Skip?

They glared at one another for a long moment, his pulse ticking like the workings of a cheap clock. "How can you be sure Jamie isn't Skip's child? Does the boy look like me?"

"Well, no." She frowned, seeming to consider something only she knew. Whatever it was, she didn't say. The teacup rattled on the saucer. "He—he looks like me."

Kane blew out a breath and paced the length of the cabin, feeling Carlie's gaze on him, sensing her rising temper.

She cut through his silence. "How was I supposed to tell you when I had no idea where you were?"

The accusation brought him up short. She was right. He'd deserted her, disappeared on purpose without telling anyone why or where he was going. He hadn't known. He'd just run and run until he could breathe again without wanting to scream or hit something. He'd been a selfish bastard in those days, reacting to every wrong he'd felt had been done to him without a thought for anyone else's feelings.

What Carlie didn't know was that he'd come back for her—only to discover she was on her honeymoon. With Skip.

His heart tightened at the memory, surprising him, shredding his long-held belief that he'd gotten over her, moved on with his life. Dear God, he couldn't, wouldn't, get caught up in wanting her again.

"What's true? What's not?" He shook his head. "I don't know what to think, Carlie."

Tears welled in her eyes. "I know this is a shock. But I hadn't anywhere else to turn. Jamie is alone with a stranger, a woman pretending to be me, with a father who has all but murdered his mother. God knows what Skip has in mind for my little boy. I'm terrified for him, but obviously coming here was a mistake. I'll go."

She set the cup and saucer on the counter and started past him. He caught her arm. "I didn't say I wouldn't help you."

"You didn't say you would."

"This has been a hell of a day, Carlie. Can you blame me for being...confused?"

"Confused? Like before?" She pulled from his grasp and stepped beyond his reach. Despite the strength of her words, she looked near collapse. "If you think it was easy for me to tell you this, you're wrong. I knew you might run out on us like four years ago."

"I wasn't running out on you." He moved closer to her. "I was running for my life. There's a difference."

"Yes, the difference was that I hadn't the luxury of running out on my life. I had to stay and face it and do

the best thing for my baby. You weren't the only one
who didn't have an ideal childhood, you know. Mine was
pure hell.''

"Yours?'' Kane blinked hard, not catching what she
meant. He knew her parents had died when she was six-
teen, knew she'd been taken in by Hugh Proctor, a local
attorney with a small practice, knew she'd been a rich
kid up until then. But her statement suggested she'd kept
things from him. Important things. "Just what kind of
hell are you talking about?''

She blanched. "That doesn't matter now. What mattered was that I wanted more for my child, so much more
than I had had. I *gave* him more.''

Kane tensed, her betrayal cutting fresh wounds through
his heart. "Did you love Skip?''

"I—I—'' She nodded, then shook her head and
sobbed. "How could it have turned out so wrong?''

She groaned, then curled in on herself as though the
pain of her heartache were too much to bear. She began
to crumple to the floor. Kane caught her and dragged her
to the sofa. He pulled her into his arms and held her as
she sobbed against his chest.

Her tears wet his T-shirt and soaked him through to
his very soul. If only he'd been less selfish, she more
honest, so much might have turned out differently. His
gut twisted with regret and impotent frustration. It was
too late to change the past, impossible to snatch back lost
time.

He'd run from fear of love and commitment, and now
had neither. She'd married for love and security, and had
gained neither. It would be laughable if not for the trauma
being suffered by an innocent child.

And now, he was dealing with a crazed woman making
crazy accusations about her ex-husband. For, her claims

that a man as unimaginative as Skip Ellison had replaced her with a twin seemed ludicrous. Kane wished he knew what he should do about her allegations. About her. About the son he might have that he'd never met.

All he could think to do was hold her more gently, more firmly. Slowly, Carlie's cries eased to the quiet mewling of a frightened kitten, and minutes later, her body went limp. Kane realized she'd dropped into an exhausted sleep. He closed his own eyes, too tired and too drained to think. He let the quiet envelop them, the steady rise and fall of her breathing wash over and through him.

Sleep, however, eluded Kane. The gentle slap of the tide against his boat no longer had its usual calming effect. Now it seemed to beat with a frantic, subtle message: *Who is his daddy? Who is his daddy? Who is his daddy?* Kane would never know who his own father was. He didn't want that for any child of his. If Jamie was his son, then, by God, no one would stop Kane from claiming him.

But he wouldn't act irrationally, would try not to frighten or hurt the child unnecessarily. He needed to know that what Carlie had told him was true, and he needed to know it now. He had to see that news broadcast for himself. He laid her gently on the sofa and covered her with an afghan. She squirmed, twitched as if to wake, then slept on.

Kane left her alone and hurried to the marina office. For once the TV was off. Maude corroborated Carlie's claim that Skip Ellison had been on TV that morning talking about his father's death and his company, and that he'd had a little boy with him and some woman who might have been his wife, but that the woman hadn't been identified by the news people.

Kane asked, "Was it a live broadcast?"

"Well, now," Maude said. "That I don't recollect."

"Could I use your phone?"

"Help yerself." She shoved a grimy beige phone toward him. "It's a local call, ain't it?"

He assured her it was, then dialed a San Diego TV station. The person he spoke with confirmed that the *EL* segment had been broadcast live from Port Luster, Washington. In fact, the station was re-airing the clip in a few minutes.

Kane thanked the man and set the recorder on Maude's VCR. "Here it comes now," she cried as the news began.

Kane didn't hear what Skip was saying. He was only interested in the little boy and the woman clutching his hand. He focused on Jamie, his heart wrenching at the misery he saw on the child's face.

"That poor young'un," Maude said. "Sure is tore up about his gramps, huh? Look how he keeps rubbin' his little chin."

Kane nodded, but he wasn't as sure as Maude about why the boy appeared so miserable.

Maude continued, "Cute little fella, all that red hair and freckles. Reminds me of Opie on that old TV show."

It was true, he decided. Jamie Ellison did resemble Ron Howard as a child. But mostly, he looked like his mother. If this boy was Kane's flesh and blood, he couldn't detect it from this tape.

The camera shifted, the view encompassing the woman now. Kane's eyes widened. "Holy—"

Something akin to an icy finger traced the small of his back. The woman holding Jamie Ellison's hand was either Carlie herself, or her clone. And it couldn't be Carlie. She couldn't have been in Port Luster and in San Diego at the same time.

"That's the woman!" Maude pointed. "Is she the wife?"

"Good question," Kane muttered.

"Say..." Maude seemed not to notice his distress. "That gal looks a little like the woman who came to see you."

Kane pressed his lips together, but didn't respond.

"How's she doin', by the by?" Maude asked. "I'm not one to jump to conclusions, but seems to me someone beat her up real bad. She's lucky to have a friend like you, Captain K. Real lucky."

Yeah, lucky. With a friend like me, she needed no enemies. But she'd found some, just the same. "I appreciate you and Pop letting me have my old boat slip awhile longer."

"No problem. Cash in the bank for us. But don't forget ya only got it fer a few days. That Alaskan schooner'll be arrivin' end of the week."

"I won't forget. *Footloose* and I will be out of here by then."

"See that you are." Her grin was warm and jovial, but he knew she was only half teasing him. They'd already leased the slip his boat occupied.

By the weekend, he'd better know what he was doing. Where he was heading. He had the unnerving sense that his days of being "footloose" would soon come to a screeching halt. He'd thought he'd wanted that a few months back, with Gina. But she'd claimed he had too many unresolved issues to make a good husband and father. No matter how he'd denied it at the time, he realized now that she'd been right. Unresolved feelings and relationships. He'd faced them all head-on once before and been beaten to an emotional pulp.

He had wrapped his heart in iron four years ago, and

in all that time nothing, until now, had so much as dented the armor. But Carlie had pierced clear through, laying open a fresh wound, and despite his best efforts to disallow it, an awful hope was taking root. God help him if it was a lie.

Kane took the videotape back to the boat to watch again. Carlie still slept; her sleep was restless. He guessed her nightmares revolved around Jamie, and he wished he could ease her mind. But could he?

Could he believe *all* that she'd told him?

He turned on his television, a thirteen-inch color model with built-in VCR. Static lighted the screen, the set no longer connected to the cable hookup at the dock. He found channel three, then pushed play, keeping the volume muted. He watched the tape four times through, reversing it and freezing it on the best shot of first Jamie, then the woman holding his hand. He studied every inch of the boy's small face over and over again, seeking something—anything—of himself in that tiny countenance.

He saw nothing.

He skipped the tape forward to the woman. Here the opposite was true. This Carleen Ellison's likeness to Carlie was incredible. Unnerving. Chilling. And it confounded him more than ever. What little he knew of her past didn't include a twin sister. Was this the part of the "hell" Carlie had lived as a child? Could that explain this look-alike?

Maybe.

But it didn't touch the surface of Skip's participation in this odd scenario. Either he didn't realize the woman was an imposter, and was the brunt of some unimaginable deception, or...he did know and had had Carlie abducted for some agenda of his own. Kane raked his hand through his hair. His cousin was a lot of things, but not a fool. If he knew the woman beside him was an imposter, then he'd never have risked a news broadcast…unless he was certain no one would call his bluff. Unless he thought the real Carlie was dead and unidentifiable.

Kane clicked off the tape. His stomach gave a queasy lurch. He itched to go back to the marina office and call Skip in Port Luster. Ask him what exactly was going on. But what could he say without putting Carlie at further risk? Without maybe causing her little boy more misery than he was suffering now? No. He had to curb his rash impulses. Whatever he did, he had to move with deliberate caution. This time, he had more to lose than ever. This time, others' lives were at risk.

"It's scary, isn't it?" Carlie was sitting up, staring at the blank television screen as though she hadn't spoken to him but to herself.

She had the afghan pulled tightly about her body. Was she chilled? Or tense? He couldn't imagine what she felt, seeing that other Carleen. Could only guess at the betrayal and rage that she must be dealing with at having someone else taking over her life. He said, "The resemblance is remarkable."

"Are you sure she isn't the real Carleen?" There was raw pain in her voice.

Kane flinched inwardly. In the past he would have gone to her, pulled her into his arms and eased her stress by making love to her. By walking out on her, he'd forfeited the right to such intimacy. Besides, he reminded himself, she hadn't really loved him. Didn't love him now. Only needed him. Needed his reassurance. "I'm sure you're you."

"Even after seeing that tape?"

"Especially after seeing it."

"But how...?" Hope filled her eyes, laced her words. "Why?"

"I can't explain it. Can't put my finger on any one thing. But I knew who you were the moment I saw you. She isn't you."

As he said it, he felt a thread or two of his tangled confusion snap and disappear. He smiled at her.

Carlie put her face in her hands and sobbed anew. Kane rose and went to her. "I thought that would please you."

"It does," she blubbered, lifting her head and wiping with the back of her hands at the tears that flowed unchecked. "Can't you tell tears of relief when you see them?"

He offered her his clean hanky and gently daubed her damp cheeks, using extra care around her tender eye. She said, "Then you'll go to Port Luster with me, to get Jamie."

It wasn't a question. It sent a cold shiver through him. Port Luster. The little harbor town on the Olympic Peninsula of Washington State. A beautiful, scenic tourist trap. His home town. Where *EL* was located. The place where all of his truths had turned to lies.

He'd vowed three years and ten months ago that he'd seen the last of Port Luster for as long as he lived. Every nerve in his body rejected the thought of returning. But despite Carlie's betrayal, despite her marrying his cousin, he couldn't look into those emerald eyes of hers and tell her that, couldn't squelch the hope that glistened there.

On the other hand, since none of the other players in this bizarre soap opera were bound to show up here—

including the most important, Jamie—he had no choice but to go with her. "I suppose a few feathers will be ruffled if I show up for Wil's funeral, but others would be ruffled if I didn't show."

"Then we'll go?"

"Yes."

"Oh, thank you, Kane." She hugged his neck, pressing her body to him with every ounce of her jubilation. Her relief. The contact, so unlike when he'd held her earlier, startled him. The passion he'd thought she'd killed four years ago roused like a sleeping monster within him, slowly, steadily, fiercely.

Kane pulled back, staring at her mouth, fighting the urges her nearness evoked. The last thing she wanted was his affection. She'd made that clear enough when she'd married his cousin. The divorce hadn't changed that. Nothing had. With an effort, he scooted back from her and stood.

She rose with him. "When can we leave?"

He took several bracing breaths, gathering his control, studying her face, then finally said, "As soon as we take you shopping for some clothes and makeup. That eye would scare Jamie."

"Oh, yes. It would," she agreed. She touched the garish shirt and shabby jeans she wore. A crooked smile brightened her expression. "And no one would believe I'm who I claim to be in this getup."

But the joy vanished as soon as the words left her mouth. Something dark and secretive filled her green eyes. Her hand went to her front denim pocket, as though to reassure herself something was still there. Something that unnerved her. She said, "I—I forgot. I haven't any money."

"My treat," Kane said, but a new doubt had woven itself into that tangled ball of confusion he couldn't quite unravel. What hadn't she told him? What was in her pocket?

Chapter Five

Carleen stared at her reflection in the mirror. She and Kane had walked into this ritzy waterfront shop an hour earlier. In her tacky kidnap outfit, she might have been a street person. He, on the other hand, resembled nothing less than a pirate of old, dressed for travel on the high seas, tanned and muscled, his dark blond hair pure white at its tips, his clothes cleaving his finer assets in tantalizing tightness.

The clerks hadn't batted an eye at either of them, but a couple of customers, drenched in gold and designer perfume, had turned up their noses, clutched their purses close, hurriedly paid for their purchases and left. Except for the store owner, they had the shop to themselves now.

She moved a step back from the mirror. Expertly applied makeup covered the unsightly bruise. Her hair was brushed into her usual style, and her new undergarments, silk blouse and lined wool-blend slacks all felt rich and somehow familiar against her skin.

A cold knot settled at the base of her spine. Only four years with Skip, with his money, and she'd grown used to the feel of silk against her flesh instead of cotton. Patched, threadbare cotton.

She shook off the black thought and spun toward

Kane, knowing the subdued green shade flattered her natural coloring like a subtle compliment, but still needing
his assurance that she looked as normal as she thought
she did. Or at least as normal as possible—given the fact
she'd apparently lost enough weight in the past seven
days that she'd shrunk a size.

Kane's full mouth tipped up at the corners, approval
keen in his deep dimples. *Jamie's dimples.* "Now, that's
the Carlie I remember."

Relief brought a smile to her lips. "Then Jamie won't
be frightened when he sees me."

The panic to retrieve her son threatened a comeback,
and her smile wobbled.

He frowned, homing in on the cause of her dismay. "I
know you'd like nothing better than to hop a plane to
Washington this minute, but we'll be in Port Luster
around noon tomorrow. In plenty of time to make the
funeral."

She nodded, grappling with her desperation. "I know.
I know…but, Jamie…I want to leave now."

"That's not a good idea, Carlie." He tilted his head,
his lips lifting sympathetically. "We'd arrive in Seattle
around midnight. Port Luster is another two, three hours
by car. Are you planning on storming the Ellison mansion
in the wee hours of the morning, demanding Skip return
your son—his son—without a speck of proof that you are
who you claim?"

"Yes." It was exactly what Carleen wanted to do. It
was exactly what she must not do. She bit down a sob
and hugged herself against an onslaught of internal shivers. "No."

Traveling through the night without sleep would ruin
her makeover, her shaky confidence. She would arrive a
frenzied, hysterical shrew. She dare not act irrationally.

Panic, she repeated like a grating theme song, would work against her, would make her claims of being the true Carleen Ellison sound as believable as Clinton not knowing Monica. If they showed up, as Kane had suggested, in the wee hours of the morning, Skip would have them arrested.

She murmured, "I must look and sound credible."

"Exactly." He seemed to want to touch her. Instead, he stepped back, holding himself apart from her, his hands stiff at his sides. "You can do this, Carlie."

The strength and reassurance in his gruffly spoken words lent her courage, buoyed her self-confidence. She nodded hard with renewed conviction and offered him a brave smile. "I will do it, Kane. For Jamie. God, I pray he's safe."

His heated gaze caressed her even as he held his distance. "He's fine. Hang on to that thought. Skip has never hurt him before—he won't do it now."

"No, he won't—not as long as he thinks he's won everything he wants." She let out a taut breath. "Thank you. For the clothes, and for believing in me, but mostly for keeping me calm."

He nodded, his expression that of a discomforted teenage boy receiving praise, then he lifted his gaze and the private torment issuing from him sent a searing heat through her.

There in his eyes was the echo of all the fervor they'd once shared, but in her heart lived the resonating pain. She mustn't react to him, mustn't allow the commiseration in his glances, the compassion in his touches, to overrule her sensibility. She couldn't afford to be passion's victim again.

The shopkeeper hovered nearby, eavesdropping, her

perfect eyebrows lifting at the bits of conversation she'd already heard.

Carleen gently pulled free of Kane's grasp and stepped back, putting physical distance between them, wishing it were as easy to distance herself from him emotionally. "Do you think your budget would handle one more outfit? I should get something appropriate for the funeral."

"Of course." He turned to the saleswoman. "What have you got in black?"

"Something with slacks," Carleen added. "Where we're going is not as warm as San Diego this time of year."

She thanked Kane again. In recent years, the generosity of others had been a lifeline against the tumbling waters of poverty and despair she'd known throughout her youth. But she didn't want to be indebted to him any more than was necessary for her to reclaim her son.

"I'll pay you back as soon as we're in Port Luster," she promised, but the second the words left her lips, an ugly thought struck her. "Oh, my God. Skip has had access to my personal accounts for over a week. What if he's closed my checking account? Torn up my credit cards?"

Kane considered, then shook his head, a lock of sun-kissed hair tugging loose to swing across his forehead. He shoved it back with his strong fingers. "We won't know that until we get to Washington, but I can't imagine he would. It's the kind of thing that would draw unnecessary attention."

She supposed he was right. Hoped he was. Wondered why it had suddenly seemed so important. The only thing that really mattered was Jamie. But if she focused on him, she'd fall apart. "At the moment, Skip has more attention

on him than he likely wanted, what with his father's unexpected death.''

Kane grew thoughtful. ''That does seem to have come
at a bad time for Skip.''

But had it? she wondered suddenly. Could Wil Ellison's untimely death have come at a more opportune time
for his son?

Kane's expression held something akin to the suspi-
cions whirling through her mind. But she knew his emotions balanced on a different plane than hers. He might
only be upset that his uncle's unexpected death left him
with a slew of unanswered questions about his own life,
and not about the cause of his uncle's death.

Kane rubbed his jaw where golden bristles were be-
ginning to sprout. ''I wonder if an autopsy is being done
on Wil.''

''I don't know.'' So, he *was* as unsettled as she about
Wil's heart attack. ''It seems the obvious thing to do,
after all—''

''Yeah,'' Kane interrupted. ''I can't imagine a less
likely candidate for heart failure. He was a fanatic about
his health.''

''Do you think Frances would sanction an autopsy,
though?''

''You mean, given her fear of scandal? It would be
risky. No telling what might show up in a coroner's report. I'd say it's a safer bet that she'll go along with
whatever the doctor put on the death certificate.''

''As will Skip and Starla.'' Carleen swallowed over
the lump forming in her throat. What a cold family she'd
married into, and how fortunate she'd been to escape. But
she hadn't escaped completely, or unscathed, had she?

Kane dipped his head toward hers. ''Do you think Wil
died from natural causes?''

It was so close to what she'd been wondering, Carleen started, but before she could respond, the shopkeeper arrived with an armload of suitable mourning wear. Shoving Kane's question into the dark corners of her mind, Carleen retreated to the dressing room.

Trying on more clothes held no appeal. She'd half made up her mind to take the first suit that fit, regardless of style or how it looked on her. Then she realized this was likely the outfit that she'd wear to confront the Ellison family the first time. Fit and style not only mattered, they were vital. Like the phoenix, she was rising from the dead. She must appear as strong and striking as the sensation she would cause.

The third suit fitted her purposes to a tee. The designer style was feminine and flattering, and disguised her recent weight loss. It was also the most expensive of the bunch. Last year she wouldn't have balked at the price. But what if she couldn't pay Kane back? What if Skip hadn't cared about suspicion being cast on him? What if he'd had the faux Carleen empty her accounts, tear up her credit cards? The ones she had gotten on her own?

Hell, what did *that* matter? It could all be straightened out…eventually. And it would be. Her stomach clenched. The real thing preying on her mind was just how heinous Skip had become. If he was capable of ordering her murder, was he also capable of killing his own father?

The internal tremors started again. She shook herself. No. Fearing Skip gave him power over her. She was stronger than that. Stronger than he'd thought. If not, she wouldn't be here now.

She stripped off the suit and reached for a set of tan jeans and a cream-colored sweater, the other new purchase. She pulled on the sweater and glanced at herself in the three-way mirror, her gaze falling on the vile clothing the kidnappers had dressed her in. They lay on the floor in a discarded heap.

Her nose wrinkled. It wasn't that these items had belonged to someone else, that they'd come from some unknown source, or that they were covered with rank-smelling, vile-looking stains. This disgust was years deep. These were the clothes she'd owned growing up. Not this particular blouse, not these jeans and that underwear, but articles enough like them that just glancing at these brought back the sensation of abrasive fabrics against her skin.

Why did the past still haunt her?

Carleen sank to the chair in the dressing room, her gaze on her reflection, but she no longer saw her present-day image. Her mind floated back to those awful years.

When they'd lived in Las Vegas, she hadn't realized how dire their situation was. But when they'd moved to Port Luster, it had become all too apparent. Her father gambled away every cent that wasn't needed to keep Jamison's Grocery Store running and to maintain the appearance of a wealthy family in a small town.

Keeping the truth secret was her job, a humiliating task for a sensitive teenager. She'd flunked gym because she wouldn't get undressed in front of the other girls. She'd rather have failed than listen to their ill-concealed giggles at her expense, for she'd had no way to conceal the hand-stitched mends in her panties and bra, or the embarrassing thinness of the overbleached fabrics. She sighed now as she slipped on her new shoes. At least her undergarments hadn't been dingy gray. But even years later, she couldn't smile about it.

She'd kept to herself, hiding her pain and shame. Most of her classmates thought she was stuck-up. She'd discouraged the only girl who'd seen through her standoffishness. She'd had to. The girl might have wanted to come over to her house, might have discovered the only room with furniture was the living room. The house, like her life, just a facade.

But the truth had been exposed, as most ugly secrets usually were, when her parents died. Then the whole town had discovered her disgrace. Her father had lost everything to his gambling—the house, its meager contents, the grocery store. Everything gone to pay bad debts. She'd been left without a penny.

Hugh Proctor and his wife had taken her in. They'd been as generous as their small income allowed. They'd seen to it that she finally had a decent wardrobe—

"Do any of those suits work?" The shopkeeper's impatient voice cut through her dark musings. They'd kept the woman past her usual closing time.

Carleen leaped up. "Yes. This one." She handed the woman the hanger with the suit she'd chosen. Then pointed to the outfit she wore. "I'm going to wear these items out of here."

"Sure. They look like they were made with you in mind. Meet me at the counter, and I'll remove the tags."

Carleen joined Kane and the shopkeeper near the front display window. He was signing the credit receipt.

She said, "Thank you, Kane."

The words seemed trite. Overused. By her. Her gratitude, however, was the only thing she had to offer at the moment. She owed this man more than the cost of these clothes. He'd given her back some hope, some sense of herself. But she couldn't tell him that—for fear of the price he might exact from her in repayment.

As they started for the door, the shopkeeper called, "Ma'am, would you like me to dispose of these?"

Carleen spun toward her. The woman was holding the

kidnapper castoffs. "I could put them in the Dumpster out back."

"Yes, please." Carleen glanced at Kane, who was putting his credit card back into his wallet. She froze. The VISA card—the one that made her so uncomfortable, the one that belonged to someone named Coral Clayton— was in the pocket of those awful jeans. She considered letting the woman toss the pants anyway, but for some inexplicable reason she felt she'd better hang on to that card.

"Wait a second." She hurried to the woman and slipped the VISA from the pocket, then tucked it into her new clutch. It was the only thing in there; the faux Carleen Ellison had her credit cards, her driver's license, her photos of Jamie.

And Jamie.

This time, instead of desperation, she felt white-hot rage. At Skip. He would pay for every indignity he'd caused her. For every tear her child had wept, for every moment of terror Jamie had lived these many days and nights.

KANE WATCHED CARLIE withdraw a credit card from the pocket of the ratty jeans, watched her put it into her new clutch, watched anger color her cheeks, fill her eyes. Something dark and cold swirled through his gut. If Carlie had a credit card, why was he paying for her new clothes?

One thought occurred to him. Maybe she hadn't wanted Skip to trace her. But if that were the case, why hadn't she told him? And why had just touching that sliver of plastic infuriated her? Myriad new doubts skittered through his mind. How much of what she'd told him was true? How much was fabrication? How much was she holding back from him?

He moved toward her, stuffing his wallet into his back jeans pocket. It was time she told him a few things—about her past, about anything and everything she did recall of the previous seven days.

"I should toss the clothing, then?" the saleswoman asked.

"Yes," Carlie confirmed.

"No." Kane watched the shopkeeper's perfect brows lift in surprise. He saw confusion and a touch of fear in Carlie's green eyes, and he knew he was right, knew something about those clothes terrified her.

"Why?" she asked, the single word like an explosion in the silent shop.

"Because," he whispered in her ear. "Those clothes are the only clue we have to whatever happened to you in your forgotten week."

He felt her tense. She touched her temples as though a headache pounded there, and directed her gaze to the shopkeeper. "Could you bag them for me."

Port Luster, Washington—that same day

WITHOUT APPOINTMENT or invitation, and without knocking, Starla Ellison Harding barged into the office of the new CEO of *EL*. The huge room reflected the persona of the man who'd occupied it for the past three years—elegant cherry paneling; rich leather furniture imbued with the scent of Panama cigars; and framed photographs of his boyhood days on his father's tuna boat, an ever-present reminder of his humble roots.

She glared at the broad cherry-wood desk that Wilcox Ellison had bought when he'd launched *EL* thirty years earlier. He'd turned a good idea into a multimillion-dollar company. He'd earned the right to sit in this office. As had she. But she'd been betrayed by the one man she'd always thought she could trust. Her father. Acid seared her stomach, just as rage fueled her steps. As far as she was concerned, all bets were off.

"Such a touching show of grief." Starla advanced on her brother, her twin. Physically they resembled one another. Both were tall and leanly built, both were tow-headed blonds, both had their mother's upturned mouth, the straight, clipped Ellison nose and cool blue eyes. But in Skip the features came together in male model perfection.

On her these same features were somehow askew. All her life she'd been described as striking or interesting or chic. Never gorgeous. She hadn't cared. Skip had the beauty, but she had the brains. Daddy had known that, appreciated and respected that. He'd called his son "the captain," "the little skipper," but she was always his "shining Star," glowing brighter, he declared, and longer than all the rest.

Last week he'd promised to reward her for that. To change his will. She'd believed him. But he hadn't done it.

Her barely contained fury heated her cheeks. Her blood pressure, she realized, had to be off the charts. Dangerous, but unavoidable, given the circumstances. The last twenty-four hours had been the worst of her life. And seeing her brother sitting in Daddy's chair, behind Daddy's desk, beneath Daddy's portrait was the cruelest slap of all in the awful nightmarish drama in which she had a starring role.

"Jealous, little Star?"

"Hardly." But even she heard the bitterness in her

voice. Skip's smile broadened. He was enjoying her discomfort, and she'd promised herself she wouldn't let him
see it—no matter what. Crap. Her emotional defenses
were weaker than she'd guessed. A bad calculation on
her part. She couldn't afford self-deception. She wouldn't
make that mistake again.

"Concede it, Star." Skip tipped his handsome head to
one side, offering her a flash of his brilliant white teeth.
The grin was as cold as the white caps in the bay that
she could see through the wall of windows to her right,
but his voice rang with fire. "I've won the ultimate
prize—and you can't stand it."

She bit her cheeks to keep from responding with something she'd later regret. Their childhood rivalry had
reached a pinnacle, and this time Skip was on top. Star
glanced up at the portrait. *Damn you, Daddy. Why did
you do this to me? Why did you encourage me to think
that I might be head of EL, when all the while you'd left
the company to this egomaniacal inferior?*

"Why aren't you home, comforting Mother?" Her
brother's tone reeked of dismissal, as though she had no
rights at this company where she'd worked since gradu-
ating from the University of Washington, as though
woman's work was holding the hands of grieving wid-
ows.

"You're the one Mother wants…and needs right now.
Not me."

"Well, I have a company to run. Mother understands
that. So, you'll have to play surrogate for me this week."
At her dark glare, Skip hurried on. "It's not like I'm
asking for a kidney or something. You know how frail
Mother is."

"Don't try laying that guilt trip on me." Under the
circumstances, Star wasn't about to retire to the family

mansion and wallow in their mother's grief. Not for Daddy. Not after his betrayal. Not now, anyway. Maybe later. "I'm not going this time."

"But she needs one of us. Now, more than ever."

"Then you go, Skip. I'm not the kind of woman for sackcloth and ashes. I have work here, too." Daddy had taught her to be tough, to act and think like a man, and, by God, she would. "Why the hell did you pull my new campaign? It's all set to run. It'll net *EL* millions."

"I disagree." He wrinkled his nose as though a disgusting odor had wafted beneath it.

Probably got a whiff of his rotten soul. Star thought she could smell it herself.

Skip said, "Selling our sportswear in discount warehouses is not the future I see for *EL.*"

"Daddy approved it."

"The old man is gone. Long live the new king." Skip stood and leaned his square hands on the desk as though branding it, claiming it, taking total possession of the broad expanse of cherry wood. "I'm making all the decisions now."

"All the wrong decisions."

"The old man was living in the past. What worked in the seventies and eighties, hell, even the early nineties, doesn't work now. We're into a new millennium. We've got to stay ahead of the pack. Can't do that by following old trails."

Star wanted to strangle him. Instead, she placed her hands on her stomach, barely rounded from the life growing within, and reined in her temper for the sake of her baby's health. "Daddy meant to change his will. He meant to leave this company in my capable hands."

"Says who? You?" Skip's cruel chuckle echoed off the richly paneled walls. Then his cold gaze settled on her. "Your condition has you delusional. *EL* was always meant to pass to me, then to my son."

She stiffened as though he'd struck her. "No. You're wrong—"

"Why don't you try to be a good loser, Star?" His grin turned even nastier. He waggled his fingers at her, gesturing for her to leave. "I've got work to do. Go see Mother."

Grief rode hard against Star's resentment. Daddy's body hadn't even been cold when Skip summoned the lawyer to read the will—the *old* will. The lawyer swore no new will had been made in the past fifteen years, swore Daddy hadn't even spoken to him about one. She clenched her hands at her sides, her nails gouging her palms. The will he read gave controlling interest in *EL* and the CEO-ship to whomever of Wilcox's children had produced the first Ellison heir.

Jamie.

Despite her delicate condition, Star wasn't sure she wouldn't commit murder if she stayed a moment longer in the presence of her jerk brother. She spun on her heel and headed out into the receptionist's office.

If Skip thought she was going to go quietly into the night, he was sorely mistaken, as well as underestimating her desire to gain that which rightfully belonged to her, that which Daddy had promised her. Whatever it took, she would break Daddy's will.

Her child should have been the first Ellison heir. No one cared about Daddy the way she did. His betrayal smarted worse than his death.

Poor Jamie. Until this morning she'd adored her nephew—just seeing the way Daddy had doted on him deepened her love of the boy. Until this morning, she'd have given her life to keep him safe from harm.

But now, after Daddy's betrayal of her and her unborn child—the grandchild Daddy would never know and dote on—she wished Jamie were dead, too.

Chapter Six

Kane placed Carleen's purchases in the trunk of her rented Dodge, then settled in the driver's seat and poked the key into the ignition. But he didn't start the car. Instead, he turned toward her, stretched his right arm between the bucket seats and gripped the back of her seat. She could see from the serious cast to his eyes that something was amiss.

What now? Dread took hold of her stomach, her muscles. The air between them felt alive with so much that had been left unspoken, unresolved. So much dangerous ground she didn't dare travel. His fingertips brushed her shoulder. She wanted to lean into the pressure of his touch. Instead, she cringed away from him, unable to deal with the need he roused in her, unable to ignore it.

Kane reached his left hand as though to stroke her cheek, stopping himself with a visible effort. He seemed awash in emotion. She recognized the warmth of his inviting mouth from reawakening memories, but the cool tightness around his eyes was unfamiliar, and frightened her.

He said, "I want answers, and I want them now."

She let out a quavery breath. "If I know the answers."

"I saw the credit card."

The heat drained from Carleen's limbs. Did he think the card was hers? Or did he know it wasn't? "What about it?"

"You tell me." His gaze snagged hers. "I know it makes you uncomfortable. Or worse." He narrowed his eyes. "Why?"

Why, indeed? If she could figure *that* out, she'd be plays ahead in this game. But she couldn't. Wasn't. "I don't know. I can't even tell you how I came by it."

"It isn't yours?"

"No." She pulled it from the clutch and held it out to him. Her hand trembled, but she wasn't sure whether her distress was his doing or the usual disquiet she felt every time she touched the card.

His hand bumped her shoulder as he took the VISA, studied it for a second, then lifted his eyes to her. They were the blue-gray of a stormy sky at dawn. "You don't know anyone named Coral Clayton?"

"No." This time hearing him say the strange woman's name stirred a flash of memory, but it slipped through her mind with the speed of light, there and gone before she could connect with it. Damn. What was it? "Do you know her?"

"Never heard of her." He studied the card, turned it over and back again. "Could she be the woman who's posing as you?"

Carleen had no way of knowing. She conveyed that with a shrug. "You think someone placed this on me for identification when my body was found?"

"It's one possibility." He hesitated as if considering something long and hard, then said, "I realized earlier today that you've told me almost nothing about your childhood."

Carleen tensed. "What could this VISA card have to do with my childhood?"

"It occurred to me that this imposter might be part of your past."

"How?"

"You said your childhood was hell, but not what kind of hell." He blew out a breath that brushed her face like a tender stroke. "Maybe I'm grasping at straws, but I can't help wondering if this imposter might be, say, a twin sister?"

"Who was adopted at birth?" She lifted her brows and shook her head. She supposed he would go on forever coming up with absurd scenarios if she didn't tell him the truth about her childhood now. "No. I can assure you if that had happened then it would have been because my father sold her for enough cash to bet on the Super Bowl."

"Your dad—"

"He had a passion for gambling like other men do for sports, or cars, or jobs."

"But you lived in that big house on Hill Street, and John Jamison bought a new Cadillac every year."

"All a front. Every other cent not needed to keep the store running, he poured into his bookie's coffers."

She told him all of it then, pent-up resentments and long-buried self-pity spilling from her with every revealed secret. The effect was like that of a huge weight slowly but surely being lifted from her soul.

As she shared her past with him, Kane lifted his hand and cupped her head; the gesture, an acute reminder of their past, was at once tender and intimate and telling. She was shattering his long-held fantasy, destroying his belief that having both parents alive and living under the same roof was always the best thing for a child. Perhaps now he would understand why she'd wanted Jamie to have more than she'd had. Why she'd decided Skip might give her child the security she'd never had.

She said, "We follow paths as adults that we've learned from our childhoods, but sometimes those paths lead us in vicious circles to repeat the same mistakes our parents made. I figured the way out was to find a new trail, or make one. But I was wrong. And now Jamie is paying for my errors in judgment."

"Don't beat yourself up. None of this is your doing." Kane's mouth and jaw were set in hard lines, but his voice held an unexpected tenderness. "Jamie is lucky to have you for his mother."

His compliment did nothing to ease the heaviness in her heart. "Right now, he doesn't have me, but some imposter."

Kane swore under his breath. "Which brings us back to who the woman is. If she's not your twin sister, could she be some other relative?"

"If she is, then she's one I've never met. I wouldn't forget someone who was the spitting image of me."

"No, I don't suppose anyone would." He grew thoughtful for a moment. "There's one other possibility—Coral Clayton could have been one of your kidnappers."

"Yes, that's true."

"If so, I don't think we can be sure there really is a Coral Clayton."

"Why not?" She accepted the VISA from him and ran her thumb over the raised lettering, as though touching it would conjure a mental image of the woman. No flash of memory came, just that same awful anxious twinge in her belly.

"No kidnapper would risk carrying anything that might give away her real identity."

"What if I got the card somewhere else?" She heard the tremor in her voice.

"Where?"

"I don't know. If only I could remember." She shook her head and blew out a frustrated breath. Should she tell him about the creepy sensation the card gave her? She considered, concluding that he might think she'd lost her mind completely. No. Maybe she'd tell him later. "God, I hate this."

"I know, I know." Again the heat in his eyes eased some of her inner chill. "But forcing your memory isn't a great idea. Either it will come back to you or it won't. Let's concentrate on what you do recall."

"Such as?"

He considered a second, then asked, "Did you use this card?"

"Oh." The multitude of laws she'd broken by signing Coral Clayton's name to charge slips would likely land her in jail at some point, Carleen realized with a sickening dip of her stomach. But she would do it again, in a heartbeat...to help her son. She wasn't sure Kane would understand that.

She pulled the rental agreement for the car from the glove box and showed it to him. "I had to. I had to get here, to you."

Alarm filled his eyes. Was he concerned about the legal repercussions? Or something else she ought to have thought of, but hadn't considered? His brows dipped low. "Was this the only thing you used it for?"

They both already knew her answer. "The motel I stayed in last night."

"And presumably the flight here."

"I guess."

His alarm had turned to something else: an urgency she didn't understand. He asked, "Do you have your airline stub?"

"I haven't come across it." Why did he want that? "Maybe it's here in the car."

They executed a quick search, in the glove box, under the seats, front and back, between the seats, then through her kidnap clothing. It wasn't there.

"I might have left it in the motel room," she suggested. "Why is it so important?"

"Because knowing where your flight originated would tell us where you were when you escaped your kidnappers."

"The Olympic Peninsula, I assume."

"But you don't know that, do you?"

"Well, no." An inexplicable shiver tripped through her. "And, as you pointed out earlier, getting to SeaTac International from the Peninsula would take a couple of hours. Maybe I was held somewhere else. Except—"

She broke off and clasped her hands to her temples as a flash of pain brought another memory tumbling into her mind, this one moving slowly enough to grasp and hold. She clutched his arm; excitement bubbled through her. "Kane, I remember something. The sea, hitting rocks, a cabin by the seashore somewhere. Yes, I'm sure of it."

She smiled up at him. "Doesn't that suggest the Peninsula?"

If he shared her enthusiasm, he hid it beneath a cautious look. "It suggests the coast. But there's a lot of that between Port Luster and San Diego."

"Yes, but at least I've remembered something. If I can recall this, maybe I'll remember it all. Soon. I might even be able to tell the police who kidnapped me."

Then she would see to it that Skip was arrested and brought to trial for his role in the crime.

Kane looked as though he thought her remembering was both a good idea and a lousy one. He reached for her hands, and she had the impression the effort cost him something. His touch wasn't one of intimacy. He was hanging on to her to keep her from bolting, to reassure her that he was there for her. For Jamie. It was something she could expect from any compassionate person. But his work-roughened hands had power over her senses: the power to imbue her with heat, the power to unearth long-denied needs, the power to wash her in emotional confusion.

She tried to pull free of his grip. He tightened his hold, and she realized his expression was dangerously grim. Her heart tripped. "What?"

"I don't want to worry or frighten you more than necessary, but it's occurred to me, perhaps a little late, that Skip may have learned by now of your escape."

"Oh, my God! My kidnappers will have told him." Fear shot through Carleen. "Do you think he'll send someone here, expecting to find me with you?"

"Would he? Does Skip know that…er, ah…?" Kane swallowed with an effort, then cleared his throat. "That Jamie isn't his son?"

"You mean, does he know that *you* are Jamie's biological father?" Carleen took a ragged breath, grateful now that he was holding her hands, keeping her anchored, sane. "He does. Out of the blue one night last year, he came home ranting about you being Jamie's father. I never did find out what triggered his accusation, but I didn't deny it."

Not for long, she hadn't, anyway. She'd barely survived the beating he'd given her after she'd admitted the truth.

Kane said, "So, we don't know how he found out, only that he knows. How like him to want the boy at all costs."

"What do you mean?"

"For as far back as I can remember, Skip was jealous of me." Kane's voice had gone flat. "It made no sense to me. He had everything. I had nothing. But anything I took an interest in, he would take up immediately and try to best me at. I usually managed to remove myself from the competition once I discovered his motives."

"Why would he do that? Why you?"

"That's what I wondered. It was why I started looking more closely at my relationship to his father, my uncle Wil. He treated me better than my dad did, was generous with words of advice, praise, monetary handouts. Hell, he even displayed my trophies in his home office next to Skip's, and my dad allowed that without so much as a word of protest. But Skip hated it. And he coveted whatever was mine."

Like her? And now Jamie? "That's sick."

Kane arched a brow at her as though to say *"Yeah, exactly."*

But Carleen had already come to that conclusion. It was why she was so worried about her son. If Kane was right, might the boy be in more danger than she'd even imagined? "What if he hurts Jamie?"

"That won't happen."

"Why?"

"Skip hasn't told anyone he isn't Jamie's father, has he?"

"Well, no. He made me swear I wouldn't, either. It was the reason he gave me the divorce without a hassle."

"Of course. That's one secret he wants *kept* secret. If it comes out, it would mean forfeiting the company to Starla."

She frowned. "How's that?"

"According to my uncle's will, the controlling interest of *EL* goes to whichever of his children produced the first heir."

"I didn't know." She gasped. "Starla is pregnant. I found out just before I was kidnapped."

"Well, now we know why Skip tried to shut you up permanently. He couldn't risk your telling Starla the truth."

"I'm so terrified for Jamie. We have to get him out of that house. Away from that family."

"Jamie will be safe with Skip. He won't harm a hair on the head of his little golden goose. I'm positive Jamie's not in any physical danger."

"God, I pray you're right."

"I am. I know that much about Skip. Please trust that."

Instinctively she did, but the emotional damage being done to her son was another matter. And it would continue, if Skip had sent someone to San Diego to kill Kane and her.

Sitting in the car on this busy street, she felt suddenly exposed, a bull's-eye. At any moment a bullet might fly through the windshield and kill her. Kill Kane. Fear burned beneath her skin. Ate her breath. She jerked around in her seat, sending her gaze over the traffic, down the sidewalk in both directions, across the street and into passing cars.

Had she been found? Had she put Kane at mortal risk? Would Skip send someone to murder them both—leaving a small boy without either of his true parents? Her skull felt as though it were shrinking. She knew the devil who lived in her ex-husband. Knew of what he was capable. Knew she might never see her son again.

"Jamie." Tears stung her eyes. *Jamie!* She had to get home to her little boy. Had to find a way to give her son his real father. She'd done them all such an injustice by marrying the wrong man. Her childhood had taught her that having lots of money equaled emotional stability. Nothing in her life had prepared her for the reality that happiness and inner tranquility couldn't be bought. She lifted her tear-glazed eyes to Kane.

He tightened his grip on her hands, an anchor keeping her grounded, lending her strength, reassuring her that they would make it through this. Together. She wasn't alone. She had a choice: give in to her terror, or hang on for her son, for her son's father.

She owed them both that much.

She mustn't collapse or allow herself to panic. An inappropriate laugh caught in her throat. How many times today had she told herself that? But this time her terror wasn't a matter of Skip playing head games with her; this time he might actually have sent someone to San Diego to murder Kane and her.

"What are we going to do? We can't go back to the boat. What if someone is there?" She gasped. "What if they destroy the *Footloose?*"

"That's the least of our worries. Besides, it's insured," he said. His tone hinted that the boat meant nothing to him, but his expression darkened, and she knew the thought of someone destroying it both worried and infuriated him.

She pulled her hands free of his. Her heart thudded. "We can't go back there."

"We have to." His voice resonated calm. He rubbed

a hand over his bristled jaw, and a mischievous glint shone in his eyes. "I'm not going to Port Luster without my shaving gear or clean, ah, socks. And I sure can't attend the funeral in this getup."

Despite her fear, she smiled at him. He was making light of this serious situation, striving to keep her on an even keel. He seemed downright reliable. Unintentionally, she reached up to stroke his whiskered chin, but caught herself and pulled back. The intimate gesture was something she'd have done automatically four years ago. In fact, even without touching him, the memory of how he would feel seared a hole through her heart.

At this moment, she almost believed she could trust him not to run out on her again. For Jamie's sake, she had to believe that. But as things stood, neither of them could guarantee they'd reach Port Luster alive. Tension filled the space between them. "We'll be cautious, right?"

"Absolutely." He started the car. "We won't spend the night on the boat. We'll get a motel near the airport."

"Good."

Dusk was falling when they arrived at the marina. Kane turned off the engine. "Stay here. I won't be long."

"No." Carleen followed him out of the car. "I'm coming with you. I can keep a watch out while you pack."

Shadows had begun to fall across the docks, and a breeze was rising, tossing whitecaps against the creaking wood. Boats slapped their bumpers, stretched their mooring ropes and filled the night air with spooky sounds that raised goose bumps on her arms and legs.

She stayed close to Kane, her nerves jangling, as they hurried to *Footloose* and scrambled aboard. When Kane started to unlock the glass door, he frowned, his hand freezing on the key. The door was no longer locked. He whispered, "Someone's broken in. Wait here."

Carleen's pulse joggled, but her limbs felt leaden. Unmovable. Her breath froze. Kane disappeared inside the boat. It seemed an hour, but he was back in seconds.

"Whoever it was has come and gone." He pulled her inside, closed and locked the door, and doused the inside lights. "Keep an eye out. I'll hurry."

Carleen did as directed. Taking deep breaths to calm her trembling body, she scanned the docks and neighboring boats for anything or anyone out of place or acting suspicious.

Below deck, she heard Kane opening and closing closets and drawers, rushing as though he, too, sensed the wind telling them to *Hurry! Hurry!*

Minutes later he rejoined her, a single duffel bag in tow. "Let's get out of here."

Kane locked the boat, scanned the marina, then helped her to the dock. They started for the parking lot. Carleen felt clammy, jumpy.

A light glowed from inside the marina office, and she could see Maude talking to a man. Carleen's pulse tripped, her heart climbing into her throat. Could the man be someone sent by Skip?

As they came abreast of the office door, it swung open. Carleen let out a small scream.

But it was only Maude. The man behind her was the one who'd been with Kane at the gas dock that morning: Maude's husband, Pop. Relief flushed Carleen's veins.

Maude eyed her appraisingly. "Well, now. You cleaned up real nice, missy."

"Thank you," Carleen managed, her breath returning slowly.

Maude switched her gaze to Kane. "Captain K, some

gent called askin' 'bout you an hour or so ago. I tol' him your trip to The Keys was on hold and that you'd likely be home this evenin'. Said he was an old friend, but he wouldn't leave no number.''

Kane nodded. "We won't be aboard the boat tonight. And I don't have any 'old friends' who won't leave their phone numbers, Maude. So, if you notice *anyone* hanging around or any suspicious lights or anything like that near *Footloose,* call the cops.''

"You got it. The outer gate'll be locked. But Pop and me'll keep a lookout all the same." She glanced at Carleen. "You think the guy who called was the one gave you that shiner?''

"Maybe." Carleen glanced away, resisting the impulse to touch her sore eye.

Maude asked Kane, "Where you two gonna be?''

"It's better if you don't know," he said. "We don't know yet, either.''

THE MOTEL WAS BLOCKS from the airport. Kane signed a phony name in the register and paid cash. Their room was on the first floor of a two-story *L*-shaped building. It had the standard motel decor, television, phone, tiny bathroom and two queen-size beds. It was a "nonsmoking" room, but stank of stale cigarettes.

"I'll take this bed," he said, choosing the one nearest the door. He dropped his duffel bag on the floor, stealthily checked the parking lot one more time, then shut and locked the door. He pulled the curtains closed, but peered out through the edge, fearing whoever was aboard his boat had lain in wait and followed them.

No one seemed to be watching their room. He released the curtains.

In the bedside lamplight, Carleen looked pale and vulnerable. Frightened. He damned himself a fool for wanting to pull her into his arms. Even if he deserved to, even if she'd allow it, he didn't trust himself to stop at comforting her. He'd hurt her. She'd hurt him. She didn't love him. How long before he understood that? Accepted that?

Maybe the only thing they would ever share again was their son.

If he really was Jamie's father. The possibility threatened to overwhelm him. He couldn't deal with it. Not without knowing for certain. Couldn't speculate, couldn't hope or plan or even embrace the wonder of being a father.

And what if he was? Could he bear having to interact for the rest of his life with this woman he still wanted with every ounce of his being? This woman who didn't love him?

"I—I'm going to shower," she said. She gathered her new clothing packages and retreated to the bathroom.

As the shower started, Kane jerked back the bedspread and dropped onto the firm mattress, clothes, shoes and all. He wanted to be ready for whatever the night might bring courtesy of Skip.

Nerves raw, he turned out the reading lamp and rolled to his side, his back to the bathroom door. He didn't want Carlie any more ill at ease than she already was, sharing this room with him. Never mind that just the sound of the water running was driving *him* nuts, his memories playing havoc with his need to stay alert to the danger that might lurk just outside this room.

His desire, a rock-hard ache, had him shifting uncomfortably in his jeans. He closed his eyes and saw her, rubbing soap over every luscious curve, every secret hol-

Little Boy Lost

low. The image increased his sweet agony, and he longed to join her.

But the thought of Skip touching her, making love to her, cooled the longing, riveting him to his bed.

The bathroom door opened. He heard her move quietly across the room; the subtle aroma of her new perfume drifted to him. He feigned sleep. But his throat closed as desire reawakened in him. His mind, unrelenting, dredged reminiscences of bittersweet moments, of pleasure and passion.

Her bedsprings squeaked, and she whispered, "Good night."

Kane didn't answer. He was afraid that if he took an opening, he'd take advantage of the situation, of this woman who'd haunted his dreams, who owned his regrets. How many nights had he longed to share her bed? To touch her naked body? To taste her? Feel her? Smell her? Make love to her? How many nights would he ache for a woman who had married another man? How many nights would her loving lies haunt him? What price had they all paid for his walking out on her?

He forced his mind elsewhere. He had to stay alert. Focused.

Soon her even breathing told him she had fallen asleep. He tried doing the same. He lay there, jolting at every creak of the building, at the occasional voice outside during the night, at every car headlight that passed through the parking lot. He got up and prowled the room, rechecked the door locks. Lay down again.

In the early hours of the morning, Carlie moaned softly, whimpering in her sleep. He turned in her direction, barely able to make out her face in the light filtering through a crack in the curtains. Was she dreaming about the hellish week she'd spent at the hands of her unknown captors? Or about Jamie?

The ball of hurt and confusion he'd wrestled with for hours clenched inside Kane. Maybe it was his lack of sleep, or maybe it was the old hurt over Carlie's betrayal with Skip. Whatever it was, he was suddenly awash in anger. If Jamie was his son, why hadn't she told him after Skip found out the truth? By then, she knew where he was. So why, during the two months she'd been divorced, hadn't she at least phoned him and leveled with him?

Chapter Seven

The plane lifted off at sunrise. Carleen knew she looked more put together than she felt. For all of her outer calm, her stomach churned with one acidic roll after another. Kane seemed unaware, introspective, his expression dark and shuttered. She could only guess at his thoughts; he wasn't sharing. He huddled in his window seat, pulled his baseball cap low over his brow, leaned his head into the pillow the flight attendant had provided and went promptly to sleep.

It reminded her that there were more ways of deserting someone than physically leaving. Granted, he'd agreed to help Jamie and her, but just how much she could depend on him remained to be seen. When she again had custody of her son, would Kane consider his obligation to her and Jamie over and done? Or would he make a good father, the kind of father neither he nor she had known, a man devoted to his child?

Would he be any more capable of commitment now than he'd been four years ago? Not to her, but to the child he'd fathered? She asked nothing for herself, wanted nothing for herself. A relationship with Kane was all-consuming, and she would not lose herself to any man again. She'd done that twice in her young life—three times, she supposed. First with her passion for Kane, second by marrying a violent control freak and third by allowing herself to remain vulnerable to that same madman.

On all counts, Jamie had suffered for her weakness of character. She couldn't let him down a fourth time. But how was she going to explain Kane to her three-year-old?

She glanced at Kane as he slept, her gaze going to his full mouth. An unbidden longing swept her, rousing such honeyed memories that tendrils of need stirred and teased. She tensed, forcing the yearnings aside with an effort. She couldn't bring herself to look away from him, couldn't bring herself to quell the sensuous shiver that only this man's passion had ever awakened in her—passion and such heartache.

Her breath felt heavy passing through her slightly parted lips. No, she expected nothing from Kane for herself. Jamie, however, would need him desperately in the future. Kane's soft snore reinforced her certainty that even if she did want more, she'd receive nothing other than help from him. He hadn't even cared about her enough to stay awake.

A thought struck her. Maybe he was just exhausted. *She* hadn't stayed alert most of the night worrying about Skip's hired killers. No, she'd dropped into a heavy sleep and had had nightmares about them. But Kane wouldn't have done that. She glanced at him. Even beneath the shadow of his cap she could see the dark smudges underscoring his eyes. He'd likely slept little, if at all, during the night.

The realization eased her anger at him. They'd awoken unharmed. Also undiscovered? Or had someone found them, and followed them aboard this plane? The acid in her gut roiled. God, why did Kane have to sleep?

The flight attendant interrupted her dark musings with an offer of breakfast. She accepted a cup of coffee, bagel and cream cheese. Anything to pass the time, perhaps still the nerves in her stomach. What she really wanted was Kane's warm hand on hers, reassuring her that Skip's henchmen were not on this plane, telling her she wasn't alone...as he had done yesterday.

What had changed during the night that she felt such cool indifference in him? She had a niggling fear she knew exactly what it was.

She ate without tasting, noticing only that the coffee was hot and bracing, the bagel dry. They filled her stomach, but added to her discomfort. Abandoned to an over-full tummy and to dealing with her worries by herself, Carleen found the flight the longest two-and-a-half hours of her life.

They arrived at SeaTac International to a morning of dark, unrelenting rain. Awake, Kane remained aloof, alert, every move and action calculated and cautious. All warmth had vanished from his demeanor. Carleen decided he'd open whatever can of worms he was sitting on in his own good time. She wasn't a chatterer when nervous, but grew quiet and withdrawn. He seemed not to notice.

The heavy rain continued through their drive to downtown Seattle, on the ferry ride to Bainbridge Island, throughout their trek across the Hood Canal Bridge and on to Port Luster.

The oppressive weather punctuated the gloomy silence that rode with them in their rented SUV. She knew Kane must have a million questions for her, but he asked none. She sensed he distrusted her on levels that strangely paralleled her own distrust of him. She also knew they were going to have to bridge that gap of trust if they were to help their son. But she could think of nothing to say to lead the way, nothing to assuage the resentments he had to be feeling, nothing to dispel the grievances she harbored. So the silence endured.

Kane slowed the vehicle and turned off Highway 104 onto the road that led in to Port Luster. The downpour had turned to a misty drizzle, patches of fog rising out of nowhere, swallowing them, then disappearing a few blocks later.

The misery of the day mirrored that in Carleen's heart. She wrung her hands in her lap. It felt as if she'd been away from this town for a year, instead of eight days. But the closer she came to her son, the more hope nibbled away her desolation. *Soon, Jamie, soon.*

As much to break the stilted quiet between them as anything, she said, "It's an awful day for a funeral. Wil would have hated it."

Kane ignored the mention of his uncle. He glanced left and right as they passed long-standing landmarks— McCray's Marine Works, Brison's Boatbuilders, Schuler's Radiators. "Place hasn't changed a whit in four years." Disdain laced his statement. "Makes a person wonder why anyone stays here."

She glanced sharply at him. Had he any good memories of this town? Or were they all awful? Painful? Resentments, old and new, were easily read in the taut lines at his mouth, at the corners of his eyes. Wil's death, her sudden appearance and the revelations she'd laid on him had obviously ripped open ancient wounds and created fresh heartaches and hurt.

Until now, she hadn't considered the cost he'd been willing to pay by agreeing to help Jamie and her. Contrition pricked her conscience. What about Kane's demons? What bothered him most about Port Luster? Wil? Skip? His aunt Frances? Her? A combination of all of them? "Do you despise this town and its people?"

He gazed at her. "Not all of its people."

She cringed inwardly at his brooding look. Would she find her name on the list of those he despised? Except for how that would affect Jamie, did she care?

No. And yet, she felt a twinge of regret at the thought that he hated her. She shook it off. He wasn't the only one with two such lists. She'd stayed here when things were bad, then worse; stayed and braved the looks, the gossip, the mean-spiritedness. Eventually, she'd earned the respect of the worst of them. Somehow that had been important to her. Somehow, Kane hadn't been able to do that.

Or was it that he hadn't needed to do that?

She blinked, considering. Was that one of the reason's she'd married Skip? To show the town she had overcome every rotten thing life had thrown at her and nabbed the golden son? The possibility rattled Carleen to her toes. Had she been that shallow? That desperate to rise above her childhood? That needy?

God help her, she had. *Oh, Jamie, I'm so sorry.* Tears filled her eyes, not from self-pity or self-recrimination, but for the child, her little boy, whom she'd harmed in ways she might never be able to mend.

The road crested, then slanted downward straight into the city center. Below, the main commerce buildings, mostly brick, hugged Port Luster Bay. After being in San Diego and Seattle, driving into this old town was like stepping back in time into a Victorian seaport. On a clear day, the view was breathtaking—shimmering blue water spreading in every direction as far as the eye could see, with Vancouver Island, Canada, across the Straits of Juan De Fuca.

But now, what water they could see through the drizzly mist that shrouded the quaint shops and eateries churned black, choppy with white c▯▯s. Carleen hugged herself against a sudden, fierce chill, as Kane drove down the main street. Despite the darkened windows in their vehicle, she feared someone would glance their way, recognize them. But few people occupied the sidewalks. Those who did had their heads ducked against the wind and rain.

Kane stared straight ahead. "Why did you wait until now to tell me about Jamie?"

The question rang with hurt, startling Carleen out of her own dreary musings. Her palms were instantly damp. This was the question she'd feared, the one thing she knew had to be eating at him. Why hadn't she contacted him about Jamie any time since Skip had learned he wasn't the boy's father? After all, Kane had sent her a postcard with his address and the name of his new business on it, eliminating her excuse that she didn't know where to find him. So, why had she not contacted him even then?

If only it had been that simple. She wasn't sure he'd understand. She drew a bracing breath. "I was afraid of Skip. He'd made me promise not to tell a soul he wasn't Jamie's father. And more than anyone else, that meant you."

"So, if this present situation hadn't arisen, you weren't ever going to tell me."

It wasn't a question, but a bitter lash of anger. Her heart clutched. "No, Kane, that's not true. I was bringing Jamie to San Diego the morning I was abducted. We were coming to find you, to tell you."

"Why should I believe that?" He glanced at her, and she saw the wariness in his eyes. "Does Jamie know I'm his father?"

"Well, no, not yet." She twisted her hands tighter in her lap.

"When had you planned to tell him?"

Her flesh burned as if from a slap. When had she meant to tell Jamie? On the plane? In a motel room? "I...I... Sometime before we got to you."

He made a derisive noise and turned his attention back to the road.

"I couldn't just leave town. Skip kept a close watch on the house I was renting. As long as I appeared to go along with his wishes, I knew he wouldn't catch on. But for the last two months I was executing my plan. I needed enough cash to make credit cards unnecessary. He might trace my whereabouts through those. So, I scrimped and saved and eventually had enough to buy Jamie and myself airline tickets to San Diego."

She released a taut breath. "I don't know why, but recently I felt such an urgency to get on my way that I ignored my better judgment and risked something that was likely my undoing.

"I needed more money. I convinced Bernie Fritz to buy an expensive ring Wil had given me to celebrate Jamie's birth. Bernie must have told Skip. I was on my way to Fritz's Jewelry Emporium—the last thing I needed to do, I remember, before heading to the airport. Then, something must have happened—and I was abducted."

Kane's expression remained dark. "You could have called me. I was in the San Diego phone book."

"I couldn't tell you about Jamie over the phone." She leaned toward him. "I hadn't kept your postcard. Didn't commit it to memory. I dared not risk Skip finding it. Or finding out that I'd heard from you. Knew where you were.''

She stared hard at his profile, willing him to understand, seeking any sign of softening in his expression, his body. None appeared. Her throat tightened with anger. He wasn't the only injured party in this mess. ''At the time you wrote, Skip didn't...well, I couldn't tell you about Jamie then.''

''Because Skip didn't know he hadn't fathered the boy? Would you have gone on keeping the lie—if Skip hadn't found out the truth?''

Would she have? Carleen couldn't be sure, but she didn't like the slimy feeling in the pit of her stomach that question caused. ''I didn't know I was pregnant until after I'd married Skip. Then, yes, I was stuck. Trapped by the awful lie. What would you have done in my situation?''

He turned toward her then, his gaze piercing, his mouth so tight the words could barely slip out. ''I wouldn't have lied.''

''I didn't lie to you.''

He didn't say it, but she knew from his expression that he was thinking, *A lie of omission is still a lie.*

Carleen fumed, her temper as fierce as the white caps in the bay. He didn't understand. Might never understand. Well, he didn't have to. As long as he didn't desert Jamie, he could remain as angry with her as he liked. She was even more angry at him.

As the SUV curved through the end of the shops and started up a steep slope, the silence returned. Carleen sank deeper into her seat, grappling with her ire, hating this mess. Hating that this man made her feel defensive when *he'd* committed the most serious offense by walking out. If not for that, maybe none of this would have happened, maybe her baby wouldn't be scared right now.

Jamie. The Ellison estate loomed ahead. Firs barricaded it from view on the side that bordered the road, hiding it from the outside world, keeping Jamie in, keeping her out. As they skirted the property, she spied the mansion's turrets and its widow's walk above the trees, and felt at that moment as though it were a touchstone.

I'm here, Jamie. We'll be together soon, baby. Soon.

Once again she wondered how she was going to explain all she had to tell the boy. How much would he understand? He'd had so much emotional upheaval in his young life already. But he wasn't the only one who would have a lot to deal with. The Ellisons were in for a real shock. A horrid scandal. And worse. Skip would go to jail for what he'd done to her.

And Jamie would need protecting from all of it. Could she and Kane manage that if they stayed at loggerheads with one another? Again, she realized she must find a way past the old resentments. They *had* to be able to work together.

"Where were you and Jamie living when you were abducted?" Kane asked, shattering her thoughts.

She shook herself, glad for the interruption, glad he was speaking to her again without the rancor of a moment ago, glad to discover her own anger abating. "I'm renting a house off Kendall, on Stone. The second to the last house on the left."

"Would any of your neighbors have seen the abduction?"

"I don't know." She hadn't thought of that. "I doubt it. My neighbor on the right is an old woman who is nearly deaf. The other is a couple who work at a restaurant that serves only breakfast and lunch. They work very early in the morning until about three every afternoon. And there's nothing but empty lots on the opposite side of the street.''

"Just the same, we should ask. Maybe one of them reported it to the police.''

Carleen laughed snidely. "Skip would have curtailed any such report to the police. He'd just have my stand-in claim the report was false.''

"Maybe. But it's something to check out.''

Kane drove down Stone, a neighborhood of quarter-acre lots, the houses all old, built in the forties or fifties. The yards were well-tended; a couple of the homes needed painting.

He slowed the car as she pointed out her small two-bedroom clapboard with the detached garage. It was gray with white trim and in this drizzle looked sad and abandoned. He pulled to a stop next to the empty lot directly across from the house. Carleen gasped at the For Lease sign in the front yard.

Kane let out a low whistle of astonishment. "They cleared you out lock, stock and barrel. I'll be damned.''

I'll be damned. The words rang in Carleen's head as if from some great distance. *I'll be damned.* Her temples began to pound with pain and she shut her eyes, gripping her skull on either side. Suddenly she was back on that early morning eight days ago, hearing the motor of a strange vehicle pull to a stop behind her car. Carleen was in the back buckling Jamie into his car seat. She'd glanced out the rear window. A van. The lettering on the side was the logo of the local cable company. Two people sat in the front.

A woman leaped out of the passenger side. She was taller than Carleen by a good three inches and had the build of someone fanatical about her body. Her raven hair was pulled to the nape and caught in a rubber band, bangs poking from beneath her baseball cap. And she carried a clipboard as she came toward Carleen, spouting some garbage about answering a call for a problem with Carleen's cable hookup.

Carleen finished with Jamie and closed the back door of the Lexus, straightening. Before she could tell the woman that she hadn't called anyone about her cable, the woman charged her, forcing a cloth over Carleen's mouth and nose. A sickeningly sweet stench filled her nostrils. She struggled against her attacker. She heard Jamie screaming, "Mommy! Mommy!"

She had struggled harder then, managing to rip the cloth from her face. "I'll be damned!" the woman cried. "She's stronger than she looks. Don't just stand there, help me!"

Carleen had broken free. Yanked open the driver's door of the Lexus, scrambled onto the front seat.

Jamie cried, "Mommy! Mommy! Mommy!"

She'd reached out to him. Their fingers touched. Then she was jerked backward.

"Stop it, you bitch." This was a man, speaking to Carleen. The driver of the van. He'd come up behind her. She couldn't see his face. She kicked out blindly. The cloth came over her nose again. She made the mistake of gulping air, and moments later all went black.

She was shaking now. Kane had put the SUV in park, set the emergency brake. He was turned toward her, briskly buffeting her arms with his palms, speaking to her. "Carlie? What's wrong? Carlie?"

She met his concerned gaze. "There were at least two of them. A woman and a man." She related what she'd just remembered.

Kane clasped her icy hands in his warm ones. Big,

sturdy and work-roughened, his hands somehow conveyed a sense of trustworthiness that his touch hadn't had four years ago. Carleen yearned to fall against him, to feel his warmth engulfing her, chasing the chill from her body. But she knew better than to believe he was offering to hold her, comfort her as though they were still those long-ago lovers. Nor could she forget his desertion.

But more than that, she feared what she'd be encouraging if she gave in to her need to wallow in his embrace.

The knot in her throat grew, cutting off her very breath.

He asked, "Would you recognize either of them if you saw them again?"

"The woman."

"Coral Clayton?"

"That's as good a guess as any."

"What about the man?"

"I didn't see him. Just heard him."

"What about his voice? Was it familiar?"

She closed her eyes, listening to the voice again and again in her mind, able to hold the shudders at bay only because Kane's grip tightened on her hands.

Gazing up at him, she shook her head. "I'm not sure I'd recognize it if I heard it again."

A cold prickling touched the nape of her neck. She glanced quickly around. No one seemed to be lurking nearby, or staring at them from behind parted blinds. And yet, she felt as exposed on this street she'd once called home as she had yesterday in San Diego when they'd realized Skip might be hunting for her.

"Could we leave here, please? I'd rather no one noticed us and called the Ellisons. The biggest thing we have going for us at the moment is surprise."

Kane dropped her hands. He wrenched the brake loose and shifted into gear, grumbling, "Surprise."

Carleen knew he hated surprises. Hated lies. It was a trait they shared, a dislike burned into each of them from their earliest days. The last week had been too full of both surprises and lies. But the exposing had only just begun.

Kane glanced at her again. ''You're positive the man wasn't Skip?''

The man was as tall as Skip, but had he *been* Skip? She'd been so certain her ex-husband wouldn't dirty his own hands, but given his brutal treatment of her in the past…was it really that far-fetched?

Her heart was racing. She gazed up at Kane and shook her head. ''Maybe it was.''

Chapter Eight

Kane chose a motel on the outskirts of town. It was nearly empty, the tourist season over, and he had no trouble procuring a room in the back of the building, away from the street and prying eyes. He told Carlie, "It's the one at the end, next to the laundry room."

"One room?" Her eyebrows arched. "How did you register?"

"As Mr. and Mrs. Kane Kincaid." The fact that she might once have been his wife, the fact that she'd chosen his cousin over him instead, still cut Kane deep, and it had been with a trembling hand that he'd signed the register as he had. But the look of aversion in her liquid-green eyes—on hearing what he'd done—cut him deeper still.

He curbed a childish urge to lash out at her. She had every right not to want him. The least he could do was face her rejection with some shred of dignity. Besides, they needed to find a way past the anger and hurt, needed to work as a team. For Jamie's sake, as well as their own.

Determined to make the first move in that direction, he softened his tone. "You were in the car. I didn't know whether or not the motel manager had seen you, but in case she had, I couldn't risk registering as a single. Should I have asked for adjoining rooms?''

''No.'' Her protest was instant. ''No. I don't want my name in any register. Don't pay any attention to me. Skip has my nerves on edge. I don't want him to find out about this and turn it into something dirty.''

Kane nodded, realizing she was still shaken to the core by her sudden flash of memory, by her uncertainty about Skip's participation in her abduction, and by returning to Port Luster to find her home emptied, all of her belongings confiscated. Perhaps destroyed.

Kane reached to touch her hair, her arm, but resisted, tamping down his urge to connect with her physically, relinquishing his needs in lieu of hers. He swore silently and shoved his offending hand through his hair, glancing around, alert to anyone watching, more alert to the wishes of this susceptible woman. ''What do you want to do?''

She considered for a long moment, strain tightening her luscious mouth, drawing his gaze to the full ripeness of her lower lip. It raised an irrational desire in him to bend to her, to kiss her, hard and long, until the tension eased from her face, her limbs, and turned to something else, something hot and jolting, a connection deeper than flesh.

But his kiss was the last thing she would want. Why was it, the more vulnerability she showed, the less able he was to resist her? Damn it, anyway. Air seemed to leech from the car. He wanted out. Needed out. Had to move. To shake free of the trapped feeling that had seized him.

Carlie seemed not to notice. She stared at her hands, at her newly manicured nails. There was a tremor in her voice. ''I could register under my own name and ask for my own room, but until we've got the law after Skip, staying alone could prove too dangerous. I want to do the right thing for Jamie, but I have to also do what is right for me.'' She gazed up at him. ''For us.''

He nodded and thrust open the door, letting in the icy wind. It felt cool and welcome against his heated face. ''A united front, by all means.''

Kane handed Carlie the room key, then opened the back of the SUV and gathered their bags. Coming in behind her, he saw that the room was large, decorated in shades of blue and white and green, which gave it a cool feel and added to the chilliness in the air. There were two chairs shoved up to a round table, an entertainment center with built-in dresser and a single king-size bed.

His heart clutched at the sight of the lone bed. He said hoarsely, ''I'll sleep on the floor.''

''Don't be silly. It's November. You'd catch cold. Besides, God willing, we'll have Jamie and be on our way out of town by tonight.''

A steady rumbling shook the wall behind the bed. Carlie frowned. Kane grinned. ''Must be the ice machine. The manager said it was in the laundry room, along with a cola dispenser. Is it going to bother you?''

''No. We won't be here that long. And I don't want to change rooms. That would draw too much attention to us. It doesn't bother you, does it?''

''Not in the least.''

The ice machine rattled to a stop with a loud *bang*.

Kane and Carlie burst out laughing. He felt the tension in his neck break up and float off with the speed of the clouds passing across the stormy sky.

She said, ''It reminds me of that dilapidated Chevy you drove in high school.''

He grinned, recalling the 1956 two-door hardtop that would be a classic now and worth tons more than he'd gotten for it when he'd upgraded to a Toyota pickup. He tilted his head as it struck him that he hadn't even spoken to her during the time he'd owned that Chevy. When had she noticed him? And his car?

"It was paid for and it ran, if a little noisily, most of the time."

"It used to make the same kind of bang when you shut it off."

"Oh?" He grinned wider.

She seemed suddenly self-conscious, as if she feared he might question her further about what else she recalled of his car, and maybe him, in those bygone years. She said, "It's getting late. I'd better change."

She gathered the bag she'd purchased at the airport and headed into the bathroom.

Kane laid his suit out on the bed. Last time he'd worn this, he'd taken Gina to Old Town for dinner in a favorite Mexican restaurant. They'd ended their relationship that night. Amazing the change his life had taken in the few weeks since then.

No regrets. Not about Gina. Except perhaps for the time she'd wasted with him. She might have spent that time with someone who really loved her, someone who would build a future with her. That someone wasn't Kane.

Carlie emerged from the bathroom wearing the black pantsuit he'd purchased for her yesterday. It hugged her figure in a flattering, yet subtly seductive way, the color giving her skin a translucent creaminess. She'd fixed her hair into some sort of fancy braid with wispy curls feathering her face. She wore no jewelry; neither of them had thought to buy any. But Kane felt certain even diamond baubles would have been redundant on this jewel of a vision filling his eyes.

His pulse skipped, then sent blood thrumming through his veins. Desire surged beneath it, threatening to strip his self-imposed restraints and overpower him. Regrets, dear God, yes. Too many to name. He grabbed his clothes and travel kit. "I need to shower and shave."

CARLEEN PACED THE ROOM, restless, anxious to get to the church to see her son...and to face her nemesis. *He'd emptied her house.* The son of a bitch had cleaned out every stick of furniture, every stitch of clothing, every one of the seashells Jamie had gathered for her from their trips to the shore. She couldn't care less about furniture and clothing, but those seashells...

Tears stung her eyes. She dabbed them away with the heel of her hand. Damn Skip. He would not make her cry. But she wished he hadn't the power to frighten her still. Did he already know she was in town? Cold slathered the base of her spine.

She stole to the windows and pulled aside the closed drapes. Aside from their SUV, two other vehicles stood in the parking lot, both bearing out-of-state license plates. Both had already been there when she and Kane had arrived.

Wind sent leaves flurrying across the damp tarmac, but the sky seemed lighter, the rain less threatening. She dropped the curtain and rechecked her hair and makeup in the mirror above the round table, then began pacing anew.

The sound of the water running in the bathroom filled her ears. She closed her eyes, trying to shut out the visions of Kane naked beneath that misty shower, but the visions resisted her efforts, plying her with images fresh from her memory banks, his body so familiar, so indelibly imprinted on her brain, so missed. And now a new element was added: speculation of the changes four years had wrought, of the new planes and definitions age and the outdoors had used to sculpt and enhance his physique.

The embers of that old passion—the passion she kept denying, kept trying to squelch—stirred with renewed energy, intent on driving other concerns and worries from her thoughts. Damn. Here was the danger of this passion she felt for Kane, the passion that wouldn't die, the passion she could barely hold at bay.

She couldn't allow this all-consuming desire for him to wash out even one of her concerns and cares as though nothing in the world but the two of them mattered. She sank onto the bed. She would not risk Jamie's welfare. Not for anyone or anything.

The phone rang. Carleen jumped, staring at it as though in a face-off with some deadly creature. Who knew Kane was in town? Who knew already? Shivers flushed her skin. Did this caller also know *she* was here?

Hesitantly, she lifted the receiver, held it to her ear and mumbled, ''Yes?''

''If you want to see your son again, don't show up at the old man's funeral.'' The voice was eerie. Disguised. Disembodied. Like something from her lost week. Something from her nightmares.

But how had the caller known *she* would answer the phone? It was as though he could see her. Her pulse tripped unevenly. She jerked around. Her gaze darted across the wall behind the bed—the wall between this room and the laundry room. Goose bumps covered every inch of her. Was someone in there, watching her?

''Who is this?'' she snapped, hysteria gripping her belly. ''Skip?''

Fiendish laughter was her only answer. It seemed to come from some great distance, definitely not the next room. Fury and relief flashed through her. "You tell my ex-husband he's going to pay if he harms Jamie." There was no response, and her anger mounted. "Coward."

Another chilling laugh burst down the line. "Stay away from the funeral, or you and your brat will both be sorry."

"No." Carleen gasped. Heat and anger drained from her, collapsing her, pulling her in on herself. "No, don't hurt Jamie. Please, don't hurt Jamie—"

But the line had gone dead. Carleen couldn't move. She clutched the receiver so tightly her hand ached, and the icy cold she'd felt yesterday returned, making her insides shake hard enough that her teeth rattled.

The ice maker started again. Its chugging motor beat like the pain at her temples. Kane emerged from the bathroom, as handsome as an Adonis as he buttoned the cuffs of his starchy white dress shirt, his hair a mass of damp golden curls, his jaw clean and slightly shiny. The details clicked into her head as though of tantamount importance—when they mattered not at all.

Kane scowled and mouthed, *Who is it?*

But she couldn't answer. Couldn't move.

He rushed to her and uncurled her fingers from around the receiver. "Who is this?"

He slammed down the phone. "Who was it? Skip? Your kidnappers?"

She didn't answer, couldn't move her mouth. Every part of her felt frozen. He pulled her into his arms. "It's okay, love."

She warmed only because she felt safe in his arms, safe as if nothing could touch her or hurt her. The sensation was odd, unfamiliar, something she hadn't felt four years ago in Kane's embrace. Barely able to register this curiosity, she noticed something more: his warmth was thawing the frozen chill that had grabbed her.

Feeling her strength returning she whispered, "Someone called."

"Who? Skip?" He asked the questions in a softer tone this time. "One of your abductors?"

"I don't know. Probably."

"How did he know you were here?"

She shook her head. "This town is like that."

Kane swore long and hard.

His fury called back her own. Bolstered by it, she related the whole conversation. "I have to do what he said. I can't risk Jamie's welfare. I won't. I can't go to Wil's funeral."

"I won't leave you here alone."

"You must. You have to go. Have to make sure Jamie is okay. Please, do this for him. For me."

"I don't want to leave you here alone."

"We don't have a choice." She pleaded for his understanding. "I'll be fine. No one is going to come after me here. There are other guests, witnesses not under Skip's control. It would be too risky."

"I don't like this, Carlie." Kane shook his head, his eyes steely with conviction. "I can't take Jamie from Skip without you."

"I'm not asking you to do that. Just make sure Jamie is unharmed. I have to *know* that. We'll wait until the mourners are at the mansion to claim him. I'll confront Skip there and demand he turn Jamie over to us. That will be less traumatic for Jamie than snatching him in front of all those grown-ups and strangers at the church or cemetery."

"Okay. But only if we compromise." Kane reached for the tie he'd left on the bed. "I'll forgo the ceremony at the church. I'll attend the graveside services. I'll stay only as long as it takes to assure myself that Jamie isn't in any physical danger.''

And to ask Skip what he thinks he's pulling.

"KEEP THIS DOOR LOCKED, Carlie, and the drapes pulled shut.'' Kane instructed. "That way, it will look like no one is here.''

"Believe me, caution has become a way of life. I won't open the door to anyone but you.'' She gently pushed him outside. "I promise.''

But even hearing the locks click into place did nothing to ease Kane's worry. He climbed into the SUV and started the engine, but before backing out of his parking spot, he checked the clock, then scanned the motel, each door, every window, and the other two cars. Nothing seemed amiss, but his nerves felt as raw as open wounds. He didn't like leaving her here alone. Vulnerable. Didn't like it at all.

But he'd promised her he'd go...to check on Jamie. He shifted into gear and headed out. The rain had stopped; the wind seemed to be dying, too, as though the grand man, Wilcox Ellison himself, had pulled a few strings in heaven for a reprieve in the nasty weather. Kane muttered, "I would have bet you were in hell, old man.''

He glanced at the dashboard clock, too aware of every minute and every turn of the tires that took him farther from Carlie. He slowed as the Episcopalian Church came into view. The parking lot was empty, the services over, the mourners either on their way, or already at, the cemetery that occupied one of the best view lots on Hill Road, half a mile beyond the Ellison mansion.

Kane drove down the main street of town again. The

improved weather had shoppers and sightseers out in droves. Or maybe it was the parade of mourners that had brought them out to stare and gape, to mill about like gossips at backyard fences.

Whatever the cause, they made maneuvering the street a work in caution that grated his frayed nerves and aggravated his need for speed.

But finally, he was passing the Ellison estate and could see the black wrought-iron fence surrounding the cemetery. The huge gates hung open on blacktopped pavement that wound through the graves as lean and respectful as a black armband; two black limousines headed the caravan of cars lining most of it.

Kane parked the SUV on the street and entered the gates. He guessed most of the town was in attendance, crowded near the twin tents. *EL* was the city's largest employer and the reason for most of the tourism. The least of what Port Luster residents owed the man and his family was respect.

And they were paying it.

The large crowd was surprisingly hushed: a cough here, a sniffle there, a few hearty sobs. Kane skirted the crowd, trudging through wet grass toward the front, where the grieving family sat.

No one glanced at him with more than a quick flick of their eyes—no one he recognized, no one who seemed to know him or even wonder who he was. He felt anonymous. Invisible. He liked the feeling. But knew it couldn't last. He needed to use these precious few moments sizing up the situation, studying his adversaries. Plenty of time after the minister finished for confrontations.

Squeezing between two women, he found a good spot to observe the family without being noticed. There they were. His mother's relatives, her older sister Frances and her two grown children, the only living souls he was sure he was related to. The nerves in his gut bit deeper.

His gaze centered on his aunt, Wil's widow. Frances Ellison had always reminded him of a precious piece of furniture wrapped in plastic, strictly to look at, not to touch. Her father, his grandfather, had loaned Wil Ellison the money to start *EL*.

Frances was royalty in this town. She sat in the folding chair as though seated on a throne, her frail, queenly shoulders squared, her gloved hands folded in her lap, her upturned mouth set as though frozen in a secret smile, her white hair a crown atop her head, and the thoughts behind her gray eyes as impenetrable as a fortress.

Starla was seated next to her mother. Skip's twin sister had none of her mother's affectations. Like Wil, she was lean and loose-boned, her own person, willing to defy conventions in lieu of her own ego. Grief had her hunched over, wiping at her eyes with a hankie that might have belonged to her father. Her face was as pale as her iced-blond hair.

Skip and Starla were a month older than Kane. While Skip had always been jealous of Kane, Star had always been decent to him. Did she know what Skip had done? Was she part of it?

He glanced at his wristwatch. He'd been gone less than twenty minutes. Was Carlie still okay? Nagging worry jacked up his need for action. He shifted his weight, craning his neck until he caught sight of Jamie. Wedged between Skip and Starla, the boy seemed too little for the grief and confusion on his tiny face. He was rubbing his chin as he'd done on the newscast.

Kane's chest squeezed. Jamie's red hair had been slicked down and combed into place, but he could see a

cowlick in the front trying to defy good grooming. Freckles bridged the boy's button nose. He was the spitting
image of his mother, right down to her big emerald eyes.
He looked so sad, so frightened, so lonely. Kane longed
to cut through the crowd and swoop him up and hug him
close. He felt such empathy with this child, such a connection with him. Was it because he was looking at his
son? Or was it because he knew too well what the kid
was going through, knew too well how it felt to be a little
boy without a mother?

God, how well he knew that feeling.

Fearing he'd be consumed by Jamie's sadness and
need and his own bitter memories, Kane shook himself
and forced his gaze to the man holding the child's hand.
Skip.

His cousin appeared as cool as a blue-ice sculpture,
sleek, clean, handsome and chiseled, all the edges shaved
smooth. If he was grieving for his father, it wasn't apparent.

Next to Skip was the woman Kane had come to see in
person, an elegantly dressed redhead, her face half hidden
by the lacy veil of her hat. A chill crept up his spine. If
he didn't know he'd just left her in the motel, he'd think
he was looking at Carlie.

His gaze jumped back to Skip. Did he know the
woman was an imposter? Or was he being duped? No.
Skip had Jamie. He was the only one who could have
had Carlie's house cleaned out. He was as guilty as sin.
But what all was he guilty of?

The minister finished. The family rose, the crowd began to disperse, and a few stragglers offered last-minute
condolences to the Ellisons.

Kane held back, then stepped forward at the last possible minute, ever aware of time slipping away, of Carlie

alone and vulnerable in the motel room. His aunt caught sight of him first. Her mouth puckered as though something sour nestled her inner cheek, but she was too aware of her breeding, too secure of the position she'd created for herself in this town, to fear him. He was nothing more than an annoyance she'd dealt with and dismissed four years ago.

She lifted her brows and composed her expression. "Kane. Wilcox would have been touched that you cared enough to show your respects for him."

"I'm not here because of Wil," Kane said pointedly.

"Well, isn't that just like you," Frances retorted, disdain flashing in her eyes. She'd never forgiven him for suggesting that her husband had had an affair with her younger sister around the same time he'd gotten *her* pregnant with Skip and Starla.

Skip caught sight of Kane then. An expression of surprise crossed his face. It was so perfect, so calculated, it stank of practice, as did the smooth, glad-to-see-you, hate-your-guts smile. "Kane. This is unexpected. And damn good of you."

"We need to talk," Kane told him. "Alone."

"Sounds serious." Skip looked interested, guileless, as though he hadn't a clue what this could concern.

"You know it *is* serious."

Skip lifted his hands, palms out, in an *I surrender* gesture and shook his head. Fire flashed in his anemic, cold blue eyes. "I don't need your bull today, pally. I'm burying my dad here. Or hadn't you noticed?"

"I noticed."

"Then show some respect. My dad treated you like a son. Have you forgotten?"

"No. I haven't forgotten anything."

"Well, this isn't the place."

"Hello, Kane." The Carlie impersonator greeted him with such stark openness that anyone watching would assume they knew one another. She moved to Skip's side and slid her arm through his. Her voice was not quite Carlie's, but enough like it that most people wouldn't detect the difference. She tipped her head the same way, moved her hands similarly, and she was wearing a huge diamond-and-emerald ring that might be the one Carlie had told him about.

"Do I know you?" Kane asked her.

She pulled in a sharp breath as though he'd offended her. Beneath the veil, she blinked hard. "Are you joking?"

"No," Kane said. "Who are you?"

The Carlie imposter sniffed.

"This isn't funny, Kane." Skip huffed.

"Especially not today," the strange woman said, managing to reprimand him while sounding hurt at the same time.

Starla and Frances had stopped their trek to the first of the waiting limousines. Neither spoke, but they watched silently from a few feet away.

"Come on, Carleen." Skip spun away from Kane, taking the woman with him. "Son." He grabbed Jamie by the hand and tugged him toward Frances. Kane was relieved that he could assure Carlie her son was in no physical harm from the Ellison clan. None he could detect, anyway.

The little boy glanced up at Kane, and for a split second their gazes connected. Kane felt a *zing* of pity and something deeper grab his heart. Did the child feel it, too—this indefinable, undeniable familiarity of spirit, of soul, of blood?

Kane shivered as though the wind had suddenly re-vived. He took a step toward Jamie, wanting to touch him, needing physical evidence that he wasn't imaging this consuming sensation. Jamie took a step toward him. Kane stopped short, such fear in his heart that he thought it might stop beating. Once before, he'd felt this same kind of inexplicable connection. With his Uncle Wil. That had proven false. He realized he couldn't bear it if this one was also fraudulent, based only on his secret knowledge, on his growing desire to be this child's daddy. Hell, was there even such a thing as a father-and-son bond—a bond that no amount of environmental influence could obscure?

Skip stepped between Jamie and Kane. "Mother, take Jamie home. And son, stop rubbing your chin. It's starting to look like you have a rash." He handed Jamie over to his mother and told her, "Carleen and I will use the second limo."

Frances hustled Jamie toward the first limousine. Starla lifted one brow, but Kane couldn't guess what she was thinking. How much did she know? All of it? None of it? Frances called over her shoulder, "Starla, we have guests waiting."

Starla nodded, pressed the man's hankie to her eyes, and followed her mother and Jamie. Kane hustled after Skip and the faux Carlie. He called, "Skip."

His cousin ground to a stop and whispered something to the woman. She scurried off toward the first limo. Skip Ellison pivoted, his expression as stormy as the day. "You know, pally, you never did have any idea of timing. What is it that can't wait until tomorrow?"

"Spare me the innocent act, Skip. I know that woman isn't Carlie. I know you had Carlie abducted. Planned her murder. And I know that you know she's alive and well—here in Port Luster with me."

Skip chortled coldly. "I don't know who that—who you have at the…Bayside View Motel, but she's not Carleen. You're the one who is delusional."

"It was *you* on the phone." Kane wanted to throttle this man. Pushing Carlie's buttons, making her worry about her son. Hell, he'd played right into Skip's hands by leaving her alone. "If you've touched her, I swear, I'll kill you."

Skip glanced at the startled faces of a couple making their way to one of the graves with a bouquet of pink carnations. "Did you hear that? This man is off his rocker."

Kane ignored the odd looks of the couple and raced to the SUV. He made an illegal U-turn. Horns blared as he passed a line of cars on the shoulder. He slowed his speed through town, his heart tearing with panic. He took the corner around the motel on two wheels, squealing to a stop at the room he shared with Carlie.

He flew out of the SUV. "Carlie!"

He was two feet from the door when he saw that it was ajar. His heart clambered into his throat. His breath clogged. God, why had he left her alone? He slammed into the room. "Carlie?"

The room had been turned upside down. Sheets and blankets were ripped from the bed. Their two bags were dumped, their clothes strewn everywhere. His feet hit something slick. A puddle. Dark and damp. *Blood?* He dropped the SUV keys. "Carlie?"

She was gone. His stomach flopped. Bile burned his throat. Spread across his tongue. He'd promised Carlie he'd keep her safe. Instead, he'd let Skip abduct her a second time. "Dear God, Carlie. What have I done?"

Chapter Nine

"Oh, Carlie!" Kane wailed and buried his head in his hands. The ice maker in the room next door rumbled, its steady *clickety-clack* chiding him for leaving her alone. The weight of his guilt pulled him down; both knees landed hard against the damp carpet.

Wetness soaked into his slacks and jerked his attention to the brown spot. Gingerly, he pressed his fingers into it. It felt sticky, and the scent was sweet and familiar. He rubbed his fingers in it again and sniffed again.

What the hell was that smell? Fear stifled his senses. Glowering, he smeared his palm through the damp spot, then sucked in a deep breath. Finally, it came to him.

Not blood. Cola. The relief feathering through him was short-lived. So what if Carlie hadn't been wounded? She'd still been nabbed. And he knew as sure as he knew his name that unless he found her soon, she'd be killed.

The thought wrenched him to his feet. Where had she been taken? His mind scrambled over ideas. The plant? Yeah, maybe there. It would likely be empty today, all employees of *EL* having been given a few days off to mark the founder's death. Or maybe her vacated rental house? No, the neighbors might report suspicious comings and goings to the landlord. Skip wouldn't risk that.

The plant, then. He raced out to the SUV. But the keys were missing from the ignition. Good God, what had he done with them? He dug into his pockets and came up empty-handed. He swore and banged back to the room. His pulse throbbed in his throat. *Where the hell were the keys?* Had he dropped them?

The mess in the room assailed him again. This time it also stopped him cold. Why, if they'd come only for Carlie, had her abductors risked leaving behind this destruction? What was the point? It was almost as though someone had been trying to find something. But what? What did he or Carlie have that anyone would want?

It hit him like a blow to the head. The clothes she'd been wearing yesterday. The credit card. He hurried to his overturned duffel bag. The plastic sack the clothes had been placed in by the shop manager yesterday was gone. And Carlie had the credit card in her purse. With a sinking heart, he knew he'd been right to want to hang on to them. Correct in thinking they held some clue to this nightmare. And now, Skip had everything…including Carlie.

His throat ached with tightness. His skin felt alive with nerves, unspent energy. He swung back to the mess of clothes on the floor near the wet spot of spilled cola. He dug through the piles, tossing everything. Where were the damn keys?

A metallic *jangle* caught his ear. *There.* He snatched up the keys from under Carlie's pale green sweater and charged for the door. The ice maker boomed to a stop. He lifted his gaze to the wall, the sudden silence chilling him.

A new sound echoed against the quiet. A soft whimpering, like a kitten mewling. Gripped, he moved closer, pulled inexplicably by the eerie noise. There it was again.

He dropped to one knee and looked beneath the bed. Nothing but a thin layer of dust. The sound came once more. Just on the other side of the wall. What the hell...?

A trap? A lure? Kane scanned the room, seeking a weapon, settling finally on a can of hair spray which he snatched from the bathroom floor. Holding the can with his finger on the aerosol button, he crept outside and crossed to the laundry room. Fear pressed against his heart.

Night had fallen hard. Wind whispered a cold, sorrowful moan in his ears that matched the sorrow in his heart. The laundry room was dark. He shoved the door inward. Then stood listening. The sound didn't come. His breath snagged. He fumbled for the switch, the can held high in the other hand. His pulse thumped his temples.

"I know you're in here." He flipped on the light, half expecting someone to jump him. Nothing happened. The room was a six-foot-square box containing the ice maker, coin-operated washer and dryer, a cola machine and a snack dispenser.

The mewling came again. Kane jerked. His gaze darted the room as he tried to pinpoint the origin of the noise. There was no window. No place to hide. No back way out. He scrutinized the room again and realized the dryer was pulled away from the wall, leaving a gap large enough to accommodate a person.

The hair at his nape prickled. He tightened his grip on the can and growled, "Show yourself!"

He leaped to the dryer and wrenched it farther from the wall.

She sat with her knees hugged to her chest, her green eyes wide with fear, her mouth falling open, the scream dying at the sight of him. *Carlie.* Her hair, in that sensuous braid, was disheveled, her perfect makeup smeared, her bruised eye visible. Bits of lint clung to her chic black pantsuit.

She was the most beautiful sight Kane had ever seen.

The anchor of pain weighing down his heart lifted. He tossed the hair spray can and reached for her, lifting her into his arms. She dropped the small purse she'd been holding clutched to her chest and threw her arms around his neck. The wallet-size bag teetered on her lap.

"Jamie?" she whimpered.

"He's fine, he's really fine," Kane assured her, snagging the purse and dropping it into his suit pocket.

"Thank God, you're finally here." She clung to his neck, her face pressed into his shoulder, her body soft and trembling. "I, I spilled my cola…went for another. Locked the door. Just walked into laundry room. Heard tires squeal…outside our room. Thought it was you, but realized it was too soon…"

"Shh." He stroked her quaking back, amazed at how wonderful she felt. "You don't have to tell me."

"Do." She shuddered. "Two men. Dark pickup truck."

"Did you know either of them? Recognize either?"

"Ski masks." Hysteria shivered her voice. "I—I couldn't get out without being seen. Heard them knocking on our door. Wood cracking. Then ice machine…couldn't hear anything. Not even voices. Pulled dryer out. Hid. Waited…sure they'd find me. Waited…for you."

Kane drew her into the room, moving with her in his arms, not about to let her go. He kicked the door shut with his foot. It bounced open. The jamb was cracked, the striker bolt broken. He carried her to the bed and laid her gently on the mattress. She sat up, hugging herself again, oblivious to the mess in the room.

Quickly, he wedged one of the chairs beneath the doorknob, hurried to the bed and swept her into his arms again. She nestled against him as though the two of them embracing on a bed were the most natural thing in the world.

Her heart thudded against his hands, but she was safe. Here with him. Where she belonged. He lowered his chin to the top of her head and inhaled. A subtle dusty scent mingled with her spicy-sweet perfume, tickling his nose, maddeningly teasing his senses. Relief and something infinitely more powerful swept through Kane, loosening every restraint he'd placed on himself, drowning every promise to himself that he wouldn't touch her romantically, dismissing every hurt he'd ever felt over her betrayal.

"Carlie," he murmured. He smoothed his hands up and down her back, pulling her near, feeling her firm breasts pressed to his chest. Blood licked hot through his veins, pooled thick in his loins. He kissed her hair, then her temple, then her cheek. She gazed at him with willingness in her emerald eyes.

"Oh, yes." Kane sighed. "Oh, Carlie, my Carlie."

She tilted her head, lifting her mouth to his, the contact a hot collision of passion too long denied, a sizzling coming together of spirits too long alone, a release of fear too great to name. He rode the swell of desire, oblivious to thought and promise and concern, feeling it build in him like a killer wave on a storm-tossed sea.

The ice machine kicked on, its steady rattle muted by the beating of his pulse in his ears, the thudding of his heart against his rib cage, the fire of his need for this woman. She parted her lips, and his tongue twined with hers, testing, tasting, renewing an old, once cherished acquaintanceship. His breath quickened with want, his hands slowed, relishing every touch, every soft curve and taut peak they encountered—

A loud *bang,* like a discharged gun, sounded. Kane froze. Sobered. "Was that a shot?" he whispered.

Carlie shook her head, and breathlessly said, "No. The ice maker."

Instead of smiling, Carlie frowned, her cheeks burning with what he'd swear was embarrassment, contrition. She pushed up off the bed, that ill-at-ease expression increasing as though her being swept up in the moment with him was the worst mistake she'd ever made. Was that how she felt?

"I—I'm sorry," she choked, still shaky. "I shouldn't have—"

"Shouldn't have what?" *Let me think she wanted to make love as much as I do?*

She didn't answer, but he saw the panic in her eyes and decided not to press her.

"Jamie," she said, as if in explanation. "We have to get him. Now."

Kane drew a ragged breath and strove to allay her hysteria. "He's not in any danger. Skip and his cohorts are using him to scare you. To keep you off balance so they can abduct you again."

And kill you. His heart squeezed at the thought of how close they'd come to that happening—thanks to his falling for their tactics.

"In my head, I know you're right, but in my heart…" She pleaded, "We have to get him out of that house, away from those people."

Kane admired her spirit, her ability to wade through the terror that still gripped her, for the sake of her son. His son? Their son? He reached to snatch a piece of lint from her hair. She flinched as though repelled by his touch, which only moments ago had had her melting in his arms.

He pulled his hand back. "You'll probably want to clean up before you see Jamie. Cover that eye again."

"Oh, God, yes."

She managed the transformation from abduction escapee to gorgeous mom in less than two minutes.

She asked, "Did you report this break-in to the front desk?"

"No. We don't have time to deal with the police. Besides, the police would side with Skip, and whoever runs this motel is in his pocket. Otherwise, those men wouldn't have known you were here alone."

It was almost six p.m. when they pulled through the white wrought-iron gates of the Ellison mansion. Outside lights illuminated the circular drive, glinted off the half-dozen parked cars, and cast eerie shadows at the edges of the lawn. Kane and Carlie strode to the double front doors.

Kane rang the bell. Beside him, he could hear Carlie fidgeting. He hadn't told her their ski-masked visitors had stolen the kidnap clothes. Didn't want to upset her further than she was at the moment. But the theft preyed on his mind, and he ached to grasp her hand, to reassure himself as well as her that they'd get through this.

They stood at the front porch waiting, anxious, their breaths puffing in the cold night air, Kane fighting the urge to take her hand. She'd made it clear she didn't want him touching her. He reached to hit the bell again, and the doors swung open. Mingled voices escaped from within, blaring in the outdoor silence.

Starla Ellison looked more composed that she had earlier, though just as pale. But if she was pregnant, the baggy black mourning dress kept her secret. She gaped at Carlie.

"Hello, Star." Carlie smiled. "Where's Jamie?"

"I beg your pardon?" Starla started to close the doors.

"You heard her," Kane said. "Where's her son?"

"*Her* son?" Starla's eyes widened. "Skip warned us you had this imposter with you. I'll admit the twinsy, look-alike makeup is pretty good, but it doesn't fool me. She's not Carleen. Why, Kane? What have we done to you to make you this vindictive toward us? Especially today?"

"Are you in on this conspiracy, too, Starla?" he asked.

"Conspiracy?" She looked flabbergasted. "You've lost your mind."

"Where's Jamie?" Carlie shoved into the house, past her former sister-in-law.

Starla caught her arm. "Hey, lady, what do you think you're—"

"God, Star, how can you do this? Where's your heart? He's only a baby. He needs me." Carlie jerked free of Starla's grasp. "Jamie?"

Guests turned and gaped at Carlie, obviously offended at her raised voice in this house of mourning. She ignored them and raced to the curved open stairwell. "Jamie?"

Shouting her son's name, she ran up the stairs two at a time, then down the long hallway, opening doors, then slamming them shut.

"Say, now, what's all this uproar?" Vaughn Harding, Starla's husband, seemed to appear from nowhere like a shadow needing sunlight to be seen. He had sandy hair, well-balanced, if bland, features, a ready smile, and the ability to melt into any background. His one saving grace, as far as Kane was concerned, was his genuine adoration for his wife. He hadn't married Star for her money.

It didn't bother Vaughn that she wore the pants in the family. He was the kind of man who would probably cherish staying home and taking care of his new child while his wife worked, who would happily change diapers and get up for those middle-of-the-night feedings.

Kane felt a pang of loss so great it wrenched the length of him. God, he'd missed it all: Jamie's first cry. The first time he'd rolled over. Sat up. Crawled. Walked. Talked. Two days ago he'd have bet it was impossible that he would ever envy Vaughn. But damn if he didn't.

He was hit with a sudden, desperate need not to miss another minute of his son's life. He grunted at Vaughn, then stormed through the downstairs rooms calling the boy's name. As he trekked from the foyer into the parlor, through the formal dining room and into the kitchen, he noticed his cousin Skip was oddly absent. He was nowhere on the main floor. Neither was the child.

He had the sinking feeling Skip was still one step ahead of them. Damn. He yanked open the door to his uncle's home office. Frances was seated behind Wil's antique desk, a phone receiver in her tiny hand.

"Quickly," she said, and hung up, glaring at Kane with those cold expressive eyes, her mouth curled at the corners in that perpetually nasty grin.

"Where's Jamie?" Kane asked.

His aunt sat straighter, folding her hands on the desk in front of her. She ignored his question. Said nothing. Kane was not about to be baited into ungentlemanly actions or behavior by her ploy. He'd leave the scaring of women to Skip.

"Where's my—where's Jamie?"

She pursed her lips and lifted her chin. "Even if I knew, I wouldn't tell *you*."

He knew she meant it. Questioning her further would

be a waste of breath. He stormed out, shutting the door with the force of his anger—and nearly colliding with a man. A stranger.

Kane said, "May I help you?"

"Just looking for the bathroom." The man had shaved his head in an apparent attempt to disguise his premature baldness. He had gray-green eyes in a face that had seen too much of the world at too early an age. Lean in a way that seemed bred in the bone rather than due to any conscientious effort on his part, he moved with the sure-footed stealth of a big cat.

He'd been standing so near the office doorway, Kane wondered if he'd been eavesdropping. Kane narrowed his eyes. "Do you know Jamie Ellison?"

"Skip's son, you mean?"

"Yes."

"Well, yes, as a matter of fact I do."

"Have you seen him?"

"Nope. Not for an hour or more."

"Damn."

"Aren't you with that hysterical woman who's racing through the upstairs calling the boy's name?" As he said it, they heard doors overhead slam. Carlie's voice was a faint shout.

Kane nodded and glowered. The man offered his hand. "I don't believe we've met. I'm Wade Newton. *EL*'s company doctor."

EL *had its own doctor?* Kane's brows lifted as he wondered again about his uncle's fatal heart attack. "Were you Wil's physician?"

"Oh, nothing like that. I don't practice medicine these days. I developed the new orthopedics for the tennis shoe line." Wade Newton raised his dark brows. "I'm more what you'd call a consultant."

Kane accepted the doctor's proffered hand and introduced himself. "I'm Wil Ellison's nephew."

"Oh, I see. Let me offer my condolences. Sudden death is always disconcerting."

"Did you know my uncle well?"

"I'm not sure what you mean. He was my employer. We had a good working relationship."

The door to the office opened. Frances marched into the hallway. She glared at Kane. "Why are you still here?"

At her rudeness, the doctor's eyebrows arched. With an abashed expression, he excused himself and walked quickly away.

Kane ignored his aunt as she'd ignored him earlier. He stalked back to the foyer.

Carlie was coming down the stairs. He could see she was more frantic than when they'd arrived. She said, "He's not up there."

Kane wished for some way to blunt his news, but could think of nothing but the truth. "He's not down here, either."

Starla stood near the doors with her arms folded across her chest. Carlie charged her. "Where's my son?"

In the distance, Kane detected the sound of sirens. His nerves tweaked tighter as he realized who his aunt had called. The police. "Where's the boy, Starla?"

"He's not here." She shrugged.

"We know that," Carlie railed. "Where is he?"

Starla rolled her eyes and sighed loudly. "With his mother."

"I'm his mother!" Carlie shouted.

Starla stared at her with disdain. "Don't pull that crap on me, you—you imposter."

Kane grasped Carlie's arm, eclipsing her next outburst. He scowled at Starla. "Where did she take him?"

Vaughn appeared from the shadows again, clamping a hand on Kane's shoulder. "Quit harassing my wife."

Kane stared at Vaughn, surprised at this show of machismo, at the strength in his grip, at the fire in his hazel eyes. He'd underestimated this man. At what cost? It struck him that he hadn't seen Vaughn at the cemetery. Where had he been? After Carlie? Was Vaughn part of this conspiracy? If so, why?

He shrugged free of Vaughn's hold and glared at the man. "Where's Jamie?"

"We weren't told," Starla answered. "You'll have to ask Skip."

Kane spun back toward Starla. "And we'll find Skip...?"

Vaughn stepped protectively between his wife and Kane. "At the plant."

Kane knew he shouldn't be surprised, but he was. "Nice to see how torn up Skip is about his dad's death. Wil would have been touched."

Heat flared in Starla's eyes. He'd struck a nerve. She resented Skip's public disrespect of her father, and maybe something more, something darker, was brewing behind those cool blue eyes. Kane had lived amid the rivalry between the twins since childhood. Starla was Skip's superior in too many ways for her not to resent Wil's leaving the lion's share of *EL* to her brother. And maybe, just maybe, she resented Jamie because he was the catalyst in all this. But would she wish him harm? Harm a small child? Real fear for his son swept Kane.

It was imperative they find the boy. Soon. No matter how they had to do it.

He released Carlie's arm, and took her hand. This time

she didn't flinch or try to pull free. Either she'd come to the same conclusion, or she'd heard the rapidly approaching sirens and realized the significance.

He rushed her through the door and outside. "Quick! We need to be gone before the cops arrive and haul us to jail."

"As soon as Vaughn and Starla tell the cops where we're headed, they'll follow. We won't have much time with Skip."

Kane started the motor. "Hell, we'll be lucky if he's still at the plant when we arrive."

"Even if he's there, he won't tell us where Jamie is. We don't have anything to bargain with—nothing he wants or needs that we can exchange for that information. And he'll never admit he knows I'm the real Carleen— that would land him in jail."

Determination seared through Kane. "If he's there, I'll make him tell us."

They wheeled out of the gates and turned toward the cemetery. Behind them, headlights stroked the top of the rise and swung across the corner of the Ellison estate. Instead of slowing as it neared the estate gates, the vehicle sped up, coming straight after them...and coming fast.

"That's not the police." Kane tensed as he realized what he was seeing in the rearview mirror. "It's a pickup truck. Hang on."

He hit the accelerator. The SUV lurched forward. The roar of the powerful engine behind rent the night air. The pickup closed the gap by ten car lengths, then five.

They passed the graveyard doing sixty. The other vehicle was four lengths behind now. Tires squealed as they rounded the first bend in the road.

"Where are we going?" Carlie's voice was taut.

Kane stared straight ahead. His grip was hard on the steering wheel as he fought to keep on the road. He had planned on taking the back way to the plant, but figured now they'd be lucky to lose this tail and make the outskirts of town.

He spoke loudly to be heard above the howl of the engine. "No one knows this road as well as I do. As a kid I used to explore these woods above the bay. As a teenager, I drove around The Point to the plant in that noisy clunker of mine. The Point road branches off in a couple of places. One of those cutoffs is a dirt track that leads to the main highway. Not many people know about it."

He gave a silent prayer that he could find it in the dark, traveling seventy-five on a night as black as pitch, through woods as dense and sinister as hell, with the devil himself on their heels.

"No, Kane. We can't go this way. The road is eroded in several places. Washed completely away in others. Look!" She yelled as a roadblock loomed out of the darkness. The pavement seemed to drop into oblivion ten feet ahead.

Kane hit the brakes. The pickup kept coming. It slammed into the rear of the SUV. Crunching metal exploded into the night. Carlie screamed. Kane stomped the brake with both feet. But the pickup had more power. It pushed the SUV forward.

Kane threw the vehicle into reverse and pressed the gas pedal to the floor. The SUV moved backward, hard against the pickup's front bumper. For a second neither vehicle moved. Then the SUV lurched forward, losing ground.

It plowed through the roadblock. Wood cracked beneath its tires. The maw gaped five feet ahead—the open mouth of a hungry monster.

Kane wrenched the wheel. The SUV slid sideways, still headed for the drop-off. His body slammed against the seat belt. Something bulky poked his side. Carlie's purse. His blood ran cold. When their bodies were found, the police would discover the purse in his pocket and take the VISA card as proof that this woman, who'd met her death with him, was an imposter. And Skip would see to it that Carlie was buried as Coral J. Clayton.

Chapter Ten

The pickup slammed into the SUV. Carleen's body snapped back, then forward. The seat belt bit into her breastbone. Glass crunched. The lights filling the SUV from behind died. The SUV lunged for the cliff.

Kane shouted, "Jump!"

Carleen tore aside her seat belt. She wrenched open the door and leaped. Solid, muddy ground met her. She rolled away from the vehicle and felt the earth beneath her lower body vanish. *The precipice.* "Kane," she gasped.

The looming black hulk of the SUV angled down past her in slow motion and disappeared. Below, far below, Carleen heard waves pounding the rocky shoreline. She began to slide, sucked down by the loose earth and mud. She grappled for a hold. A rock. A bush. Anything. But all she found was slimy ground. She dug her fingertips into the damp earth. It stopped her slow descent.

But she knew it wouldn't hold her for long.

Below, trees cracked and popped like brittle toothpicks as the SUV plunged through them. A second later, a resounding *crash* echoed up from the rocky shore. Fear pounded in her heart. Her clothes and body slick with mud, she squirmed to hold her position. Useless. She began a downward slide. She was going to die. Going to plummet to her death. Bile burned the back of her throat. She grabbed for a handhold. Nothing. She slid backwards. Completely over the edge now and sinking.

In the distance, she heard the dying whine of a siren. Likely the police had finally arrived at the mansion. Too far away to do her any good. Too late.

On the flat above her, the door of the pickup banged open. Carleen's blood ran cold. Footfalls approached the cliff, led by a beam of light. A flashlight. She dug her nails deeper into the eroding dirt. She held her breath. Behind the bead of light, she made out a shape in the darkness. A man. He leaned out over the cliff, fanning the beam far below, across the SUV.

She peered up at him. He was close, his face hidden by shadow. He leaned down. Carleen's whole body clenched, as though trying to make itself smaller. Invisible. She pushed her face into the dirt. *Please, God, don't let him shine that light on me.*

Her lungs burned with unspent air. She pressed her lips, holding it in, and prayed Kane had rolled into the underbrush and would escape unharmed. That if she died, he would find Jamie and prove his fatherhood. That he would raise their son. Jamie.

She should have told Kane about their secret signal. Then Jamie would trust him immediately, would know she'd sent Kane for him.

A sob filled her mouth. She bit it back with a shudder. Blew air from her taut lips. Sipped a teeny breath. Her body slipped another inch. The sound of sucking earth seemed a thunderclap in her ears. She strained to hear the man. He was still there. Above her. She braced for his shout of discovery, and heard him grunt in satisfaction.

He'd found her. Fear burned her nerves. Scorched in her belly. She lifted her gaze and blinked through mud-coated lashes. She expected his foot would smash down on her head and shove her to a rapid death. But the man and his light were walking away. Carleen clamped off a gasp of relief. She exhaled a long, painful breath. Gulped in a lung full of cold, delicious dirt-rich air. The door to the pickup slammed shut. The motor revved, then the sound slowly faded into the chilly night.

"Kane?" Her voice was a croak. The effort cost her precious ground. "Kane?"

Had he fallen? Gone down with the SUV? Oh, dear God, no. Her throat squeezed. She started to slide again. She poked her toes into the earth and halted her descent. She lifted one hand, raising herself up a notch. Hope came alive in her. She moved her feet. First the right. Then the left. Thrusting them into the soft earth, gaining new footholds. She reached up. Caught a small branch. She pulled herself higher. Another six inches and she'd be safe.

"Kane?"

He didn't answer. Again she wondered if he'd managed to get out of the SUV. Her breath came in hard puffs, fogging the air. She labored another inch higher. Her pulse roared against her ears, muting the sounds of the night. The earth holding the branch loosened. She squealed. The twig came free in her hand. She flailed at the empty space above her. Screamed. Gravity pulled. Her back arched. She began to topple. She cried out again—

A hand clamped her wrist. In her panic, she grabbed the arm above it, no longer caring who it was. The instinct to live was overpowering. But the mud made her as slippery as an oiled pig. She felt herself sliding again. Terror clenched her heart. "Help!"

"Carlie, hang on."

Kane. Oh, thank God. He caught her other wrist, his hold precarious, but it was her only hope. She quit struggling. Worked her feet into the mud and strained her leg muscles to assist as he dragged her up the side of the cliff.

He landed on his back. She collapsed on top of him, panting and slick with mud. He felt solid and reliable and wonderful beneath her. She clung to him, feeling his chest rise and fall, reassuring her that they were both alive, that they had survived against the worst odds.

She didn't know whether to laugh or cry.

Overhead, clouds parted, and for the first time that evening, the moon shone, sending long rays of light down on them. Carleen eased off Kane and sat beside him, sobbing in relief.

He struggled to his elbows. "Are you all right?"

"I'm alive." She tried to grin and failed. Her voice came out quavery and weak. "Don't think anything is broken. How about you?"

"I'm fine," he claimed, but in the sketchy light she could see a gash on his forehead above his left eye. He noticed her frown and reached for the cut. "I hit a rock or something when I jumped from the SUV. I think it knocked me out for a few minutes. I'll be okay."

"That wound needs cleaning."

"We both need cleaning. Come on." Kane got to his feet and pulled her up. "We have to get out of here. Find somewhere warm and safe."

"In case you didn't notice, we've lost our only transportation. Our clothes. Our—our everything." Hysteria swirled through her, crept into her voice. "Just where do you propose we go?" Rising, she realized her body felt achy. Probably black and blue under her muddy clothes. But she could walk, if a bit stiffly. "Not back to the mansion?"

"No." He told her about the call he'd heard his aunt make. "I thought she was calling the police. Now I'm not so sure."

"But I did hear sirens, and I'm almost certain they stopped at the mansion."

He considered that for a moment. "Well, if Frances didn't call the guy in the pickup truck, someone at the mansion did. And whoever was in that pickup thinks we're dead."

"They'll know otherwise in the morning."

"Yes, but until then, we need to disappear."

Disappear? Like Jamie had disappeared? The frantic need to find him whirred through her like a rusty drill, widening the hole in her heart. Where was her son? "Where could that imposter have taken Jamie?"

Kane found a hanky and gently wiped the mud from her eyes. "I don't know, love. But I'm sure she won't harm him."

"I want him back," Carleen cried into the chilly night. "Now."

Kane stopped and grasped both her upper arms, bending until his face was level with hers. "I want him back, too. But Skip is one step ahead of us all the way. The only chance we have of getting Jamie back is to quit reacting to everything Skip throws at us. We have to set out a plan and follow it."

His tone, more than his words, penetrated her frustration and fear. She forced herself to breathe deeply for several moments and consider what he'd said. As her head cleared, she realized he was right. Up to this point they'd been playing by Skip's rules. Falling into every trap he'd set. That had to stop.

"What do we do?"

"Regroup. Get a plan." He glanced toward the washed-out road and waved a hand. "Tell me about this area. When was it closed?"

"Last month. Excessive rainfall in October washed out this road. The cabins on The Point have been condemned—the few residents who lived in them year-round were forced to leave."

"Really?"

She didn't like the glint in his eye. Didn't like the way she figured his thoughts were racing. "There's no longer any way in or out. The shore road is cut off, too."

"But not, I'll wager, the old lane I told you about—the one to the main highway."

"You aren't planning on hiking to the main road down that lane tonight, are you? There've been cougar sightings in these woods since the end of September. Several deer killed. Besides, The Point road is unstable. What if it caved in on us?"

"Is The Point that precarious?"

"I don't know."

He scowled. "Look, I'm not planning on taking any chances that we don't have to take, like trying to make the main highway in the dark. Don't want to do it on foot, but we might not have a choice. Nor do I intend to be dinner for some wildcat. But we need somewhere safe, somewhere out of this cold. Town is no longer an option."

"Are you suggesting—?" She glanced behind them at The Point. But, of course, that was exactly what he was suggesting. She shivered and hugged herself. The heat of adrenaline had started to wear off, making her more aware each second of the cold of the night and her damp clothes. More aware of the fact that they were moving farther and farther from her son. "But what about Jamie? What kind of plan is this?"

"It's not. We can't get to Jamie tonight. Or without some serious planning. Look at us. How far do you think we'd get like this? We need to rest. Dry out. Clear our heads."

Carleen wanted to protest again, but he was right. "Okay."

"Good. It's just a short walk…" He took off his jacket and placed it around her shoulders. She protested. He insisted, then pulled aside a tree branch. "We'll forge our way through here to the other side of the road, and 'borrow' one of those abandoned cabins."

She feared The Point would be the first place Skip would look in the morning—after discovering the SUV contained no dead bodies—but for now, she supposed, it was their only choice. Sticking close together, they ducked into the woods and skirted the washed-out area, battling wet foliage and roots and soft spots, moving gingerly, the moon their only light. Ten minutes later, damp and chilled to the bone, Carleen stepped out on the old uneven pavement, Kane beside her.

Wind whined up the deserted street, a thin whistle like the shrill bleat of a tripped alarm. The road was potholed and crumbling at the edges. Streetlights leaned precariously, unearthed by the shifting ground deep beneath the surface. The wires linking them were slung low and swayed in the breeze.

How isolated The Point had become in one short month; how quickly nature reclaimed her own. Just as rapidly, Jamie and her world had gone from safe and sane to a nightmare without rhyme or reason. And now she and Kane were risking God knew what new menace in order to stay alive another day.

"Should we whistle or sing or something?" she asked.

"No," he said, close against her ear. "I don't want to attract attention from any living creature that might be lurking in these woods. The sooner we're indoors, the happier I'll be. Come on."

His hand was at the nape of her neck, guiding her gently but firmly down the road. She sent her gaze flying from side to side as they hurried along, alert for any unwanted shadows or the glowing eyes of a wild animal. She shuddered and hugged his jacket to her, shoving her hands into the pockets. Her fingers collided with something hard. She withdrew it and studied it in the feeble light. "My purse?"

Kane dipped his head toward hers and spoke softly. "You had it in the laundry room."

"I did?" Yes, she supposed she had. She would have needed change for the cola. It seemed a small prize in all that she had once again lost. Her new clothes were in the back of the SUV. Gone for good. This new suit ruined beyond repair. But she was alive to fight another battle, and next time she would win.

"Uh, guess I should have mentioned it sooner, but...well—" Kane cleared his throat. "The men in the ski masks stole the kidnap clothes."

"What?" She stopped and stared at him. "Why?"

He cautioned her to lower her voice. "I'm not sure."

She could tell from his tone that he knew darn good and well they'd intended on putting those clothes on her dead body. Anger flashed through her, chasing away some of her cold.

He said, "I'm certain they wanted the credit card, too. At least they didn't get that."

Carleen blanched. Though she didn't say it, she had the odd sensation that keeping Coral Clayton's VISA was the worst thing she could do. Why? A quick sharp pain hit her temples. She winced. Why did that happen whenever she tried to remember her lost week?

A sign creaked in the wind: Hermann's Hideaway. In the dim light they made out a driveway. But instead of slowing, Kane kept walking. She felt weary beyond anything she'd ever experienced. Shivering with cold. And hunger. And fear. "Aren't we going to stop here?"

"It's a double-wide. No fireplace. With the electricity turned off all over The Point, we'll need some way to keep warm."

She nodded and moved closer to him. As cold as she was, he had to be even colder, with only a dress shirt between him and the biting wind. They hastened down the road.

The next sign was four blocks farther: Digby's Digs. The driveway was overgrown, blocking any view of the cabin. Kane steered her through the bushes. "This is the place."

"You know this cabin?"

"It belongs to Elmer Digby. I used to go crabbing with him when I was a kid. He found me alone on the beach once, struck up a conversation. He was more of a grandfather to me than my real one."

Once past the brush that all but blocked the driveway entrance, the lot opened to a cliffside view of the bay. The buildings consisted of an A-frame cabin, a makeshift storage shed and a detached building that could have served as a double-car garage. Here the wind was fierce. Something sickly sweet wafted on the air. Carleen wrinkled her nose.

"Frankly, I'm amazed they got the old guy to leave," Kane said. "He's lived in this cabin for fifty years."

"Maybe this property is one of those sliding down the cliff?" she suggested, praying it wasn't.

"God willing, it will stand one more night."

As they neared the back porch, the sickly sweet odor worsened. Carleen turned her face into Kane's side. "What is that?"

Kane sniffed. "Smells like…blood."

He halted. Hugged her close, his gaze scouring the drive ahead. Carleen's fear leaped higher. "What is it?"

"A deer." Kane swore. "Fresh kill. Cougar. Could be lurking nearby. Scared off by our approach."

Carleen gasped.

"Come on. Let's get inside." Kane speedily located a key beneath an old anchor that rested beside the back steps.

She was trembling hard by the time he shut the door behind them. It was dark, the temperature degrees cooler than outside. Old pipe tobacco scented the air. She stood, hugging herself, fighting to stop the chattering of her teeth.

She was dirty and wet and shaking from the chill. She could see nothing in front of her, except, in her mind's eye, her son's frightened face. Her spirit flattened, shriveling like a dried pea, withered and sere. Desolation swelled inside her. The sensation was somehow familiar. Her head thumped with sudden pain. She winced and clasped her temples.

Mud flaked about her hands. Jamie's face faded, and in its place came another, a woman's face, the face she and Kane had decided belonged to Coral Clayton. The black hair and dark eyes were inches from her as Carleen struggled awake from her drug-induced stupor. Something shiny and silver caught her gaze. A gun.

"Get up," Coral had said. "I'm all done baby-sitting your whiny butt. You've got a date with a man in black—and I'm not talking about Tommy Lee Jones or Will Smith." Her wide lips split with a vicious grin. "But the Grim Reaper."

She'd grabbed Carleen by the arm and wrenched her from the bed. The room had spun, but Carleen could see it more clearly now, as though a curtain had parted in her brain. A cabin of some sort. Log walls. Seashells on the windowsills. Like Jamie's shells. Who would listen to his seashells with him? Who would know what that meant to him? How it comforted him? *Jamie.* She must have said his name aloud. Coral hit her across the face. "Shut up. And get marching. We're going for a little ride."

Fear flushed Carleen from temple to toe, and the vision vanished, leaving a lingering, if dulling headache. What had happened between her and Coral Clayton? Her teeth chattered with renewed fervor, and deep inside a trembling started as though her whole body were going to quake apart. She hugged herself tighter and blinked against the internal onslaught, feeling she was in as much danger of dropping off this emotional precipice as she had been earlier of plunging off the cliff.

Kane was coming toward her with a glowing candle. In the flickering light, his handsome face was streaked with mud, his warm eyes full of such concern. It was too much. The last thing she could handle—that sympathy issuing from those glorious blue orbs. She bit back the need to cry, but couldn't halt the two tears that fled from her eyes.

"Hey, hey... What's this?" His voice was tender.

"My God, you're trembling. Come on. The fire's starting to heat the living room. We've got to get you out of these wet things. I've even found a couple of blankets we can wrap up in while our clothes dry."

Carleen didn't struggle, didn't protest, just let him lead her into the living room. The furniture was gone. Kane had set lighted candles on the brick slab that held the freestanding wood-burning stove. A couple of tattered blankets were heaped on the multicolored shag carpeting; a pan of water was heating on the stovetop.

If it was warmer in this room than the back porch, she couldn't feel it, couldn't stop the shakiness controlling her body. Kane guided her to the edge of the stove. Even this close to the flames, she felt no heat.

"Come on. You need out of these wet clothes." Kane undid the suit jacket, then her blouse, his fingers clumsy in the struggle with damp fabric and small buttons. She made no effort to help. Couldn't have helped if she'd wanted to. He shoved the garments back over her shoulders, exposing her bra, brushing her breasts in the process and skimming the teeniest speck of heat over her naked flesh. He peeled the jacket and blouse down her arms and off. Mud and grit clung to her skin. He hung her garments from nails that Elmer had apparently pounded into the bared ceiling beams.

Next Kane opened the zipper of her slacks and tugged them down. She felt grimy, even beneath her underclothes. Mud and grit had penetrated everything. He grabbed up one of the blankets, wrapped it around her shoulders, loosened her bra and eased it off, then her panties. He reached into the pan on the stove and extracted a rag, then slowly, gently bathed her face, her body. There was nothing sexual about his actions—they were just those of a caring friend. A nurturing soul.

When she was clean, he buffed the blanket over her damp skin, then pulled it tight against her, urging her to sit on the floor in front of the stove. Sinking down, she clutched the rough fabric to her. It smelled of damp house and wood smoke, but at that moment was as welcome as if it were the softest flannel, blown dry in a field of roses.

The plate-glass windows rattled in the wind. There were no drapes, and with the night pressing in, Carleen felt exposed. She wanted to blow out all the candles, but hadn't the strength.

"Brr," Kane said as he stripped off his own muddied clothes, washed all over, then wrapped himself in the other blanket. He sank to the floor beside her. Their clothes loomed above them like phantoms keeping watch, constant reminders of the nightmare they were living.

"We'll be warm soon," Kane said. "Then I'll check and see if Elmer left a can of chili or ravioli or soup behind. We'll eat like royalty."

His attempt to make her laugh tore at her heart. Who would try to make Jamie laugh? Who would talk to him, explaining or answering all the "why" questions his busy mind conjured. Who would hold him? Comfort him?

A sob twisted her throat. She felt herself crumbling inside, needing, but not finding, a lifeline to hold on to, and knowing she'd die without one. Burning hot tears filled her eyes and slid down her cheeks. Her shoulders began to shake and a sob, like the cry of a wounded animal, spilled out into the room. First one, then another, and another, until they wrenched her body.

"Oh, babe." Kane's arms went around her, and she sank into him, against him, hungry for the contact of another person—this person, she realized with a jolt. If not her son, then only Kane. The tears came harder, all the pain and loss and fear she'd tamped down bursting from her in a rush of release. He held her, gently rubbing her back with his solid hands, the heat of his fingers finally able to warm her gelid blood.

Kane murmured as he stroked her, his voice a gentle lilt like the mellow song of a night bird soothing her ragged nerves, shrinking her distress. Her tears subsided to a soft snuffling, the red-hot sting of them spent, the sobs no longer wracking, no longer strangling her. Even her chest had stopped heaving.

Kane held her tighter, his head braced on hers, his mouth soft in her hair, his breath warm against her ear, his kiss a tender glance to her neck. She lifted her head, and their gazes met and held. The candlelight reflected in his blue eyes, a pale glow that didn't conceal the stronger smoldering need in their depths.

He lifted his hand to the side of her face, feathered his fingertips down her cheek. ''Oh, Carlie, I—''

''No.'' She shushed him, and traced his mouth with the pad of her thumb. ''Don't talk.'' *Don't make promises. Don't tell me you won't let me down this time.* All she wanted from him right now was to feel, to lose this numbness from her heart, from her limbs, from her brain; to make love with him until she felt whole again—as only he could make her feel.

She shoved her hands into his hair on both sides of his head and pulled him gently to her until she could reach up and touch her lips to his. They were firm and warm and familiar, and her body responded as though they'd never lost contact, never spent as much as an hour apart. Showers of delicious tremors poured through her, chasing off every lingering chill, and swirling her pulse, flicking butterfly strokes of pleasure through her.

His arms came around her with a fierceness that she

hadn't expected, hadn't prepared herself for, but that she welcomed with every ounce of her being. He deepened the kiss, plunging his tongue into her mouth, shoving the blankets off, his naked body golden in the candle glow.

She shivered, but not from cold, no longer cold, but hot and melting, turning liquid and fiery inside, her need for him a rush as hard and fast and all-consuming as a flooding river.

"Oh, Kane," she murmured, reaching to touch him, running her hands over his shoulders, down across his taut nipples, into the dark golden hair on his chest and on his flat, muscled belly to the denser, darker hair below. Then she touched him, curled her hands around the hard, sleek length of him, and her sigh met his in a tangle of need.

He pulled her to him, kissing her mouth, then lowering her onto her back, the blankets nestling her, as he found her breasts, her nipples, her belly and lower. His tongue flicked knowingly over every intimate inch of her, touching with assurance and persuasion, leaving her wet and frenzied, aching to join with him, at the edge of release. "Oh, please. Oh, Kane. Now."

"You don't have to beg, love." He lifted above her, grinned at her with such joy that it filled her heart, then kissed her lips and slid inside her, filling her, the friction electrifying. Her body tensed and a quick climax shuddered through her, tingling clear to her toes and clenching her inner muscles. Kane groaned her name and lifted his hips, moving easily back and forth, up and down, every thrust branding her, making her his in some inexplicable way, and always carrying her higher and faster up this mountainous peak of passion. Carleen didn't give thought to the possible hurt she might feel later for having capitulated, for having given in to this complete rapture. All she knew was that she felt herself coming alive again, as though renewed by the very rhythms of life, by the sweet agony of their joining.

Kane's body tensed and he gasped her name at the same moment as release exploded through her, hot and trembling and exquisite, turning her limbs liquid.

For a long moment neither spoke; they just gazed at one another. Then Kane eased off her, settling beside her, pulling her close and covering them both in the blankets as the chill of the cabin stole over them once again.

They lay nestled together. Then Kane sat up on one elbow and gazed down at her lovingly. "I've missed you so much."

Outside, a cry like a woman's scream filled the night. The cougar. The sound was eerie, lonely, as lonely as the longing inside Carleen. Apprehension clawed at her heart.

She'd missed Kane, too, missed their lovemaking, but feared saying it out loud, feared the words would hold some power over her, cause this wonderment to all go away, to repeat the awful pattern of the past. For once again, Carleen realized, they had given in to the passion they roused in one another. And once again, they had used no protection.

Chapter Eleven

The morning sky held heavy clouds, dark with the promise of a nasty storm. They'd risen at first light and dressed, their clothes dry; the mud had flaked off with ease, the aftereffects of their lovemaking not as easily brushed away.

Instead of the cocky, possessiveness Kane had shown toward her four years ago whenever they'd made love, instead of the insatiable urgency to repeat the act again and again, this time once seemed to satisfy him. Only once. They'd slept wrapped together for warmth, for comfort, but that was all.

This morning he'd seemed eager to dress, to distance himself from her physically, to shed temptation—was even now scouring the house for some outerwear he hoped Elmer had left behind. But they had more to fear this day than the sharp wind. During the night, every time Kane had reached out onto the back stoop for wood, she'd worried about the cougar jumping him. And soon, very soon, Skip would discover the empty SUV and send men to scour The Point for them. Men with guns, no doubt.

She shoved the dark thoughts away and worked her hair into a braid as best she could without brush or comb, her mind straying back to Kane and his odd behavior since making love with her last night. Was he afraid she'd expect a commitment from him that he wasn't willing or ready to give? They hadn't discussed it, would likely never discuss it. Last night, he'd given her what she'd wanted and needed.

But it didn't change the fact that she'd taken too long to tell Kane he was Jamie's father. Didn't change the fact that Kane had run out on her once, and might again. They still had not spanned that gap of trust. Without trust, all they had were unresolved feelings—plus a slew of other worries to face and deal with.

Besides, Kane hadn't said he loved her, only that he'd missed her.

Guilt niggled Carleen. She wasn't being fair. He, at least, had admitted he'd missed her. That was more than she'd done. She'd held her silence around her as tightly as she'd held the shabby blanket. The only person she'd ever said ''I love you'' to without reservation or hesitation was her son. Not her son's father, not ever. She hadn't even dared tell him she'd missed him.

She paced the room and stared out at the water churning in the bay below. She'd made love with him, risked her heart and possible pregnancy for the chance to connect with him in the way only he made her feel whole and alive, and yet she couldn't put her feelings for him into words. Couldn't admit how important he was to her. Had always been to her. Some lessons she'd learned too well in childhood.

As long as she didn't care about someone, her heart couldn't be broken. But it *was* broken. So what had she gained with her silence, except the biggest heartache of all?

And now that silence seemed to trap her, hold her distanced from him. And him from her. She shivered and rubbed her hands together, snatched one of the blankets from the floor and wrapped it around her like a cape. Kane had kept the fire going into the wee hours, but it was out now and the room was losing heat rapidly. They'd dared not relight it; the smoke would give away their location.

"Look what I found." Kane strode into the room, holding out to her a heavy-duty canvas jacket that might once have been sage green, but over the years had been stained to the color of rhododendron leaves. He wore its twin. "They aren't pretty, but they're warm. Put it on. We're leaving."

"But we haven't made a plan." She donned the overly large jacket. It smelled musty, but doused her chills. Sleeping on the floor had left Carleen more aware than ever of every bruise and scrape she'd gained in the last ten days. The biggest ache centered in her heart, but she knew if she concentrated on that pain she'd revert emotionally to where she was last night before she and Kane had made love. That wouldn't do. She needed to remain strong for Jamie. "What are we going to do?"

Kane carried the candles from the brick hearth to a kitchen cupboard and thrust them in. He came back for the pail of water, emptied it in the sink, then quickly disposed of it in the same cupboard. "First, we're going to the police, and reporting what happened last night."

The thought of the police set butterflies whipping through her stomach, but she couldn't tell him. Like so many other things, she couldn't explain it to herself. Her mouth dried. "Is that your plan? How you intend to get Jamie?"

"No." He gathered the blankets and hastily folded

them. "I don't think the police will help us without some physical proof that you're Jamie's biological mother."

Her brows lifted in surprise. "Jamie's my proof. He'll know me."

"Oh, my God." Kane groaned. "Exactly. That's why Skip didn't want you at the funeral. Jamie would have instinctively known you. Cried out for you. It's why Jamie's been taken somewhere that we can't find him— because he will instantly put the lie to Skip's imposter."

The truth of his words galvanized Carleen. Her body jerked. "Stupid…" She swore, furious with herself, feeling her loss more deeply and more cruelly than ever, as though she'd had Jamie within her grasp and dropped him. The hole in her heart widened. "I should have—"

"No. Don't go there," Kane warned. "Self-recriminations are a waste of our energy and time. We need to be wiser, more prepared in the future."

An hour ago, they'd dined on tuna fish and soup—not usual breakfast fare, but sustenance. Right now, the remains of her meal churned in her stomach, threatened to come up. Carleen hugged herself, gathering and releasing several bracing breaths. The ill feeling subsided, and her head began to clear.

He was right. *Wiser, more prepared.* They had to give each other every foot-up available to them. "Kane, if something should happen to me—"

"Don't say that. Don't even think it."

"Listen to me. This is important." He stopped protesting, and she continued, "Jamie and I have a secret greeting we give one another whenever we're feeling sad or scared or lonely. For his sake, you need to know it."

Kane put his hand through his mussed hair and quirked his mouth, making a face that reminded her of their son and was both endearing and heart-wrenching at the same time. "Okay. Tell me."

"For some reason since he was about a year old, he's worried the skin under his chin with his forefinger and thumb when he's falling asleep, the way other kids worry the silky edge of a favorite blanket." Carleen demonstrated on herself as she spoke, gingerly tweaking the taut skin beneath her chin. "If he's on my lap, he does it to me. It's become our special, private signal to each other, a silent kind of 'Hello, glad to see you' gesture that only the two of us know the meaning of. It's safe, you see, as no one else has ever paid particular attention to it or questioned either of us about it."

Kane narrowed his eyes. "He was doing that yesterday at the funeral."

"And during the news conference, remember?" At the memory, tears stung her eyes.

Kane nodded.

"If anything happens to me," she choked, "and you have to go for him alone, if you touch your own chin the same way, he'll know you're to be trusted. He'll know I sent you to him."

In her heart of hearts, she realized, if worse came to worst, it might be the only comfort she would ever give her child again. She prayed it never came to that. Panic reared through her at the possibility. "God, Kane, what are we going to do?"

"We need the law on our side."

"But you said the police wouldn't—" She broke off, confused, struggling with impotent rage and helpless frustration.

"We'll go to the police eventually, but right now I was thinking more about your patron, Hugh Proctor. Is he still living in Port Luster?"

"For another few weeks." The attorney who'd taken her in when her parents died was retiring next month. Moving to Florida. "But at the moment, he and Phyllis are in Orlando. They're buying a house. They've been gone for, ah, two weeks, I guess." It struck her suddenly why Skip had made his move against her when he had. The Proctors would know the imposter wasn't her—and that probably meant the woman would stay away from Port Luster until the Proctors had moved. Stay away with Jamie. Panic threatened to engulf her anew.

"Damn." Kane scowled. "Is there any way we can contact him?"

She wrestled down her anxiety. "His secretary might get in touch with him for me. Or give me a number where he can be reached."

"Okay. Good. Once he hears your story, Skip will never manage to pass that woman off as you. We've got to get to a phone."

"What about the cougar?" Apprehension burned through her veins.

"I don't think he's hungry anymore."

"Maybe not, but what if he's a she? A mother with cubs she thinks we're threatening?" She shivered at the idea. "And what about Skip's men?"

"I'll be cautious, but there's no choice. We can't stay here indefinitely."

He'd be cautious? Not *they*? What exactly did that mean? "What are you up to?"

"I'm hoping one of the residents left behind a car or truck or motorcycle we can use. I'm going to check out all the properties. I'll be back as soon as I find something."

"Oh, no. You're not leaving me." Again. Running out. What if he didn't return? Like last time? She couldn't bear that. "If you do find a car, you'd waste precious time coming back for me. And I'd go nuts worrying about you."

Would you? his look seemed to ask.

She swallowed against the knot in her throat, wishing he'd ask her aloud, wishing she had the courage to tell him without his pushing the issue.

"Okay," he said, handing her the two blankets. He grabbed the fireplace poker, little enough protection against men with bullets or the fierce claws of a wildcat. "We'll do this together."

Hugging the two blankets to her thudding heart, she followed Kane outside. Wind bent the fir trees and sent dead maple leaves scurrying across the ground. As they approached the garage, gulls and crows took flight, cawing and squawking in anger at having their frenzied feeding disturbed. The plucked deer carcass was grotesque in the morning light, but before she could turn away, she heard and saw flies buzzing in a congealed puddle of blood, spotted a single, large paw print in the mud near the half-devoured head.

Her stomach flipped. Kane propelled her past the gruesome sight. He flung open the double doors of the rickety building Elmer Digby had used to store his old pickup truck and station wagon. The interior smelled musty. All that remained there were a few gardening tools and an old oil spot on the concrete floor. He grimaced. "Guess that would have been too easy."

He pointed toward the cliff, keeping his voice low. "Come on. We'll follow along there. If Skip's men are on The Point, we'd risk more chance of bumping into them on the road."

Carleen hurried after Kane, unhappy with all their choices. Below, she could see where the old road had washed away. She eyed the surf with apprehension. It seemed to tear at the shoreline like a hungry monster munching a savory meal. Her foot landed hard on a loose mound of soil.

Pebbles rolled down the hill, hitting with a resounding pinging. A low trundling noise followed as larger rocks slewed down. The ground beneath her trembled. Carleen squealed. Kane grabbed her and wrenched her back, just as a large chunk of the bluff broke off and disappeared. A fissure split the ground near their feet.

She and Kane scrambled farther out of harm's way. Gasping, she cried, "That was too close."

"It's my fault. I guess I didn't believe it was this unstable." He steered her toward the main street, staying just inside the property line. The bushes that bordered the road would protect them from detection. They soon arrived at the next lot. Parked beside a fairly new-looking log cabin was an old Jeep Wagoneer. Carleen's hope soared. She started to charge toward it.

"Wait." Kane grabbed her arm, his voice frantic, hushed. "We don't know who that belongs to. Someone could be inside. The owner, maybe. Or it might belong to someone else, someone walking The Point looking for us."

In her eagerness, she hadn't thought, had just reacted. Her pulse tattooed against her temples. They hunkered down beside a giant rhododendron bush and watched, leery, ready to bolt. The seconds moved like hours. Her body ached with tension. But after five minutes no one had appeared.

Kane cautioned her, "Stay here. I'm gonna see if anyone's inside the cabin. If not, I'll try and start the car."

He sneaked to the back of the log cabin and peered in a couple of windows. Coming back, he kept low, moving with deliberate caution. He shook his head at her, then stole over to the Jeep on the driver's side. She saw the door swing open. He ducked inside, disappearing from her line of vision. She held her breath. Willed him to hurry. A metallic *pop,* like a spoon hitting a metal pan, jolted her. A second later, Kane scrambled out of the Jeep, shoved the hood open and peered into the engine compartment. His curse echoed on the wind.

Behind her, Carleen heard a rustle in the underbrush. She pivoted. Caught a glimpse of something tan, like a flash of fur. The cougar? She scooted to Kane's side.

"Motor's missing," he said.

"Oh, n—"

Her response was cut off by a man's shout. "They're not in here."

The speaker came stomping out of the log cabin. Carleen's heart stopped. She couldn't see the man. Which meant he hadn't seen them. The person he'd called appeared in the driveway. She bit back a gasp.

Kane grabbed her. They ducked around to the front of the Jeep. He peeked through the Wagoneer's windows, then dropped back down beside her. "They didn't see us. Yet," he whispered. "We've got to hide."

He pointed to the giant rhododendron. They raced back and gingerly plunged into its depths. They crouched among the wet leaves. Carleen's insides trembled so hard she feared she'd give away their hiding spot. Thank God for the warmth and camouflage of Elmer's old coats. Thank God for Kane's quick thinking and rapid reflexes, and the fact she wasn't facing this terror without him.

"Hey," one of the men said. "Did you mess with this Jeep?"

"Nope. Didn't touch it. Why?"

"'Cause since I went into the cabin, someone's opened the driver's door and put up the hood."

"And," the other added, "dropped this here blanket."

Carleen gasped. Indeed, she now carried just one of the blankets. Kane put his arms around her, pulled her close and murmured in her ear, "It's okay. They don't know where we are."

"Look," one of the men called to the other. "A footprint. Small, like a woman's. She ran this way. Up toward the top of the rise."

Carleen blanched, buried her face hard against Kane's thundering heart, and prayed with all her might that the men wouldn't find them. She heard their footsteps approach, then stop. In fascinated horror, she lifted her head. She could see them now. Both carried guns—one, a rifle slung across his arm, ready to be raised and fired; the other, a revolver of some kind with a long barrel— something like the one Coral Clayton had had.

The men were dressed in army fatigues with neon-orange vests. Hunters. Ski masks hid their faces. She recognized neither. Slowly, they came abreast of Kane's and her hiding place. Carleen couldn't breathe. Couldn't move. The taller of the two men turned, staring into the rhododendron bush. She swore he was staring right into her eyes.

Her blood ran cold.

The rustling she'd heard earlier sounded off to her right. The man jerked toward it. "That her?" his companion asked.

The first man poked his rifle into the bush. "Naw. Musta been a squirrel or something."

"Let's look up this way. She can't be far ahead of us."

The second the men disappeared from view, Kane

hauled Carleen up and out from under the rhododendron. They fled in the opposite direction, keeping to the trees, and down to the next lot. This property had a concrete slab for a trailer or motor home, and a huge pole building with metal siding and roof.

They approached with caution, both aware that the two men they'd encountered might not be alone. A small pile of bones, like those of a rabbit or squirrel, were scattered in front of the gaping doors of the metal pole building. Shivering at the sight, Carleen stepped over the bones and into the dark, windowless space.

Her eyes adjusted after a tense few seconds. The dirt floor muffled her steps, but nothing could contain her disappointment at discovering it was as empty as Elmer's garage.

Kane's breath was ragged. His face was as dark as the day. "Both roads are washed out, yet all of these residences have been emptied. Seems to me the lane I told you about was used as an exit route."

She frowned, holding a stitch in her side. "That means Skip will know about it."

"Probably." His expression mirrored the growing concern inside her that they might not make it off The Point alive.

He said, "There's one other cabin on this side of the road. If we don't find a car there, we'll cross the street and work our way up the other side." He kept his voice calm, trying, she thought, to soothe her nerves. But he tapped his foot with the fireplace poker, giving away his own tension. "If we don't find a car there, we can risk either the old lane, or return to the hill behind the cemetery the way we came here last night."

"We'll cross that bridge when we reach it."

"Okay. We'd better get going. Those men'll be back soon."

They slipped outside, listened for their pursuers, heard nothing, then started through the woods again. They'd gone less than ten feet when they heard the men, running from the direction of Elmer's cabin. Excited. Expecting to find them. Knowing they'd find them.

Kane pushed her toward the path to the next lot. "Hurry!"

Carleen froze. Kane rammed into her. She pointed. A cougar perched in the shadows of a fir, on a branch directly above the path. Her heart thumped her chest. Had it been stalking them? Realizing they'd seen it, the cougar growled low in its throat, crouching, ready to pounce.

Behind them, the men were getting closer. They were trapped. Between the men and the cat. Between the crumbling bluff and the stand of trees.

She muttered, "What do we do now?"

Kane clasped her hand and tugged her toward the firs. "This way. Run."

With the fireplace poker, he slashed a path through the bristly branches and out onto the road. The noise alerted the men. They called out in glee. Ran more quickly.

The cat moved even faster. Anticipating Kane and Carleen. Reaching the road first. Carleen let out a cry when she saw it. But hope surged through her again. Between the cat and the men, there on the pavement, its doors hanging invitingly open, stood the big, black pickup truck with the broken headlights that had shoved the SUV over the cliff last night. That had almost ended their lives.

The filthy, mud-splattered truck was the best thing she'd seen in ages. What sweet irony that this weapon of destruction might now be their salvation.

They exchanged a look, connecting mentally. Of one

mind, one thought, they flew to the truck. Clambered inside. The keys were gone. Kane bent, yanked down a couple of wires from beneath the dashboard and touched them together. The engine chugged, then started with a powerful grumble.

Despite the cold, both door windows were open. They heard the men shouting angrily. Saw them emerge onto the road ahead, their guns lifting as they halted.

Kane yelled, "Hang on and keep down."

Carleen banged her door shut. A shot split the air. She ducked, spotting the startled cougar disappearing into the underbrush.

Kane shifted into four-wheel drive and stomped the gas pedal to the floor. The truck shook and lurched forward. Another shot rang out, then another. A bullet zipped past Kane's head and out the passenger window. Carleen squealed and shuddered and held on tight.

Kane drove off the road and through the first driveway. More shots rang out. Metal pinged. Kane zigzagged, purposefully making the truck a less viable target. At length, he pulled back onto the road. Carleen peeked through the back window. The men were charging up the road, still shooting, the bullets falling short.

Across from Elmer's lot, Kane plunged the truck between a stand of cedar trees and onto what looked like an abandoned logging road that had recently been reactivated. In several spots, fallen trees had been sawed through and moved aside to make travel possible.

"Are you okay?" Kane asked, his voice loud inside the noisy truck.

"Yes." She struggled into a sitting position and rolled up her window. "How about you?"

"Great!" he shouted, sounding like a man high on the adrenaline of meeting death head-on and escaping by the skin of his teeth. "Did you recognize either of those guys?"

"No," Carleen said.

"Me, neither." Kane pulled down the visor and handed her a sheaf of papers. "See if there's some identification among these. A registration or insurance form. Let's find out who these yahoos are."

Kane slowed the pickup to an easier speed.

Carleen searched the papers. "Receipts. Nothing with a name on it."

She wrenched open the glove box and dug through more papers to the bottom. Her eye caught something that made her heart leap. She pulled it out, tested it and smiled. She turned toward Kane. "No registration. But I found a prize."

He glanced at her.

Grinning, she held it up for him to see. A cell phone. "And it has a full charge."

Chapter Twelve

The pickup bumped along the dirt road, bouncing through one chuckhole after another, slowly winding around and down. Firs stretched to the sky, cutting off the dark clouds and keeping the rain that had begun to fall from touching the windshield.

Jostled but still grinning, Carleen dialed Hugh Proctor's office in Port Luster. After the third ring, a familiar, gravelly voice said, "Proctor, Dutton and Reese."

Proctor, Dutton and Reese. How many times in her life had she heard those familiar words? Carleen calmed, feeling on solid ground for the first time in eleven days. A tiny fly of heat flitted about her heart. "Thelma?"

"Of course."

There was an odd note in the familiar voice that swatted the heat from Carleen's heart. "It's me, Carleen."

"Well, yes. Hello…again," Thelma said. "Forget something, hon?"

Hello…again? Forget something? When had Thelma last spoken to me? Carleen's stomach pinched. *Or thought she'd spoken to me?* Recently? Today? Did that mean Jamie was still somewhere in Port Luster? She cautioned herself against false hope, but it was fruitless. Her mind, her heart latched immediately onto any speck of hope where her son was concerned.

"I'm sorry about the connection. I'm using a cell phone."

"Yes, I can tell. You should have the muffler on that Lexus checked. It's sure noisy."

"Th-that's where I'm heading," Carleen lied. Kane glanced at her curiously. She shook her head at him. She wanted to put her hand over the receiver and discuss what she'd just learned with him. Instead, she concentrated on keeping her voice even. "I was wondering if you had a number where I might reach Hugh and Phyllis."

"What?" Thelma hesitated. Then she laughed, her voice deep and throaty from forty years of smoking. That voice gave the image of a sexy siren, where, in fact, she resembled someone's kindly, if dumpy, grandmother. Neither image was anywhere near the real Thelma, who'd never married, secretly confiding that she had enough of men every day at work. When she got home, the only housemate she wanted waiting for her was her cat. "Is this a joke?"

"No," Carleen answered cautiously, feeling a deep uneasiness.

"Honey, what the hell is going on?" Thelma laughed again. "Did you lose the number I gave you five minutes ago?"

"Oh." Carleen covered her mouth, cutting off her gasp. *Five minutes ago.* Her hope soared. She warned herself to stay calm, striving for something to say that would sound plausible. Logical. She forced herself to laugh, too. "No. But I ran out of the house without it. Totally scatterbrained today."

"Ah, you poor thing. Probably that news report has you upset, hon."

The phone signal cut out. Had she heard Thelma correctly? A news report? What news report? Carleen frowned, then decided to go along with Thelma as though she understood, counting on her to elaborate. "I suppose you're right."

But Thelma mentioned nothing more about the news report, apparently assuming Carleen knew to what the allusion referred. She rattled off a phone number. Carleen wrote it down on the back of one of the receipts, asking Thelma to repeat it twice as the phone signal faded out again, then restored to clarity moments later. "Thanks, Thelma. Sorry to bother you twice."

Kane wrenched toward her at the word "twice." His brows lifted questioningly.

"You're never a bother, hon."

Carleen could hear hesitation in Thelma's voice and knew the woman was about to offer some advice or a mild rebuke. Carleen exhaled impatiently. She was in no mood for a lecture, no matter how well meant. "Thank—"

"It's just that Hugh and Phyllis...well, you lived right in town these past four years, and yet they hardly ever saw you." Thelma plunged on. "Oh, they realized you were busy with your life and with your darling little boy, but they're very fond of you, hon. And Jamie is as close as they'll ever come to a grandchild. Forgive me for rambling, I'm just trying to say that since they're moving to Florida next month, well, it would be wonderful if you could manage to keep in touch with them on a more regular basis this time after you and Mr. Ellison remarry."

After you and Mr. Ellison remarry?

The thought turned her stomach. But she supposed she shouldn't be surprised. It made perfect sense in the scheme of things. The truck hit a huge puddle and shoved her sideways against the door frame. She winced, swallowed her distaste over Skip's plans to "remarry," and her own guilt for keeping Jamie from the most decent people she knew, and thanked Thelma.

She disconnected and gave Kane a rundown of the call. The tiny lines around his eyes deepened, and she wanted to reach up and soothe them away with her fingertips, to curl against him and let his strength imbue her. But she hadn't the breath to request he pull over and hold her. She barely choked out, "Does 'she' really sound that much like me?"

He shook his head, denial in his eyes, but he seemed to realize only the truth would help her now. He made a face of concession. "Yes—and no. There's something in her tone that's very near yours, but it's just…different."

Enough the same, however, to convince Thelma she'd been talking to me. She hugged herself, that loss of self filling her again. How? "How could she sound like me?"

Raindrops smudged the windshield now, like tiny teardrops, like a child's teardrops. Carleen bit back her own tears of anger and frustration and concern for her little boy.

Jamie's precious face flashed into her mind, tugging along all of the worries she couldn't bear. No. She couldn't get lost in thoughts of the things he needed to have done for him—tying his shoelaces, brushing out the cowlick on his crown, getting his shirt on properly after he'd put it on wrong side out. Thinking that she wasn't there for him would drive her insane. She wouldn't be able to go on.

She had to keep his image close, but only to give her strength. A mental aid to shake off her helplessness.

The truck slewed sideways. Kane gripped the wheel

harder and eased his foot off the gas. He divided his gaze
between the narrowing lane and her. "Too bad we don't
know where the imposter called from or why she wanted
the phone number of the Proctor's hotel in Orlando."

The track ahead ended abruptly at a creek that was six
feet wide. The bank of the stream was a three-foot drop
into white-capped water that rushed over and around pro-
truding boulders.

"Hold on," Kane advised.

Carleen braced herself, one hand flat on the seat and
the other clutching the door frame. He downshifted. The
truck lurched and slowed to a crawl.

To keep her mind off how deep the stream might be,
she said, "Skip probably wants to find out when Hugh
and Phyllis are due home."

"Uh-huh." Kane was concentrating on driving. He
dunked the front tires into the water with caution. The
truck groaned, dipped, lifting the seat high. Carleen slid
forward. She wedged her feet against the floorboards, her
hands against the dashboard. The rear tires plopped into
the water. The truck bounced hard. She rocked back in
the seat, fearing a sudden influx of cold water, but the
boulders kept the cab of the truck high and dry.

Carleen released a taut breath.

The truck bounced and rocked, but forded the creek
with a minimum of splashing. When it had climbed the
opposite bank and was headed down the dirt lane once
again, Kane continued the conversation where he'd left
off. "The imposter could have asked Thelma when Hugh
was due back."

"But she didn't or Thelma would have mentioned it.
I didn't think to ask that, either."

"You're operating under a different set of variables
than Skip and his fake fiancée. They need to make sure

the faker gets out of town and stays out until the Proctors leave for good.''

''Yes, I know. The sooner I talk with Hugh, the better.'' Carleen dialed the number of the hotel in Orlando. The Proctors had checked out. Last week. Once again desperation scraped tiny claws across her brain. She bit the inside of her lip, the pain like an elixir warding off the frustration before it overtook her completely. ''If they're home, why didn't Thelma tell me?''

''Maybe she doesn't know.'' Kane shrugged. ''Call the house.''

She poked in the number and pushed the send button. The phone made an odd beeping noise. She read the screen. ''Damn it all. We're out of range. The call won't go through.''

''We should be back in range as soon as we clear these trees and reach the highway. It's just ahead.''

An awful thought struck her. ''Do you think we can expect a reception party there on 104?''

Kane eased off the gas pedal and brought the truck to a stop. He glanced at her, looking as if the thought hadn't occurred to him and he was kicking himself for not considering it. Concern stood hard as steel slivers in his blue eyes. ''If those yahoos on The Point had another phone with them, then maybe.''

Every good feeling she'd had about them actually escaping Skip's dragnet fled. ''What are we going to do?''

He pressed his lips together, thoughtfully, then said, ''Be grateful this truck has four-wheel drive and a full tank of gas. And that I used to know this area like the back of my hand.''

He veered to the right and headed down an ill-used branch of the dirt road. It was even more rutted and bumpy. About a half-mile in, Kane found a cutoff that

was little more than a footpath through the firs and ce-
dars. At a shot-up forest service sign, he turned left, sending the truck down and over sodden ground, dense
patches of shed pine needles and rotting stumps and logs.

Carleen's right hand clutched the door tightly, her left
gripped the phone, her lifeline to the outside world, to
the only other person who might help her regain her son.
Her gaze was riveted to the screen, watching the scan
mechanism slide through time and again—and find nothing.

The truck pitched sideways. Her gaze ripped from the
screen. The damp ground was inches from the passenger
window, the tires on her side of the pickup sinking in the
soft earth. She gasped. The steady engine groaned on,
and the truck suddenly righted itself.

She glanced through the windshield, wishing an end to
this arduous ride. Between the trees, she caught sight of
moving traffic.

Highway 104.

Kane steadied his hands on the wheel and gave the gas
pedal a firm tap. The pickup surged up and out of the
woods. Rain slapped the windshield, sending fir needles
and other debris flooding away. He drove onto the wide
shoulder of the road, and let out a heavy breath. But the
tension in his body was like a living thing in the cab of
the truck. He twisted in the seat, checking the highway
in both directions.

She'd expected him to turn toward the Hood Canal
Bridge, back toward Port Luster. Instead they were facing
west. "Where are we going?"

"Port Angeles," he said, easing on to the road. "We
need to dump this truck pronto—in case Skip's men have
managed to contact him and he's reported it to the police
as a stolen vehicle."

"Would he risk that?"

"We can't gamble that he won't."

She hugged herself. "Why P.A.?"

"Maybe Sequim, then. I just want to go somewhere we can get some clothes that don't make us look like we live on the street—pick up a different ride, and something to eat that will stick to our ribs. We can't afford to lose this battle from weakness."

The last thing Carleen wanted was something to eat, but she knew he was right. She also imagined her black eye was once again exposed for the world to see. She wouldn't mind picking up a hairbrush along with the makeup. "There's a Smart-Mart in P.A. with a parking lot big enough to 'lose' this pickup truck in. I doubt anyone will pay it much heed for the rest of the day. Maybe longer. There's even a car dealership right across the street."

"Just what I had in mind." He smiled ruefully. "How's the phone?"

Carleen studied the screen again. It was no longer roaming. She re-called Hugh's home number and hit the send key. It began to ring. To her relief, Hugh answered the phone himself. His commanding voice was a salve to her weary soul. He'd rescued her once and been her hero ever since. But Thelma was right. She'd not kept in touch with them as she should have since she'd married Skip. At Skip's insistence.

Skip hadn't wanted her associating with anyone in town. Not unless they were the Ellison's social peers. She'd gone along, rather than suffer a beating. And after the divorce, she'd feared Skip would take out his wrath on the lawyer if she confided her fears to either Hugh or Phyllis.

So once again, she'd held her silence.

But the days of silence were over. She explained the situation to Hugh. As he listened, he was in turns shocked, disbelieving, protective and outraged. His voice grew suddenly cautious. "Don't say any more. Phyl and I will meet you at—" he paused, then added "—your favorite restaurant. You know the one you used to like to go to on Sunday afternoons."

"THE DEER PARK MOVIE THEATER is where I liked to go on Sunday afternoons," she told Kane. "Hugh sounded worried, like he suspected the phone was bugged."

The theater parking lot was almost empty at noon on this Tuesday. They pulled the pickup into a spot near the video rental area. Here, the truck couldn't be seen from the highway. They waited half an hour before the Proctors arrived in separate cars: Hugh in his ancient black Cherokee and Phyllis in her aged silver Continental.

They pulled up on the driver's side of the pickup. Carleen and Kane abandoned the truck, stepping out into the rain that now fell in sheets. Hugh emerged from the Cherokee, tugging the collar of his overcoat high up his thick neck. Hugh was the opposite of Carleen's father in every way. Short, stout, with thick, dark hair graying at the temples, he was shrewd and clever, and, she would bet, still had his first dollar.

He grinned at them both with a flash of even white teeth. "Great to see you, Kane." He had always liked Kane.

He frowned at her appearance, at her black eye, then pulled her into a bear hug, and whispered in her ear, "Now don't you worry, Carlie. We'll get your little boy home."

Carlie? Until this minute, no one but Kane had ever

called her that. It was like others saw her differently than she saw herself.

"Hey, we're getting drenched," Hugh said. "As far as I could tell, no one tailed us from P.L." He pressed the Cherokee keys into Kane's hand. "Follow me."

They left the locked pickup parked at the theater, and drove into Port Angeles to the pier on the waterfront, where a simple ferry ran from there to Victoria, British Columbia. Several restaurants were within walking distance of the ferry dock. They parked in one of the various public lots and chose a small café that advertised thick steaks and fresh seafood.

It was nearly empty—the weather, and the fact that it was two o'clock. The minute they were inside the door, Phyllis exclaimed about Carleen's black eye, her bedraggled outfit, then wrapped her in a comforting hug. Phyllis was a fanatic about her weight, often bragging that she still wore the same size six she'd worn when she and Hugh married forty years ago. She either didn't care about Hugh's weight, or couldn't control his eating and exercise habits.

Her hair was still a fresh brown, all specks of gray banished by her hairdresser. She'd never been particularly motherly, but then, if Carleen were honest, she'd never encouraged any such behavior in Phyllis. By the time they'd taken her in, Carleen had reached the point where she no longer risked emotional rejection from anyone.

Her only divergence from that path had been Kane. And *that* had proven her undoing.

They chose a table in the rear that gave them a clear view of the door. They ordered, saving conversation until the waitress departed. Beneath his trench coat, Hugh wore a jogging suit—not something Carleen had ever seen him in—that attested to how quickly he and Phyllis had left to help them.

How could she have treated this wonderful couple so callously? Had she been afraid they'd let her down, too? Guilt stitched across her heart, threading a patchwork of regret. She'd shortchanged herself, as well as her son.

Hugh shoved the silverware to one side as though getting ready for a strategy meeting; he was a man used to being in charge of every situation. "First thing, after what you two went through last night, I don't want you using a credit card for anything."

"But—" Kane began.

"No, no. You'll take the Cherokee for as long as necessary. I realize you'll also need clothes and other sundry items." Hugh took out his wallet and peeled off two thousand dollars in hundred-dollar bills. "Don't argue. From now on out, we're a team. We work from a strategy."

"Which is?" Carleen asked, a lump forming in her throat at the generosity of this man, at the fear that nothing they did would best Skip.

Hugh's gray eyes narrowed and the wisdom in their depths shone. A case, after all, was a case, and every case required his sharpest legal knowledge. He was nothing if not practical. Brutal honesty was his way of life. His motto. He didn't believe in giving anyone false hope. He offered her none now. "If we go for the longer, usual way, it won't be an easy case to prove. Your word against Skip's, as it were."

"Yes, but I have custody of Jamie." She was tired, bone weary, easy prey to the desperation that she barely managed to hold at bay. Where was her little boy? Her baby? He needed her. And she needed him. "I'm his mother."

"Well, it appears Skip has another Carleen to call you a liar."

"But you and Phyllis and Kane will tell the judge I am who I say I am."

"And Frances and Starla and Vaughn will testify for the other Carleen. And from what Kane says, she's the spitting image of you."

"But Jamie will know me."

"He's three years old. A judge could be convinced that he's easily swayed or confused."

"You make it sound hopeless."

"No, no. Don't start thinking that way." He placed his hand over hers. "We just need some physical proof."

"Such as?" Kane asked.

Hugh looked right at Carleen. "Have you got finger-prints on file anywhere?"

"No."

"Are you sure? Not for a passport or security clearance or a bank for some reason or other?"

Carleen shook her head. "Is that my only hope?"

"No, no. But I'm trying to leap a few steps, take the fastest avenue. What I have in mind is to get some DNA testing. That would prove beyond a doubt you're Jamie's real mother."

"But we can't make Skip produce Jamie for DNA testing." Carleen could hear the hysteria in her voice. "And believe me, he won't do it voluntarily. In fact, he'd make sure he put off such testing until he could get me killed."

Hugh nodded, scowling. "We don't need Jamie. Just some of his hair would do. From a brush or comb."

"I don't have any."

"But you could get some from his room at the mansion."

"No," Kane barked. "We can't go back there. That's not an option."

"Okay." Hugh grew thoughtful again.

"Maybe I could try," Phyllis suggested.

"No." Hugh shook his head. "I can't imagine the Ellisons allowing either of us near the child, let alone into his bedroom."

"Then it's hopeless." Carleen bit back tears.

"No, no. There's always more than one way to skin a polecat. If we can't get the DNA to prove you're Jamie's mother, then we'll get DNA that proves you're Carleen Jamison."

She considered what he was saying. "Are you suggesting I have one of my parents exhumed?" The idea turned her stomach.

"No, no. I was thinking about those relatives of your mother's in Las Vegas."

"Aunt Lola?" Carleen pressed into the café seat. She hadn't seen or spoken to her mother's sister since moving to Port Luster. Nor had Lola Banks or either of her children responded to the telegram Hugh sent at the time of Carleen's parents' deaths. Not so much as a card.

Apparently, Aunt Lola still nursed whatever grudge had caused the rift between Carleen's mother and herself. Carleen doubted any of the Banks family would be glad to see her, let alone willing to donate some blood to help her out. She shook her head. "Do you really think she's likely to help me, Hugh?"

"Do you have any other relatives besides the Banks family?" he asked. "Anyone on your father's side?"

Carleen shook her head again. She had a bad feeling about this. "Not that I'm aware of."

"Well, maybe your aunt knows other relatives," Kane suggested.

"Maybe." Hugh grew thoughtful. "But I'd think since this is your mother's sister, her DNA would be strongest."

"I don't even know if Aunt Lola and my cousins are still in Vegas." She plowed her hand through her hair, tearing the braid loose. "Hell, I don't even know if they're alive."

"I'll find that out for you as soon as we eat."

Carleen wasn't sure.

"Well, it's up to you." Hugh placed his napkin in his lap, as the waitress approached with their food. "I can apply for an exhumation, but even with your permission that could take a while. In fact, every other option will take time. And time is in short supply at the moment. The DNA is the quickest way I can think of to resolve the matter and make Skip produce and turn Jamie over to you."

"Then, of course, it's what we'll do," Kane said, staring long and hard into Carleen's eyes. At length, she nodded, knowing that by accepting this she would have to leave the Olympic Peninsula, leave Washington State, leave Jamie longer in the hands of a strange woman, and fly to Las Vegas.

After devouring a goodly chunk of fresh salmon, Hugh called Thelma and put her to checking on the whereabouts of Lola Banks. She had the information before he finished his dessert. "Lola Banks is still at the same address. Same place I sent the telegram about your folks."

He handed Carleen the slip of paper, then he called and secured seats on a flight from Port Angeles to SeaTac Airport with a connection to Vegas, and arranged to meet them at the airport in two hours to give them the tickets.

First, however, Kane and Carleen stopped at the Smart-Mart for clothes and those other sundries Hugh had mentioned. When the salesclerk bagged their mud-smeared, torn clothing, Carleen was reminded of the other clerk in the other store and the other clothes that were now in Skip's possession.

She glanced around at Kane, and her breath lodged in her throat. He'd chosen faded jeans, a white dress shirt and a pale blue-and-black tweed sports jacket, the contrasting colors deepening his tan and bringing out the blue of his eyes. She'd chosen a similar outfit, her jacket more black than blue. To her surprise, she felt more comfortable than she had in her ruined designer suit, felt as though she were finding out for the first time in her life who she really was.

At the makeup counter, she'd covered the bruised eye and fixed her hair. Staring at her reflection, she had noticed that something seemed different about her, as though a different woman lived below the polished surface she showed the world, and pieces of that top layer were being scraped away, revealing a glimpse of the real Carleen beneath. Was her real self closer to being Carlie than Carleen?

Kane gathered the tags from all the items they'd selected, then they went to the checkout counter.

As they stood in line, Carleen thought about her life, realizing that she'd spent it as a victim, first to her father, then to her passion for Kane, then to Skip. It had taken losing her son for her to shake off the learned behavior of years and years, for her to start to figure out what she really wanted and needed in order to feel happy and whole and secure.

She understood now that she'd had a chance at all of it. Once. But she hadn't recognized that, hadn't trusted that, and had reached for the brass ring instead, only to find herself trapped on the same merry-go-round of misery.

Had wisdom come too late for her?

The cell phone, which Carleen had placed in her newly purchased shoulder bag, rang. She jumped. The phone rang again. She rounded toward Kane.

His eyebrows spiked. "I'll take it," he said.

She dug the phone from the purse. It vibrated in her palm like a vile black rodent. She handed it to him, gladly.

He snapped it open and pressed it to his ear. "Yeah."

She watched his expression darken. He closed the phone and swore. Alarm crept across her spine. She asked, "What?"

"Come on." He pivoted and headed back through the store. Passing a rack of baseball caps, he grabbed two and plopped one on her head, then donned the other.

She felt a strange fluttering of dread beneath her heart, and didn't argue with him or ask, "Why the hats?"

She hastened to keep pace with Kane's longer strides. He filed into the Home Electronics department, walking straight back to the Home Entertainment section and the wall of various-sized televisions all flashing the same MTV music video. He stopped at one of the smaller sets, and changed its channel to the Northwest News station.

A woman's photograph filled the screen. Carleen froze, her gaze fixed on the set. *It was the face of the woman who'd abducted her, the woman from her flash of memory.* What was she doing on the news? Moving like a zombie, Carleen stepped closer to Kane. He cranked the volume a turn.

The anchorwoman's voice slapped tinny against Carleen's ears. *"The body found in an Oregon seaside cabin this past weekend has been identified as Coral Juanita Clayton.''*

A seaside cabin. Carleen blanched. She'd been sure she'd been held in a seaside cabin. Had it been a cabin in Oregon? Her mouth dried. Bits and pieces of memory splashed through her mind like manic, pulsating strobe lights. She recalled the gun, the rust-colored stains on the clothing she'd been wearing in that San Diego motel room. Had it been blood? Coral Clayton's blood? Was that why Skip wanted those clothes? She felt an icy blast of foreboding.

Was that the reason she was so frightened when she touched the credit card—because she knew something about the dead woman's murder? Had she been there? Somehow been involved?

Kane clasped her hand, holding her erect. The newscaster continued, *''An eyewitness is cooperating with police and helped come up with this composite sketch of the suspected murderer, who is being sought in a statewide search. If you've seen this woman, please call the 1-800 number at the bottom of your screen.''*

Carleen now understood Thelma's earlier reference to the news report. She felt the world around her blacken and disappear, felt the crowd of shoppers turn into eyes, all staring at her, as though she alone stood exposed beneath a brilliant spotlight.

The police sketch looked exactly like her.

Chapter Thirteen

A fugitive! How soon before someone notified Oregon that their fugitive was in Washington? Carleen had never felt more afraid of permanently losing her son. The feeling that she'd waited too long to discover her true self, to take control of her life, clutched her belly.

"We need sunglasses. The bigger the better." Kane had switched the television channel back to MTV, vanquishing the newscast as though she'd dreamed it up, and dragging her away from the Home Electronics department.

But the police composite sketch still played on the screen of her mind. Was she guilty? Had she taken another's life? God, why couldn't she remember? Her desperation drove the elusive memories deeper into the dark abyss of her mind, and spiked a throbbing pain at her temples.

She glanced at Kane. Why wasn't he bombarding her with questions? Surely he had to be wondering if she had murdered Coral Clayton? She moved beside him on leaden legs, her body numb, her brain spinning with ugly possibilities, worse fears. She might as well have been a mannequin standing stock-still as he selected sunglasses for each of them. He bit off the tags, then hustled her back to the checkout line. In their caps and sunglasses, they seemed one of the crowd, average blue-collar shoppers, the kind that were the backbone of Smart-Marts country-wide.

Still, she caught her lower lip in her teeth, knowing with uncontrollable dread that they would be remembered by the sheer fact that they'd handed the clerk a stack of price tags instead of merchandise. They paid cash for their purchases, and hurried outside to the Cherokee.

The cell phone rang again. Carleen jumped. Kane cursed and dug it from his coat pocket. Instead of answering, he turned it off. The nerve-shattering rings silenced. He leaned close to her, his eyes visible through the dark lenses. "Skip can't trace our whereabouts. He's just playing more head games."

"What if they've found the truck?"

"Impossible. But even if they have, we'll be gone before they start searching P.A."

Even with Kane's assurances, the next hours passed in terror for Carleen—boarding one plane, then another, fearing, if not Skip's henchmen, the public. Every second, she expected to be recognized from the police sketch. She moved through the crowds with her head low, the sunglasses and baseball cap hiding most of her face, ever aware that her very attitude made her look suspect.

But in her heart, she knew her greatest fear was that she'd look at Kane and see in his eyes that he was wondering whether she'd killed Coral Clayton.

Just as she was wondering that very thing.

Hugh had gotten their tickets in his and Phyllis's names and supplied them with phony picture IDs to match. Carleen had no idea he even knew someone who would or could make false credentials. She would never have guessed Hugh would bend the law, even for her. She'd underestimated him at every turn.

When the plane for Vegas lifted off from Seattle, she finally began to breathe without trembling.

Kane pressed his shoulder against hers, leaning low and speaking lower. "We need to talk."

Here it comes. "About…?"

"Your Las Vegas relatives."

Carleen swallowed against the lump in her throat, but she couldn't look at him. Couldn't allow herself to be drawn into the comfort he was offering. She didn't want pity from Kane, not ever. She pulled into herself, closed her eyes and considered what she recalled about her aunt and her cousins.

As though he refused to accept her emotional withdrawal, Kane took her hand and pulled her closer to him. "Tell me, Carlie."

Oddly, the warmth issuing from him gave her the strength to confront her fear. Bracing herself, she peered up into his eyes. They were a brilliant clear blue, and she saw herself reflected there. Nothing more. Nothing less. The anxiety subsided enough to allow her to breathe without pain.

He said again, "Carlie?"

Carlie. Yes, she was starting to feel more like Carlie than Carleen. Acknowledging that, she sensed a breaking inside, heard a teeny noise like stitches popping from a seam, and something loosened around her heart, leaving her feeling freer. She hated to think how briefly she might own and enjoy this wondrous sensation.

The tiny lines around Kane's sensuous mouth flexed and deepened. "Was it that awful?"

"Awful?" Carlie laughed coldly. Her pulse jittered. "When I lived in Las Vegas, I was truly innocent. I thought my father was the most generous and loving man. No, I wasn't just innocent,'' she amended. ''But naive.''

She lowered her voice. Admitting and facing painful truths to Kane was one thing, having them overheard by strangers tinted them another shade of ugly. ''My mother and her sister came from a dirt-poor family. My father inherited a lot of money from a wealthy uncle when I was eight. I don't know when he started gambling. But he tossed away that fortune as if it was a pile of non-winner pull-tab stubs. I didn't learn about his addiction until we moved to Port Luster.''

She licked her lips. She'd never told anyone this, but telling Kane seemed right, somehow. ''When Dad inherited his money, we moved into a big house with a pool. God, how many years I spent longing to go back to that house, to the happiness I *thought* my family had shared there.''

Carlie shifted in her seat, glanced out the window, then back at Kane. ''My aunt had Tammy-Faye Baker's heavy hand with makeup and a figure like Pamela Anderson Lee. She and my cousins, Angie and Richie, used to come over every day to swim. Aunt Lola always wore the skimpiest bikini, and her skin was golden tanned. She was the most gorgeous creature I'd ever seen. I wanted to be just like her when I grew up.'' Carlie laughed at herself. ''I realize now there was something cheap and flashy about her that appealed to my little-girl imagination.''

Kane smiled and touched her cheek. ''I wish I'd known you then.''

Carlie bit her inner lip. His own childhood had, in different ways, been as hard as hers. But she doubted they'd have been friends. Kids who were hurting tended to steer clear of others who were also victims. She gave him a bittersweet smile. "More often than not, my aunt and cousins stayed to dinner. Then things suddenly changed. I don't know what happened. But if I had to speculate, I'd guess my father must have started losing money at a rapid rate.

"One day when I came home from school, the pool had been drained. It was never refilled. Aunt Lola and my cousins quit coming to our house. Once a week, Mother and I went to Lola's. She lived a long ways out of town, in a trailer park. I don't remember much about the place, but they had no pool and it was hot and uncomfortable there. Then just as suddenly as the Banks quit coming to our house, we stopped going to theirs. I never knew why. Mom wouldn't tell me. In fact, she became so irritated with my questions on the subject, she forbade me to mention any of the Banks to her."

Kane tipped his cap brim back, and his expression said he more than understood the frustration of unanswered questions. "And you've never gotten in touch with them since your mother died?"

"Hugh sent a telegram, but it went unanswered. I didn't get as much as a card from my aunt or my cousins. And, of course, none of them showed up for the funeral." She squeezed Kane's hand. "I'm so afraid Aunt Lola won't help us."

"I think when she hears your story, she will."

"I wish I knew what caused the rift between my mother and her. What if she holds whatever it was against me?"

"What if she doesn't?"

"What if she won't speak to me?"

"What if she will?"

"What if she won't?"

"We aren't going to give her the chance. We're going to show up unannounced and catch her off guard."

Carlie knew he was trying to ease her mind, to get her to take a positive attitude, even though both feared what the police search and Coral Clayton's murder could mean to them and to Jamie. "What if Oregon has expanded the search for me to other states? What if CNN or one of the other national news shows has picked up on the hunt?"

His face paled beneath his tan, but he just shook his head and kissed the back of her hand. "Then we'll be going to jail."

"Kane, don't joke." She hadn't thought about the trouble he could get into. "I don't want you arrested as an accessory."

"I'm a big boy. I know what I'm doing. Let me worry about myself."

But who would take care of Jamie if they both ended up behind bars? No. She couldn't dwell on that. One thing at a time. Aunt Lola, first.

"We'll be landing soon." Kane peered out the window. "Here's praying there are no surprises waiting for us down there."

Evening had fallen, and as she glanced outside, her breath caught. Below, the valley was spread with lights as far as she could see, like a million diamonds and emeralds and sapphires and rubies laid out on a black-velvet swatch, there for the plucking, a lure so strong few could resist. But Carlie had lived here, and she knew the lure was what did the plucking in this town.

McCARREN INTERNATIONAL AIRPORT was alive with tourists heading to the casinos, stopping to play the slot machines before gathering their luggage. Kane and Carlie had no bags to collect. They moved with the flow of foot traffic heading through the concourse to the main building.

Dread kept pace with Carlie. Every uniformed man they encountered caused her heart to leap, even though most were pilots or security guards. But it wasn't only the cops that had her continuously glancing over her shoulder. Though they seemed to have eluded Skip and his hired killers, he might have discovered by now exactly where they'd gone. She'd spotted no one, but her neck prickled and her nerves ached, and the raucous crowd noise aggravated her headache.

She caught glimpses of smiling faces, snatches of rousing laughter, and wished she could join the celebration these folks seemed to be enjoying.

Instead she kept her head ducked, and hurried alongside Kane. They seemed to be the only two not having fun, and the realization increased her fear that they stood out, would be remembered, noticed, turned in to the police.

And what about Hugh and Phyllis? Would Skip go after them? Had he already been to their home, forced them to reveal her whereabouts? God, would this fear ever end? The tightness in her chest worsened, making her light-headed. "I can't believe she's still living on Linden, in the same mobile home park."

"It's a sign that our luck is changing for the better," Kane whispered close to her ear, a soft brush of air that warmed her and tempted her to lean in to him.

She resisted, wishing she could believe their luck was taking an upward swing. She shook her head. "I never knew you were an optimist."

He blinked, sobering. "There are a lot of things we don't know about each other." His gaze seemed to ask if they would ever reach a time or place to share their secrets. He cleared his throat and cast a surreptitious gaze around. "Let's get out of here before Lady Luck decides we don't deserve her blessing."

They secured a taxi and were soon headed through the incredible light show that was The Strip, the unimaginable gridlock, slowly making their way to the edge of the desert, to the aged trailer park where Lola Banks had lived for as far back as Carlie could remember.

As their taxi pulled through the arched entrance of The Chimes, Carlie was surprised that she actually did remember the place. The years and the weather had stripped it of what little dignity it might once have claimed. Vapor lights illuminated the narrow streets and the clustered mobile homes. Number sixty-two was in the middle of the park, a single wide, a peeling metal box as inviting as an open tin of sardines left to bake in the unrelenting sun. There was no yard, just a few wild cacti and clustered rocks pushing up out of the sand beside the trailer's foundation.

As Kane and Carlie stepped from their taxi into the cool night wind, the door to the trailer banged open and shut. Beneath the porch light, a buxom redhead in a petal-pink chiffon dress, satin purse and matching satin pumps clambered out of the mobile home. A fur stole bobbed against her shoulders like a loping coyote. She gave a happy whoop, then hurried off the leaning stoop and across the pavement so quickly the small wheeled bag she pulled flopped behind her. "So, you came to pick me up, girlie. Will wonders never cease?"

Even with the shock of Lucille Ball hair and the sagging face, Carlie knew her aunt; there was no mistaking that walk, that mouthy quip, or that liberally applied makeup.

Carlie swept off her hat and sunglasses. She had no idea what her aunt was talking about, but before she could say a word, Lola Banks brushed past her, making straight for Kane, her hand extended in anticipation of his.

"I'm so pleased to finally meet you, Mr. Ellison. Skip. I just wanna say thank you for my new duds. Especially this." She stroked the stole. "Lordy, I'm looking forward to this move. Oh, my, the Olympic Peninsula sounds like heaven on Earth. Only got a couple of boxes for your movers to ship. I'm not taking anything else. You've made an old woman mighty happy—and a good choice for a wife with my Angie, here."

"Angie?" Carlie said, choking as realization hit her like a tidal wave. "You think I'm Angie?"

Laughing, Lola Banks peered at Carlie. "Now, don't you make jokes with your mama, girlie."

Lola tossed her bag into the cab.

Carlie caught her aunt by the shoulder, halting her climb into the taxi. "Aunt Lola, I'm Carleen, John and Merline's daughter. This is Kane Kincaid. And you'd better tell us what Angie is doing impersonating me."

"Yeah. Where is she?" Kane grabbed the taxi door and pulled the wheeled bag out. Lola puffed up indignantly. Kane leaned close to her. "From your act a minute ago, there's no doubt she's here in Vegas, but where?"

"Carleen? No. Carleen's d—"

"Dead?" Carlie finished for her.

Confusion grabbed her aunt's features. Then fear. Looking aghast, she stumbled back. "I—I don't know what you're talking about. Either of you. Get out of here. Leave me alone."

Abandoning her bag, she fled back toward her trailer,

shoved aside a ceramic frog and grabbed up the key tucked beneath it.

Carlie reached her before she could get the key in the door. "No, Aunt Lola. We're all going inside, and you're going to talk to us. Your daughter has my son, and we're not leaving here until you tell us where she is."

Lola Banks backed up to the door. Her blue-shadowed, mascara-laden azure eyes were wide with reluctance. Her ample chest heaved. A long moment passed, then she sighed, the fight gone out of her like a deflated puff spider. "Gonna live in some fancy-schmancy mansion in Port Luster. Yeah, sure. Stupid old fool," she mumbled. "I knew movin' outta this hellhole was just a bona fide fantasy. A total fake. This is probably fake, too." She drop-kicked the stole across the room. "Nothing that good ever happens to Lola Banks."

Inside, the trailer reeked of misery and stale cigarette smoke. Even with the lights on, there was no color to the room, as if the sun and heat had sucked it all away, along with the spirits of those forced to call it home.

Lola stalked to the kitchen. She plucked a metal ash-tray from a cupboard and a pack of Winstons from her satin purse.

Two hat-sized cardboard boxes reposed on a rickety kitchen table. Carlie moved toward them, drawn by some indefinable force. The boxes held framed and loose photographs. The only things her aunt was taking to her new home on the Olympic Peninsula?

Carlie lifted one of the photos—two young girls, a brunette and a redhead posed on the edge of a swimming pool. She showed it to Kane.

"Angie and me. At my house. She's younger by two years." Carlie thought about her now. A memory coming to her without struggle or headache. "I don't understand. We look nothing alike."

Lola laughed. "Merline and I didn't, either, but you'd have to be deaf and blind not to notice the same timbre in our voices, the similarities in our gestures. You and Angie always had that, too."

Kane released a low whistle. "Then with Skip's help, it was probably pretty simple to teach Angie to impersonate you. But the facial changes had to require extensive plastic surgery. There will be scarring, and that will help prove your case."

Carlie felt a flick of relief. "I don't understand why she put herself through the torture of multiple plastic surgeries."

But the answer was all around her. For the money, of course. Money. The desperate lack of money. Carlie eyed her aunt. "What caused the rift between you and my mom?"

Her aunt lifted an eyebrow. "Why am I surprised Merline didn't tell you?"

"You tell me."

Lola lit a cigarette, inhaled, then blew smoke in a ring above her head. It was no halo and she was no angel; her tough voice and hard, seamed face attested to that. "John Jamison. The devil himself. Lord, but Merline couldn't see what a snake he was. He had more lucre than God, but I was an embarrassment. That tight SOB had nothing to spare for his wife's sister, a widow, stuck in this dump. For all he cared, I could work like an alley cat. How was I supposed to keep my son and daughter fed and clothed?"

Carlie was outraged. "My mother used to write you checks. I remember."

Lola chortled with disdain. "Oh, Merline's 'I'm glad

I'm not you' generosity. Guilt and pity. That's what she felt for me. I tolerated it because paltry as those checks were, they helped keep the wolf from our door. Then John put a stop to that money. Merline could have stood up to him for my sake, but she wouldn't. For all she cared, my kids and I could starve to death.''

Carlie cringed beneath the hatred in her aunt's eyes, the hatred and spite garnered and nurtured by her father's greed, by the very poverty that had been these relatives' daily fare. The same poverty she and her mother had endured.

Lola sniffed with disdain. ''You're the same as them. As John and Merline. I made sure my kids knew never to trust any of you. And I was right. After your folks died, you never sent a penny to help us out. You're as mean as your old man.''

There was no sense, Carlie decided, in telling her aunt there had been no money. Lola wouldn't believe her. ''Where's Richie?''

''Don't you say his name.'' But the fight behind the words died quickly, and Lola seemed to melt into herself even more. Tears welled in her eyes, caught in the mascara and slipped black trails down her cheeks. She stubbed out her cigarette and lit another. ''Oh, he had big dreams, that one. He was getting out of here and making a name for himself. Well, he escaped all right. Enlisted in the army the second he turned seventeen, for all the good it did him.''

She wiped her tears with the sleeve of her chiffon dress, not noticing that her makeup was smearing the delicate pink in shades of a rainbow bruise. ''He was killed in the Middle East—an accident, the Pentagon claims. Friendly fire, rumor has it. But I can't prove it.

Or I'd sue Uncle Sam 'til his striped jacket was as blue as his lying lips.''

She glowered at Carlie, seeming to blame her for this, too, as though the money her family withheld from the Banks family somehow contributed to Richie's tragic, senseless death.

Fury at the whole situation flooded Carlie. The legacy of her father's greed was again extracting too heavy a price. Being paid by her son. She understood holding a grudge. She would never forgive her aunt or Angie for the harm they'd done and were still doing Jamie. He didn't deserve the nightmare they'd made of his young life. If they didn't help her now, she'd see that they were both arrested as accessories in the crime Skip had perpetrated against her.

Kane had been pacing the living room, listening, snooping. Apparently unsatisfied with his covert search, he said, "How did Angie meet Skip Ellison?"

Aunt Lola raised her eyebrows, and once again found courage in her anger, calm in her cigarette. "You'll have to ask Angie. That's not my story to tell."

Kane's neck grew red. "Damn it all, where is she?"

Her aunt took a long drag, then said around an exhale of smoke, "At one of them fancy-schmacy hotels on The Strip."

"Which one?" Carlie demanded, feeling so close to her son, yet so far away.

"I ain't telling you that." She pulled on the cigarette again.

"The hell you're not." Kane's voice held a menacing tone. He withdrew the cell phone from his pocket and flipped it open. "The Oregon State police are, at this moment, searching for a woman who looks exactly like your daughter. I think I'll call and let them know she's here in Vegas."

Lola smirked. "You're bluffing."

"No. He's not."

Something in Carlie's tone seemed to convince her aunt. The smirk twisted into a frown. Her aunt tapped the ash from her smoke, her hand shaky. "What do they want this woman for?"

"Murder." Kane's eyes were dark in the dim light.

Lola looked stunned, nearly dropping the cigarette. "My Angie never killed nobody."

"Maybe not, but given her upbringing, I'll wager she's real well known to the cops in this town."

"That's not my fault." She took a last pull on the cigarette and dropped it with the other into the ashtray. "I did the best I could by her."

"I'll bet you did." Kane grinned coldly. "All the same, I think the local police would probably be interested in the fact that she's completely changed her appearance and her name, and is currently impersonating her cousin. There can't be a legal reason for that, now can there?"

Lola blanched, and Carlie knew Kane had struck home.

But her aunt wasn't through. She sputtered and pointed at Carlie. "Maybe the Oregon cops are looking for this one."

"Maybe," Kane agreed, shrugging. "Let's call and let them decide."

He punched numbers on the cell phone keypad.

Lola shrieked, "No. Don't do that. Don't you ruin my girlie's wedding night, and her only chance at happiness."

Her only chance at happiness? Built on my misery. Carlie felt sick.

"Wedding?" Kane glanced up from the phone, eyebrows raised.

She glanced at her watch. "I've gotta get going. She's marrying Skip Ellison in two hours time."

Oh, my God, Carlie thought, hugging herself. Jamie *was* in town. Her hope rose like smoke from that tin ashtray. With luck, they'd reach him before Skip or the police could stop them.

"Where is Angie?" Kane threatened with the phone again.

Grudgingly, Lola Banks dug a slip of paper from her purse and handed it to him. He called another cab, and soon they were headed down The Strip, past one casino after another, one new theme hotel after another, the grid-lock holding the taxi to the speed of a slug.

Carlie was sure she could have walked faster than the cab was moving. Trouble was, the sidewalks were jammed, so it wouldn't really be any quicker to walk. Every revolution of the tires tried her nerves. Stay calm, she counseled herself, but it did no good. She'd waited too long to get Jamie. Too long to see his precious face and touch her chin in their favorite, secret greeting.

Ahead Carlie saw something that looked like the Sphinx. "That's it," Aunt Lola called. "That Egyptian place."

"The Luxor," the cab driver clarified.

As the taxi neared the drop-off area, Carlie noticed there were several Las Vegas police cars parked ahead of them. Had they finally caught up with her? Her stomach clenched. *God, please, don't let me come this close to getting my son back just to yank the rug out from under me.*

They entered the lobby, a breathtaking expanse with marble floors, majestic pillars, gigantic Egyptian statues, water fountains and palm trees. Police and guests were everywhere. The noise level was brutal, a mishmash of voices and electronic gambling machines.

Carlie wanted to run back outside and into another cab, drive as far from here as she could get. If not for Jamie, she would have, but he was here, somewhere in this hotel. And she wasn't leaving without him.

Kane asked Lola, "What's Angie's room number?"

Lola shrugged. "She said to ask at the front desk, and they'd direct me." She started past him.

Kane caught her arm. "We're not going to do that. First, we're going to find out what the police are doing here. Then we'll call your daughter from a house phone, and she can give us her room number."

Carlie followed Kane and Lola into the huge casino. Smoke floated on the air, burning her nostrils and eyes. The *clink* of coins and the *clang* of slot machines battered her ears. Kane waylaid a cocktail waitress, a shapely Hispanic woman dressed in a short black velvet outfit with golden bands that complemented the hotel's Egyptian theme. Carlie removed her sunglasses, but kept her cap low on her forehead.

"What's up with all the cops?" Kane asked, his tone that of a curious hotel guest.

The pretty woman gave him an admiring once-over, obviously approving of what she saw, and roused a twinge of ire in Carlie. She tamped down the inappropriate jealousy, confounded that she felt possessive about Kane. They'd made no promises, no commitments beyond rescuing Jamie.

The waitress said, "I'm sure you understand the hotel doesn't want us talking about that, sir."

Kane nodded and shoved a hundred-dollar bill into the tip cup on the tray she carried. She smiled and lowered her voice. "But, I'm sure my boss didn't mean I shouldn't tell you, sir. It's going to be in all the papers by morning, anyway."

An odd dread leaped into Carlie's throat. "What is?"

"Please, may I take your drink order?" she urged in a melodic voice. Lola ordered a gin and tonic. The waitress said, "It seems some celebrity got herself shot to death on the fifteenth floor of the pyramid."

"What?" Carlie hugged herself. Everywhere they went these past twenty-four hours, violent death seemed to follow. "Who?"

Instead of answering, the waitress insisted she order first, her pencil poised above her pad. "What'll you have, ma'am?"

Carlie wanted to scream, but Lola had a salacious gleam in her eyes. "What celebrity?"

"Not so much a celebrity as a society dame. Some rich guy's wife," the waitress said. "Ex-wife, actually. But they were going to be remarried in one of Mandalay Bay's chapels tonight."

Lola drew a sharp breath and her voice came out in a scratchy whisper, as though she no longer wanted the dead woman's name, but couldn't stop herself from asking. "Whose ex-wife?"

Carlie felt dread sweeping up like an evil fog. It seemed to her that the waitress's voice took on a singsong tone as she added, "That mucho wealthy dude who's the new CEO of *EL*."

"What?" Kane looked as numb as Carlie felt. "The murdered woman was Carleen Ellison?"

"Yeah," the waitress nodded, then began moving away. "That's right, but you didn't hear it from me."

Chapter Fourteen

"Oh, my God, Jamie!" Carlie caught the waitress's arm, and spun her around; the tip cup skidded across the tray and over its edge, sending coins and bills spilling to the floor. The waitress yelped.

"Angie!" Lola screamed. "You killed my Angie." She pointed to Kane and Carlie. "Murderers! Murderers!"

Gamblers glanced up from their preferred games to witness the hysteria. But no one came to help Lola.

Carlie's heart was crashing and skittering as wildly as the coins. "Did the murdered woman have a little boy with her?"

The waitress dived for her tip money, wrenching loose of Carlie's grasp.

Lola, her face glowing crimson, stopped screeching, staggered around and stumbled out of the casino, tottering like a drunk on her pink pumps.

"What room was the murdered woman in?" Carlie asked, dropping to a squat to get the waitress's attention.

"Please," Kane pleaded, offering another hundred-dollar bill as an enticement.

The waitress greedily snatched the money and stuffed it into her bra. "Fifteenth floor of the pyramid, up Inclinator 4—that's the elevator. I don't know which room, but nobody mentioned a kid.''

"Come on." Kane helped Carlie up. "We'll find him."

His confidence bolstered her. She wanted to reach up and touch his face, to reassure him of the same thing. For she could see the worry and concern she was feeling for Jamie reflected deep in Kane's wonderful eyes. She slipped her hand in his; they were a force united with a single purpose. They started toward the lobby, only to stop cold.

Her aunt was returning with a couple of policemen in tow. "Kane, look."

He swore, and tugged her around. They darted through the enormous maze of gaming tables and mechanized slot machines, into the hallway to the Giza Galleria, and followed the signs to Inclinator 4. The elevators were in a small hallway with a guard posted in the middle, checking room keys. They hung back a moment, waited for a large group of guests, and fell in step with them. As they entered the hallway, the elevator to their right opened. Kane flashed a credit card. The guard nodded, and he hustled Carlie inside with a group of white-haired women.

Terror rode hard along Carlie's nerves, fed by the fear that whoever had killed Angie might also have killed or injured Jamie, that the cops would stop them before they could reach him.

She also ached to ask Kane who he thought would have shot Angie and why. It made no sense. Unless…unless Skip thought he had one too many Carleens. Her insides trembled, the elevator's sideways motion increasing the ill feeling in her stomach. Maybe his henchmen meant to kill her and had mistakenly killed Angie.

The ascent was at a snail's pace, the elevator stopping on nearly every floor to disgorge another matron.

After the fourteenth floor, three women remained. Carlie couldn't talk to Kane about her fears, could only return his worried glances and think how grateful she was that he hadn't run out on her. She'd be insane by now if not for his strength and support. She'd underestimated this man on every level. Done him such injustice that given a lifetime, she doubted she could make it up to him.

On the twentieth floor, police and crime-scene workers were everywhere. A uniformed policewoman with short brown hair and probing brown eyes stopped Kane and Carlie the second they stepped off the elevator. ''If you have a room on this floor, I'll need to see a key.''

Shaking with fear, Carlie dodged the woman. The cop caught her by the upper arm. ''Hey, what's your hurry?'' She studied Carlie, recognition, if not placement, registered in her astute eyes.

Praying it was because of Angie and not the Oregon search, Carlie, her guts quivering, plucked off her cap. The officer's eyes widened. ''You look just like the vic—''

''Then apparently, the dead woman *is* my sister,'' she lied, her voice as shaky as her hands. ''My twin.''

The policewoman sucked in a breath. Sympathy issued from her dark eyes. ''I'm very sorry, but you don't want to go in there, even if I would allow it. Which I won't.''

Carlie felt cold and close to tears. She nodded, finding it difficult to speak. ''Jamie? Was he with her?''

''Jamie?'' The officer shook her head, obviously making no connection to anyone named Jamie.

Kane interceded. ''Our three-year-old...nephew. He might have been with my wife's sister.''

"No. No child."

"Are you sure?" Carlie's voice broke; the possibility that Jamie might have been wounded or abducted was more than she could bear.

"Ms. Ellison checked in alone, and the maid has confirmed only one person occupied the room." The policewoman glanced from one to the other of them, suspicion growing in her eyes. "Should we be concerned about her little boy? Maybe you should speak to Detective Sykes now instead of later."

"N-no. Th—that's not necessary," Carlie stammered. "If you're sure Jamie wasn't with her, then he's likely with his father's family. I just wanted to know that he hadn't watched his mother being murdered, and then been given over to strangers to wait for family to claim him."

The officer nodded, finally seeming to believe them.

Carlie nearly collapsed with relief. Jamie had been spared the horror of watching her cousin murdered. He hadn't been killed, or wounded, or abducted. The only downside was that she and Kane still didn't know where he was. With Skip, for sure. But where? In this hotel? Another hotel? Where? Damn it all. Her knees wobbled, and she gripped Kane's arm for support.

Kane swept her up, pulling her to his side as though her grief had overwhelmed her. "My wife and her sister were very close. She's barely had time to process her loss. Her first concern was for the living. For the boy. We haven't spoken with any of the Ellisons yet, but I'm sure that's where we'll find Jamie."

He started backing toward the elevator. The policewoman asked, "How did you know about the murder?"

"We were checking in and the registration clerk recognized us as family. The manager took us into his office and broke the news.''

She nodded, but a lingering suspicion laced her voice. ''Don't forget, Detective Sykes will want to talk with you. What's your room number?''

''503.'' Kane eased Carlie back and pushed the down button on the elevator panel. ''My wife needs to rest now. We'll be in our room. Sykes can find us there.''

The second the elevator doors closed, Carlie hugged Kane. Adrenaline rushed her veins. ''My God, you were brilliant. I was terrified she'd insist on handing us over to Detective Sykes.''

''You were pretty brilliant yourself.'' He kissed her hard on the mouth, and showers of delight fell through her, but he pulled back too soon. Regret was harsh in his eyes. ''I'd pursue this, but we've got to get off on the fifth floor.''

Carlie felt cold at his withdrawal, felt a loss of warmth and fire so sudden it sent shudders through her.

The elevator doors slid open.

As they emerged into the empty hallway, she said, ''I was so sure Angie had Jamie. Damn Skip. Where are they?''

''He's got to be around here somewhere. He thought he was getting married in an hour. We'll go downstairs, use a house phone and get his room number.''

They hurried down the hallway that was open on one side, overlooking the IMAX theater and shopping court. He opened the stairwell door. They ducked inside and descended to the lobby floor. In the casino, amid the horde of gamblers and guests, they soon found a house phone.

Kane called the front desk. ''Skip Ellison's room, please.''

He listened. "Really? What about Frances Ellison? No, hmm. What about Vaughn Harding? Okay, thank you."

He hung up and frowned at Carlie. "None of the Ellison family is registered, nor were they registered and checked out."

"Maybe they're at The Mandalay Bay. That's where the wedding is taking place."

"Yeah, that makes sense. I spotted a raised, covered walkway to Mandalay Bay somewhere around here."

Carlie's belly churned as they headed back through the casino, between and around the gamblers, the tables and machines. They skirted a baccarat table, and Kane halted, gesturing for her to retreat a few steps.

Her heart leaped into her throat as she skipped back. "What is it?"

"Aunt Lola at ten o'clock."

They peered around the corner of the baccarat table. Lola, a highball at her elbow, slumped at a nearby bar looking like a melted birthday cake with all the candles and frosting sliding off. Despite everything, Carlie felt sorry for her aunt. She understood the desperation misery could inflict. And she saw how the payment for the wrong choices out of that misery had cost her aunt both of her children. Just as Carlie's own wrong choices had cost her Jamie. But Jamie was still alive. *She* still had hope.

They edged away before Lola saw them, eluded an eager police officer who might have been searching for them, and made a stealthy exit outside into the cool night breeze that felt wonderful against her overheated cheeks.

"We should have taken the tram to the Mandalay." Kane took off his hat and ran his hand over his sun-kissed hair. He was starting to need a shave, golden bristles on his jaw catching the gleam of overhead lights. "It's above the Giza Galleria."

Carlie wasn't thrilled about going back inside, but they had no choice. "Okay."

As they turned back toward the wall of doors, a familiar face caught her attention. Carlie froze and gripped Kane's arm. "Getting into the airport shuttle. It's Vaughn."

His gaze followed hers. As they watched, Starla's husband boarded an airport shuttle bus.

Kane glanced at her with alarm. "That's odd. Why was he acting like a thief in the night? I wonder if the police know he was here. If they questioned him."

"Or if he was here looking for us."

They moved back through the hotel and up to the tram level, melding in with the crowd. Kane glanced at her, his brows furrowing. "Do you think he's part of Skip's conspiracy?"

"I'm only sure he wasn't one of the men in the ski masks."

"Yeah, but that doesn't mean he isn't involved up to his understated necktie. He'd do anything for Starla."

Anything? Carlie wondered, not liking all the implications that popped into her mind. "Do you think he killed Angie thinking she was me?"

"Why would he expect to find you in Vegas?"

"Maybe Skip forced Hugh and Phyllis to tell."

"I suppose that's possible, but Angie's death seems at odds with Skip's desire to make everything look like an accident."

They boarded the tram—a sleeker, newer version of the monorail in Seattle—taking a back seat and keeping their voices low.

"You're right," Carlie said. "Shooting a bride on her

wedding day screams drama. It smacks of a crime of passion, not the premeditated way Skip has been trying to kill us.''

Kane nodded, stretching his arm along the seat behind her as the tram began to move. ''I mean, why wouldn't Skip just get rid of Angie quietly, hide the body somewhere it would never be found, then claim the phony Carleen duped him, and that she ran off to places unknown to avoid arrest? But this—this is going to cause a scandal, and an automatic exposure of Skip's culpability.''

Carlie considered, agreeing with him, but another idea also occurred to her. What if Angie's death benefited someone else? ''Maybe Starla and Vaughn wanted Skip to get caught, to be arrested for Angie's murder. That would eliminate him as the CEO of *EL.* And give Starla control of the company.''

Kane frowned. ''So, Vaughn might have killed Angie knowing she was the imposter.''

''Well, he sure isn't in Vegas to attend a wedding.''

''Which means he knows there won't be one.''

The tram stopped at the Mandalay Bay Hotel, and minutes later they found themselves in another casino, just as crowded and noisy as the last one. They crossed its expanse and emerged in an area of elevators and specialty shops, and finally found a house phone.

Kane called the registration desk, inquired about the Ellison family and learned they were not there, had not been there.

''Apparently everyone except Aunt Lola and Angie knew there wouldn't be a wedding.'' Carlie shook her head. ''Strange and stranger.''

''We need to call Hugh. See if he knows anything about all this.'' A police officer strode past. Kane's face tightened. "But not from a pay phone. If his line is tapped, the call could be traced."

They rode an escalator to the Beach Level, stole outside, wandered along the deserted walkway and plunked down at an outdoor table. Mexican music from a nearby restaurant drifted on the night air. Kane produced the cell phone. "The battery is low. You'll have to make it quick."

Her gut was already roiling without the added stress of a time constriction. She dialed Hugh's home number. He answered right away. "Carlie, is that really you?"

"Of course. Kane and I are in Vegas."

"Oh, thank God."

"Why, what's going on?" The acid in her stomach burned. "Is it Jamie?"

"No. Jamie is fine. Honestly. I've seen him. I just left the Ellison mansion. He's fine."

"Oh, thank you, Hugh," she said on a sob. Holding her hand over the receiver, she quickly relayed the good news to Kane, then asked Hugh, "What were you doing at the mansion? Did Skip try and get you to tell him where we are?"

"No."

"Good. Because we have awful news."

"About the other Carleen?"

"Then you know?"

"Yes. The family was informed an hour or so ago."

"Did you also know she was my cousin Angie Banks?"

"The family claims she was you. Until I heard your voice, I feared they were right."

Carlie swore. The phone crackled, the signal breaking up. The charge was getting weak. Rushing, she told him about their meeting with her aunt and their discovery that her cousin was the one impersonating her. "We were with Aunt Lola when we found out about Angie's murder. She went hysterical and is telling anyone who will listen that we killed Angie. She has the police looking for us now. But Kane and I had no idea she was the one impersonating me or where she was until after we met with Aunt Lola. We've got to get back to the airport and out of Vegas as soon as possible."

"You—be—cautious." Hugh's voice broke up again.

"Of course." Carlie shook the phone and the reception cleared. "Is that why you went to the mansion—because of Angie being murdered?"

"No."

Why was he being so evasive? She'd told him the phone was losing power. Could she not even trust Hugh? Maybe Skip was with him now. Threatening him. But why—if the Ellison family had only been told an hour or so ago about Angie—weren't any of them in Vegas to attend the wedding? Something was very wrong. "What's going on, Hugh?"

"Angie isn't the only one who was murdered today."

"What?" She reeled back. "Who else?"

"Skip."

Carlie almost dropped the phone. "When? How?"

Hugh paused. "He was found in his office this afternoon, dead from a broken neck."

"Oh, my God." She blinked, incredulous. "Who's doing this?"

"The police suspect you and Kane." The reception faded and cleared again. "You should know that they found something of Kane's next to the body."

"What?"

"They wouldn't tell me."

"Well, that's just impossible."

"Is it?"

"Oh—no. I'm sure the killer could have gotten something out of his suitcase from the SUV."

"What?" Kane asked, his eyes wide. "What the hell is going on?"

Again Carlie used precious air time telling Kane what had happened.

Hugh called her name, and she pressed the phone to her ear again. "The police are looking for you both now. So, I repeat, my dear, that you must be very careful. Come straight here when you arrive. I'll go with you to turn yourselves in." His voice began to break up worse than ever. "Skip—" *crackle* "—no longer—" *crackle* "—obsta—" *crackle* "—DNA—" *crackle* "—Jamie—" *crackle* "—best—" *crackle* "—prove—" *crackle* "—innocence—" *crackle* "—police—" *crackle* "—whole story and let them—" *crackle* "—look—" *crackle* "—Skip's cohorts—"

"Hugh?" Carlie called. But the phone had gone dead. She closed it and stared at Kane. "I don't understand this. Someone is trying to frame you and me for these murders. But why? What's left to gain?"

"I don't know. But the answers have to be in Port Luster. That's where this mess starts and ends." He wrenched to his feet and held out his hand to her. "We've got a plane to catch, love."

She took his hand and stood, then offered him the phone. "Battery's spent. Might as well toss it out."

"No way." He stuck it into his pocket. "Someone should be able to tell whose phone it is by the number programmed to make it ring."

"I guess we'll need it then, because the police are already building a case against us." She told him about

Hugh insisting they go straight to his house and then to the police when they reached town.

"Bull." Kane tightened his hand around hers. His expression was fierce. "First thing we're going to do when we get back to Port Luster is pick up our son. He can stay with Hugh and Phyllis while we straighten out this legal mess, but I don't want him in that snake pit with that nest of vipers a minute longer than necessary."

THE AIRPORT WAS crawling with police, checking every flight for Kane Kincaid and Carleen Ellison. But the police had no photographs of the suspects and as Hugh and Phyllis Proctor, Kane and Carleen had no trouble boarding their flight.

As the plane lifted off, Carlie tried to sleep the way Kane was doing. But her mind wouldn't relax. How could it be possible that Angie and Skip had both been murdered? That Kane and she were the prime suspects? Neither of them would commit murder.

Pain tweaked her temples, and roused the fear of what she couldn't recall of her lost week. In truth, she wasn't sure she *hadn't* murdered Coral Clayton.

But she knew one thing for certain. She was ready to face that possibility now, to deal with the consequences for her bad choices, to pay whatever penalty and move on.

She laid her head against the small airline pillow and closed her eyes. Oddly, her headache dissolved, and as though something had unlocked a floodgate in her brain, her memory began to return.

Chapter Fifteen

Awareness came to Carlie through a thick haze. She lay on a hard surface. Like a floor. She heard Jamie whimpering nearby. Heard a woman tell him to hush. Her eyes felt glued shut—the residue of whatever she'd been knocked out with. She wrested them open. Her stomach lurched.

Her cheek pressed hardwood planking. It seemed familiar. Precious seconds passed before she identified it. The living room floor in her own rental house. Jamie. Where was he? She tried to sit up. Couldn't move. The drug? No. Duct tape. It bound her arms to her sides, her ankles together, sealed her mouth.

Dear God, please don't let them hurt Jamie. But she feared they might. Feared this was a kidnapping. Feared Skip and Wil would not deliver whatever ransom asked for Jamie's safe return. Oh, God. She wrenched against her bonds to no avail. She couldn't see Jamie. Only heard him crying. She struggled harder. Hot tears burned her cheeks.

Voices. Concentrate on the voices. A man and a woman. No, two women. They moved through her line of vision. Coral and a redhead. She frowned. The redhead wore the ecru sweater and slacks Carlie had been wearing when the van pulled behind her Lexus. She also had Carlie's hairstyle.

Carlie blinked. Her head spun. She peered at the redhead again. She felt woozy, ethereal, as though she were outside her body gazing at herself. The other redhead laughed. Carlie's laugh. Cold climbed inside Carlie. The other redhead squatted down. Carlie jerked. Her heart slammed her rib cage. This woman was her twin.

What the hell was going on? Something more than a kidnapping. Something she couldn't fathom. Fear for her son tripled. She struggled harder against the tape. The redhead smiled, an evil lifting of the lips. Carlie's lips. Carlie shrank from her. The redhead poked a needle in Carlie's neck. Injected a stinging liquid. And almost instantly, the blackness reclaimed Carlie.

Angie. Carlie took a deep breath and shifted in the airplane seat. Angie had stolen her clothes, her perfume, her earrings, her diamond-and-emerald ring, her very identity. She'd spoken with a voice so like her own, Carlie had imagined herself speaking without being able to move her taped lips.

But now—now it was all so clear, no longer confusing. Angie. My God, the likeness had been staggering. Convincing.

But Angie was dead, and no matter what the Ellison family claimed, the autopsy would prove she wasn't the real Carleen. She wasn't a natural redhead. Her eyes were not green, but hazel. She would be wearing colored contact lenses. And she would have the telltale signs of recent plastic surgery.

The coroner would find and expose these things. Carlie no longer had to prove her identity. But somehow, regaining that identity didn't give back the peace of mind and well-being she'd expected.

Was Angie wearing the diamond-and-emerald ring when she was shot? It didn't matter. Carlie didn't want it back. She'd learned a tough lesson from the Banks family: money and all of its trappings couldn't bring a person real happiness. Let them bury the ring with her cousin. Or give it to Aunt Lola.

Carlie leaned her head harder against the airplane pillow and tried to see the man's face who'd been with Angie and Coral. It still eluded her. Maybe she'd never gotten a good look at him. Damn. He was still out there. Still a threat. And given that both Angie and Skip had been killed, he was lethal.

Lethal, lethal, lethal. The word echoed through her mind.

She squirmed in her seat. The memory she'd recalled in Elmer Digby's cabin came again.

Coral Clayton's face, the black hair and dark eyes, hovered inches from Carlie. Carlie struggled awake from the heavy dose of drugs Angie had injected into her. Jamie. She could no longer hear him. Panic started up in her. Where was he? Something shiny and silver caught her gaze. A gun.

"Get up," Coral growled. *"I'm all done baby-sitting your whiny butt. You've got a date with a man in black— and I'm not talking about Tommy Lee Jones or Will Smith."* Her wide lips split with a vicious grin. *"But the Grim Reaper."*

"Where's Jamie?" Carlie asked.

"Shut up," Coral barked. She grabbed Carlie by the arm. Yanked her from the bed. The room spun, but Carlie could see it clearly enough. A cabin of some sort. Log walls. Seashells on the windowsills. Like Jamie's shells. Where was her little guy? Who was listening to his sea-*

shells with him? Who would know the comfort the shells gave him? ''Jamie.''

''Shut up!'' Coral raised her arm and slammed the butt of the gun into Carlie's face. Pain shot through Carlie's cheekbone and eye. Coral shoved her. *''March. We're going for a little ride.''*

Light-headed, Carlie started past Coral. But Jamie needed her. She wouldn't go willingly to her death. Wouldn't leave him to God knew what fate. She grabbed for the gun.

Coral yelped. Startled. They struggled. Coral was in better shape and hadn't the disadvantage of being weak from drugs. But Carlie had the advantage of being a protective mother. Adrenaline pumped through her limbs, giving her unexpected strength.

The gunshot exploded in the small cabin. Carlie's ears rang. Cordite bit her nostrils. She felt something wet and warm on her hands. Her shirt front. Smelled the coppery tang of fresh blood. Dear God, she was going to die. Oddly, there was no pain. Only an eerie numbness.

The surprised look on Coral's face didn't register for a few seconds…until Coral began to fall away from her, and Carlie saw the crimson splatter on her chest, the scorched hole on her blouse. Coral's finger still wrapped the trigger. But the gun clattered to the floor when she landed on her back.

Carlie kicked the vile weapon out of Coral's reach. Turned her over. The exit wound was huge. Blood spilled out at a rapid rate. Carlie grabbed a pillow and pressed it to the wound. Nothing stemmed the flow of blood. She needed an ambulance. A quick search produced no phone. No cell phone.

She had to go get help. Carlie ran out to the car. Keys were in the ignition. On the dashboard, she spotted a

*VISA card and an airline ticket to San Diego. Apparently
Coral had her escape planned.*

*Carlie tore down a dirt lane. It ended at a paved high-
way. She turned right. A mile down the road, she found
a small grocery store, squealed to a stop by the pay
phone and called 9-1-1. She gave the best directions she
could to the cabin, then started back to wait for the ambulance and the police.*

*But halfway there, she felt a wave of paranoia. What
if the police didn't show up? What if her clone and the
unknown man arrived first? Coral Clayton had meant to
kill her. Someone had put her up to that. Someone who
now had her son. Skip. She couldn't do this alone. But
who…? Her gaze fell to the airline ticket. "Her" airline
ticket. The one she'd bought so she and Jamie could go
to Kane.*

*Kane. She made a U-turn, and somehow—God knew
how, given that the drugs in her system had her feeling
drunk and disoriented—she got to an airport and used
that ticket. Her obsession to reach Kane had saved her
life.*

And while she'd fled, Coral Clayton had died. Dear
God, she had killed someone. Not on purpose, but that
didn't matter. Coral Clayton was still dead. From a gunshot, just like Angie. Carlie shivered. Minutes ago, she'd
thought she was ready to face and deal with the consequences of her lost week. But that was before she knew
she'd taken another's life.

Tears burned her eyes. Her own life would never be
the same. She would lose Jamie, if not permanently, at
least for the years in prison she would surely be given
by a judge and jury.

But she would lose Kane forever. The realization
ripped through her like a newly sharpened saw blade.

How could she have thought the passion she'd always felt for Jamie's father wasn't worth pursuing? Worth embracing? All of her wrong choices had led her back to Kane—and now she'd have to let him go.

She glanced at his sleeping face, the tender curve of his mouth, the golden whiskers on his chin, and her heart swelled with such love that the tears in her eyes spilled down her cheeks. Telling Kane she'd killed Coral Clayton would be the hardest thing she'd ever done in her life. But how could she tell him now? Burden him with yet another worry? Her throat closed.

She would tell Kane when Jamie was safe at Phyllis and Hugh's, tell him and Hugh at the same time, and would see what the future held from there. But she feared she already knew the outcome.

She shoved away the thought. Couldn't deal with it now. She lifted the cap and scrubbed her weary face with her hands. Had Oregon's statewide search been extended to Washington yet? Would she be arrested at the airport? Before she and Kane could reach Jamie? No.

Think about something else.

What about the man she couldn't remember? Was he on this plane with them even now? Or had he taken a plane to Port Luster before them? She rubbed both temples, but could dredge no memory of the man.

AT TWO A.M., Kane and Carlie drove onto the Ellison estate. Rain misted the windshield and wind battered the Cherokee. A few dim lights shone inside, as though not everyone had retired.

Kane said, "Looks like we're going to have to be careful."

Careful? Every instinct and impulse coursing Carlie's body urged her to charge up the front steps, hurry inside and grab her son. But that path promised disaster. No one in this house was going to hand Jamie over to her. They thought her an imposter. They'd call the police. She wasn't ready to face the police. Not yet. Not until she and Kane turned themselves in, with Hugh.

With an effort, she corralled her need for haste and forced her thoughts to the possibilities at hand. "I didn't keep a key. Did you?"

"Nope."

"Then what's the plan, Stan?" She blew out a frustrated breath, hating the rain in her eyes, hating being this close to her son, yet locked away from him. Jamie was so near, she could sense him. She rubbed her chin, as though the airwaves would carry the private signal to him. It gave her heart.

"We'll sneak in—" Kane urged her through the wet lawn to the far corner of the mansion "—find Jamie and sneak out."

"But the alarm system…" she protested, fearing his so-called plan would die before it even started. She moved as swiftly as the slick grass allowed. "How do we manage that?"

"I think I've got that covered."

She had no idea what that meant, but prayed he knew what he was doing. They crept through the bushes and shrubs; branches and leaves slapped their bodies, flinging drops of water. Her shoes and clothes absorbed the wet and rain like thirsty sponges, and a bone-deep chill sank into her flesh.

The house and the night seemed intent on making this as difficult as possible. The sensation hardened Carlie's resolve. She'd taken all the misery she was going to from this house and its occupants. The night be damned. She'd had enough.

Kane pointed to one of the windows in his uncle Wil's study. "The night of our senior prom, Skip and I got drunk and rowdy and didn't come home until hours after Frances's curfew. She locked us out. Bolted the doors. Changed the alarm code. So, we jimmied this window. We managed to break the lock and set off the alarm. It created such a clamor, it could have roused the cemetery denizens. Wil thought it was funny as hell. In defiance of Frances, he never fixed it. Actually had the alarm in this window bypassed."

"Wasn't that dangerous, leaving the mansion vulnerable like that?"

"Wil Ellison liked a little danger in his life. You must have discovered that, living in this house with him." Kane stepped close to the brick wall and placed both hands on the window frame. "I still can't believe a heart attack felled a man in his great physical condition."

"If Frances knew about this window..." Carlie said, terrified they'd be caught before they reached Jamie. "She might have had the lock replaced since Wil's death."

Kane pushed upward. The window slid silently open. No alarms went off. He nodded with satisfaction, but his movements were urgent. "Quick."

She had no time to enjoy the momentary relief. He boosted her through the window. She landed on Wil's hardwood floor with a squeal of her rubber-soled shoes. Kane scrambled in after her. The office was in total darkness, but much warmer than outdoors. The roar of her pulse slammed her ears, and the scent of their wet clothes filled her nostrils, along with a softer, sweeter scent. What was it?

Kane switched on the flashlight he'd brought. He gave her hand a reassuring squeeze, then motioned toward the door. She had taken one step when she realized she was smelling Frances's perfume.

Carlie frowned. Reached to warn Kane. Too late. The desk light flared. Kane jerked in alarm. He lunged ahead of Carlie, blocking her body and her view.

"I knew you'd come here." Ice hung on Frances's words. "The criminal always returns to the scene of the crime."

"What crime would that be, Auntie dearest?" Kane took a step toward the desk.

"Stay where you are. The police are looking for you. I'll just call them now."

Carlie moved from behind him. Frances sat at Wil's desk, a regal vision in black, her white hair like a crown. One hand rested on the phone. In the other, she held a tiny gun, so small it might have been a toy. That she knew about the window and the bypassed alarm was obvious.

They should have realized she'd known they'd come for Jamie. Should have known she'd be expecting them.

Spotting Carlie, Frances gasped and dropped the lifted receiver. In the dim light, her lined face was the color of ash. "How—?"

Carlie frowned. She'd swear that Frances had not been expecting *her*. Why? Didn't Skip's mother know anything about his abhorrent plot to replace Carlie? Hadn't Frances been in on it? Carlie started forward. "Where's my son?"

Frances shook herself. "Oh, my God, you're the imposter. Starla told me you were being escorted about by Kane. I had no idea you were so like my deceased daughter-in-law."

"Ex-daughter-in-law. And I'm Carleen Jamison Ellison, not an imposter."

"The hell you are!" Frances huffed indignantly and lifted the phone receiver again. "When my son wouldn't buy that story, you murdered him. I don't know what good you think breaking in here will do you. You're not taking my grandson from me. I lost him once, but that isn't going to happen again."

She laid the handset of the phone on the desk and began dialing, the gun leveled in their general direction as she focused on hitting the correct numbers.

Carlie lunged across the desk and hit the disconnect button. Frances reared back. The arm holding the gun flew up, the barrel pointed to the ceiling. Kane caught Frances's wrist. He peeled the gun from her grasp.

"No, no, no," she wailed.

"We didn't kill Skip." Carlie set the receiver back on the base of the phone. "He's been trying to kill us."

Frances rubbed her wrist and laughed disdainfully. "What's that—your trial defense?"

Carlie glared at the woman. Her patience with this subject was gone. "I'd hardly have been capable of breaking his neck."

"Perhaps not, but that brute is certainly capable of it." She pointed to Kane.

"You've lost the game, Frances." Kane glared at her. "We have proof that Angie Banks, Carlie's cousin, was hired by Skip to pose as your ex-daughter-in-law for the purpose of gaining sole custody of Jamie." He told her what they'd discovered about Angie and pointed out what the autopsy would prove.

"You're as big a liar as she is." Frances sniffed, reaching for the phone again. "No one is going to take my grandson from me. I'm going to raise him to be a proper gentleman, like his father. Starla will run *EL* until Skip's son is old enough to take it over."

"Skip wasn't Jamie's biological father." Carlie took the phone from her this time and moved it across the desk out of her reach. "Kane is."

Frances's eyes narrowed and red splotches appeared on both cheeks, giving her pinched face an eerie, mask-like visage. She hissed, "You're as mad as they come. Jamie has the same boot-shaped birthmark that his great grandfather, Wil's father, had. It's an Ellison trait."

Kane and Carleen exchanged a look of shock. Kane grinned and touched the spot behind his right ear where his own boot-shaped blemish nestled. "You mean *this* birthmark?"

He came close to the desk, into the solid light, and pulled his hair back to show his aunt.

Frances screamed. "No. It's not possible. I checked when you were a baby. You didn't have any birthmark. I'd have seen it."

Kane smoothed his hair back down. "My dad told me it wasn't much more than a red splotch until I was about five, and by then, even though we lived under your roof, you paid me no attention. Besides, I started wearing my hair over my ears."

"No!" She grasped the arms of Wil's high-backed leather chair and glared at Kane. "That birthmark doesn't prove you're Jamie's father. Skip could have passed on that birthmark to his son."

Kane shrugged. "I'll have a DNA test done to confirm whether I fathered Jamie, but since the birthmark comes from Wil's father, it does prove Wil was *my* father. Doesn't it, Auntie?"

"Absolutely not. My husband did not sleep with my sister. At the time you were conceived, I was pregnant with Skip and Starla. Wil wouldn't have risked every-thing for a cheap fling with…with anyone. Not with my sister.'' She sobbed. Her expression was bitter, and her denial had the ring of someone trying to convince herself, someone who had spent years trying to convince herself.

"Wilcox Ellison was my father. I'll be damned.'' Kane's voice was a mix of emotions: awe and disbelief…and belief. "You've done everything in your power to make sure I never found out, too, haven't you, Frances.''

But Frances wasn't listening. Her head was in her hands and she was weeping. Frances had been betrayed by two people she should have been able to trust: her husband and her sister. But instead of forgiving either of them, she'd taken years of vengeance out on their love-child, Kane.

"Let's go get our son,'' he said.

They left Frances sitting at the desk, and cracked the study door open. Kane peered out. A pale night-light shone in the hall, spilling over Kane and illuminating his face, his eyes. Something had changed in him, grown more positive, more confident, as though a missing piece of himself had been suddenly and unexpectedly returned to make him whole.

He gazed down at her. "All clear.''

He touched her cheek, a silent promise in his eyes that they were in this together. No matter what. Carlie felt her confidence in him burgeon. He'd been with her through it all. Hadn't deserted her or run out when things got too tough. He'd grown into a man she could trust, trust with her life, with her son's life.

They crept down the hall, passed the guest bath, then neared the kitchen. Their damp soles made an occasional squeal on the hardwood flooring. After the first such scare, Carlie set her feet down with deliberate caution. A light shone from under the kitchen door. Voices echoed within. Carlie and Kane froze. Listened. *Starla and Vaughn,* Kane mouthed to her. Carlie nodded.

She doubted Frances would recover from her shock fast enough to stop them, but someone else might. Urgently, she gestured for him to keep moving. They slipped past the kitchen, into the back stairwell and up to the second-floor landing.

"Jamie's room is the third on the right," Carlie whispered. As they approached, she noticed the door stood ajar, as inviting a sight as she'd ever seen. Caution fell away from Carlie. She'd waited too long for this moment. She charged into her son's room, Kane one step behind her.

Someone stood over the sleeping boy. A man. He was pouring something from a bottle into a cloth, like the cloth she'd had held over her nose the day her son was taken from her. She cried, "He's trying to drug Jamie."

The man started, jerking back and glaring at the interruption.

She plowed into him, knocking him sideways. He dropped the bottle and stumbled back from the boy's bed. Carlie sobbed, sinking to the bed beside her son, holding back the urge to scoop him into her arms. He'd had too many frights. She wanted him to see who was holding him, to fully realize he was finally safe.

Gingerly, she touched his precious face, gazing lovingly at the spray of freckles across his button nose, smoothing his cowlick, caressing the boot-shaped birthmark behind his ear that was identical to the one behind his father's ear. "Jamie, Jamie, it's Mommy."

Jamie opened his sleepy green eyes and glanced up at her. His eyes widened, and his thumb and forefinger went automatically to his chin. She smiled at him and rubbed her own chin.

"Mommy." A startled, joyful expression captured his freckled face. "Mommy." Jamie jumped from beneath the covers, scrambled into her lap and snuggled against her chest. "I knowed you'd come home, Mommy."

"Always for you, baby." Hot tears flowed unchecked down her cheeks.

Jamie reached up and clutched the soft skin at her chin, gently rubbing as though the contact brought him untold comfort. The hole in Carlie's heart shrank with every stroke of his tiny finger and thumb.

"If you'd hurt him—" Kane grabbed the other man by his shirt front and rammed him against the wall. "I thought you didn't practice medicine, Dr. Newton."

"I don't...anymore." Wade's gray-green eyes were huge beneath his brushy brown eyebrows. Beads of sweat popped out on his shaved head.

"What'd you do, lose your license because you killed off your patients?"

"No." But Wade blanched and guilt flashed across his face.

"I swear I wasn't hurting the kid."

Kane's voice grew more menacing. "What's on that cloth?"

"Nothing. I was using it to apply some salve to the boy's chin. He's been rubbing it raw. I decided it would be easier to apply while he slept. The poor kid has had enough distress today."

"You can tell it to the police," Kane growled.

"Oh, the police will be hearing a story, but not the one you think." Vaughn flicked on the bedroom light; he'd appeared silently, as though he could move without making sound. He held a gun aimed at Carlie and Kane.

Unlike the toy-pistol Frances had threatened them with, this one was huge, gleaming and deadly-looking.

"Mother has phoned the police." Starla strode into the room behind her husband. "Don't worry, Wade. It will be Kane and this imposter who will be arrested tonight. Not you."

Carlie hugged Jamie close, keeping his eyes from the gun and covering his ears. But her heart felt heavy with fear. If the police came now, the boy might be forced to stay with the Ellisons, and that, she realized with a mother's instincts, could cost him his life.

For the only thing that made sense of Skip's death was that *EL* was the coveted prize in this horror. And at the moment, as Frances said, according to Wil's will, now that Skip was dead, controlling interest in *EL* belonged to Jamie.

But Starla and Vaughn obviously had other ideas about who should control the multimillion-dollar company.

Carlie focused on Vaughn. Would he use that gun on a child? Pretend to shoot Jamie accidentally while trying to stop her, an imposter, from kidnapping him? She had to warn Kane.

She shifted on the bed and folded her body over her son's, shielding him.

"Leave the boy in the bed." Vaughn waved the gun. "The rest of us are going downstairs."

"No." Carlie shook her head vehemently. "I'm not letting him out of my sight again."

Heavy footsteps rapidly approached the room. Hugh Proctor stopped in the doorway, his sharp gaze taking in the situation. "God, this is just what I hoped to avoid."

Carlie gazed over her son's head at the man who might have been her surrogate father. What was *he* doing here?

A *zing* of pain hit her temples, and from out of nowhere came a vision she'd thought she hadn't seen: the face of the man who'd helped abduct her.

Chapter Sixteen

Kane eyed the silver pistol in Vaughn's hand, mentally judged the distance between himself and the other man, and abandoned the idea of tackling him. He was too far away, with Carlie and Jamie in between. He wouldn't risk their lives. His hand dipped into his jacket pocket, curling around the tiny gun he'd taken from Frances. He'd use it only as a last resort.

"Hugh," he said, anxious to defuse this precarious situation, more anxious still to remove his son from imminent danger. "I don't want my—Jamie to spend another minute in this house. Carlie and I had nothing to do with Skip's death, but it's my bet one of these people did. Most likely Vaughn."

"What?" Vaughn's innocuous expression turned to one of horror, as though doing anything to cause Starla pain was repulsive. But he kept the gun leveled at Kane's chest. "That's absurd. He was my wife's brother."

"Then what were you doing in Vegas?" Kane palmed the small gun. "Did you kill Angie Banks?"

"Who's Angie Banks?" Vaughn frowned.

"Vaughn went to Vegas," Starla interjected, "to tell Carleen about Skip."

''Yeah.'' Vaughn waved the gun again. ''But you'd already found and killed her.''

''Put that revolver away, Mr. Harding, before it accidentally goes off,'' Hugh growled, and moved toward Vaughn. ''There's a child present. You're about to have one of your own. I pray you're a better father than you are an uncle. Give me that thing.''

''No, Kane,'' Carlie shouted, her eyes wide with terror. ''Don't let him.''

Everyone spun toward Carlie. Everyone...except the man who'd helped kidnap her. Kane felt another's hand on his, someone trying to grab the pistol from him, someone using Carlie's distraction to make his final move. Wade Newton.

Chapter Seventeen

Carlie shouted, "Wade was in on my abduction."

Wade might have been a magician using smoke and mirrors. His hand moved quicker than the eye. His reflexes surpassed Kane's. He came up with the gun. Leaped away from Kane and landed beside Carlie and Jamie. She wrapped her arms protectively about the boy, keeping his face buried against her thundering heart, his eyes from the barrel of the tiny pistol pressed hard and gelid against her temple.

"You and the kid are coming with me," Wade growled, all trace of any attempt at culture gone from his voice.

"No way." Kane, like a wall of fury, stepped toward Wade, shaking his head, his hands curling and uncurling at his side.

"Don't, Kane, please," Carlie pleaded, terror icy in her belly, fiery along her nerves.

"Step away from them." Vaughn lifted his larger gun, but it shook in his hand, whatever bravado he'd shown earlier gone. "Or—or I'll shoot."

"Don't be a damn fool, Vaughn," Hugh grunted. "You could hit Jamie or Carlie. Put that gun down."

"If you don't shoot her, I will." Wade thumbed back the hammer on the small gun.

The *click* echoed in Carlie's ear. A sickening heat licked through her. "Please, Vaughn, do as Wade asks."

Vaughn lowered the gun.

Wade tsked. "Not good enough, pal. Put it on the floor and kick it to me."

Hesitantly, Vaughn complied.

Keeping the tiny gun jammed against Carlie's temple, Wade leaned down, lifted the larger gun and stuffed it in the waistband of his pants. "Now, all four of you get against the closet.

Hugh, Vaughn and Starla quickly obeyed. Kane had venom in his blue eyes. That he wanted to take Wade down was written all over his face.

Wade snarled, "Get over there, cowboy. You don't want to do anything to jeopardize their lives, do you?"

Carlie could see Kane's mind churning. All he needed was an opening. She prayed he wouldn't find one. He could be shot. Killed. Or Wade might take Kane's defiance out on Jamie. Fear dampened her hands, her underarms. Dried her mouth. "Why are you doing this, Wade?"

It made no sense to Carlie—this man had no motive she could fathom. He didn't enlighten her.

"Take me, instead," Kane pleaded. "I'll be less of a liability than a woman and a child. More of a shield, if you need one."

Shock spiked through Carlie. No. She didn't want to exchange her life for Kane's. But Jamie... He needed to be safe. And Kane was willing to give his life for their son, for her. What greater show of love could a woman ask?

"Listen to him," Hugh advised. "All hostages are not equal. Carlie and Jamie will slow you down."

Wade considered, then nodded. He exchanged the small gun for the large one. Gestured Carlie and Jamie to join the others, insisted Kane take her place on the bed. Then he reached down beside the nightstand to where the bottle he'd dropped had fallen. He brought up a roll of duct tape.

The sight of it galvanized Carlie. *He'd meant to use it on Jamie,* she realized, understanding how close she and Kane had come to losing their son. Hatred raked through her. She wanted to rip the gun from his hand and pistol-whip him. "Why are you doing this?" she asked again.

Again Wade ignored her. He tossed the roll of tape to Hugh. "Sit down, every one of you. Not you, old man— you bind their hands behind them, then wrap their feet together. And make it quick."

What was taking the police so long? Carlie wondered. Hadn't Frances called them? Where was she? Still feeling sorry for herself in the den?

The sound of ripping tape filled the room, and Jamie began to cry. Carlie held him tighter. She knew he was recalling the last time she'd been bound with this tape. She rubbed his back, keeping her voice low and soothing.

Hugh moved fast. He bound her hands in front of her, so she could hold Jamie. But Jamie cried. "No, Wichie bad. Bad man."

Wichie? Jamie couldn't pronounce certain letters yet. Wichie likely meant...Richie? Carlie lifted her gaze to Wade, astonishment sinking through her as she studied his face as she hadn't done in all the time she'd known him as Dr. Wade Newton. There, above his left eye, slicing through one dense eyebrow, was the white line of an old scar. Shock riveted her. He'd gotten that at her house, when they were kids.

"Richie Banks."

His mouth curled in a vicious grin. "Hello, cuz."

"Cuz? You're Carlie's cousin? Lola Banks's dead son?" Kane shook his head. "Do you know your mother thinks you were killed in the army? In the Middle East?"

"Yeah, well, she was gonna have a real surprise when she got here." Wade's words were bitter. He waved the pistol at Kane. "Tie up the old man, now."

Kane bound Hugh's hands and feet as loosely as possible. He bent down and kissed the top of Carlie's head, then ruffled Jamie's hair. The boy glanced up at him, and again he felt that unspoken connection between them. He rubbed the skin beneath his chin. Jamie sniffed and a half smile touched his scared face and lifted Kane's spirits.

"Come on, cowboy. Don't try anything funny." Wade jerked Kane by the arm. "We're going down to my car and getting out of here."

Kane let himself be led into the outer hallway, grateful that no one in that bedroom was now in danger from the madman behind him. "I know why you did this."

"Put a sock in it."

Kane walked with deliberate care. He didn't want Wade deciding to shoot him here in the house. Didn't want Carlie or Jamie hearing shots and being frightened more than they were already, didn't want Jamie more traumatized. But he couldn't seem to stop talking. "I figure you and your sister devised this plan to pay Carlie back for the hell her father put your family through. I guess you figured she owed you all big-time."

"Damn straight." Wade was opening each door they came to in the long hallway. "Where's the old woman?"

"I don't know," Kane answered, stopping while Wade

scanned a room. "Where'd you get your medical degree? In the army?"

"Nope. Never got one. I took my pre-meds in the army, then I got a medical discharge—lower back injury." They moved to the next room, and Wade repeated his search. "Couldn't afford civilian medical school."

"I suppose that was Carlie's fault, too?" Kane resisted the urge to try to overpower Wade. Wade wasn't as tall or as strong, but Kane had seen how light he was on his feet, how swift. And Kane doubted he'd hesitate to use that gun, which looked as though a bullet from it would make a torpedo-size hole through a man.

"Shut up and keep walking."

"Sure, that was Carlie's fault, too. That's what got you started hatching this plan, isn't it? I'll bet you faked your credentials, wrangled an introduction to Skip and convinced him to hire you as a consultant for *EL*. And you used the opportunity to get the lay of the land, to get close to Carlie without her realizing who you really were. That's when you started plotting how to get hold of the Ellison fortune."

"Where is that old woman?" He slammed the next door.

Kane saw the staircase ahead, felt time running out. "When Skip confided how unhappy he was at home, you must have grabbed the opportunity and set him up. Probably on a trip to Vegas, you pointed Angie out to Skip, mentioned how similar she and Carlie were, mentioned how nice it might be if he could just 'replace' the unsatisfactory Carlie with a more compliant model."

They were at the master bedroom suite. The door was ajar. A bedside lamp glowed from within. Wade kicked the door fully open. He peered inside and called, "Frances?" She didn't answer.

He shoved Kane toward the end of the hall.

Kane said, "Then you let the seeds of the plot expand in Skip's mind. Eventually, he approached Angie, and, of course, found her more than willing to play along. He paid for the plastic surgery, divorced Carlie on the quiet. Then, when all of Angie's scars were healed, had Carlie kidnapped."

"You think you know it all, don't you, cowboy." Wade sounded impressed, but there was something else in his voice. The need to brag, to best Kane. "Well, there's a couple of things you don't know."

"Like?"

"Like Skip finding out he was sterile and his figuring out you fathered his kid. Like how I made sure Skip would be as rich as Angie and I deserved. Can you figure that one out, smart guy?"

On the landing, a four-foot porcelain vase his uncle had brought home from a trip to China caught Kane's eye. He stared at it as though it were trying to speak to him, to tell him something. And then he knew. He jerked around. "You killed Wil."

Wade chuckled and tipped his head once in acknowledgment. "I lied to you the other night. I did get myself a falsified medical degree and I have been *EL*'s plant doctor for the past two years. I was actually pretty good."

"Wil trusted you?"

"Why not? My degree looks real. Not that he ever needed anything more than preventive treatment. Like weekly vitamin shots. Only last time, I injected Wil with digitalis. I had enough medical training to know it would cause him a fatal heart attack."

Kane shuddered at how little life meant to this man. How little *his* life would mean. He ought to keep mum, quit needling Wade, but it was his only weapon at the moment, the only way to hurt him. "Looks like you and Skip both underestimated Carlie. What happened? Did Skip want out?"

Wade gestured for Kane to get moving. "He had his son, he said. He didn't need another wife. He wanted the faux Carleen to disappear the way the real one was supposed to have."

"Skip didn't know Angie was your sister?"

"No. The bastard wasn't getting rid of the Banks siblings. He was our ticket to Easy Street. Snapping his neck felt so good. Only, after I calmed down, I wasn't sure how we were going to collect that ticket. But then I figured, hell, Angie could be a rich widow as easily as a rich wife. Easier. As easy as faking the wedding license."

They'd reached the stairs.

"Then why—" Kane glanced back again, twisting his body and placing one foot on the first riser "—did you kill your sister if she was your passport to riches?"

Frances Ellison emerged from the open doorway of the master bedroom. She charged Wade from behind, swift and lithe for her age. Before Kane could warn him, she barreled into him. Wade pitched forward.

The huge gun flew from his hand and the small one from his waistband. He careened past Kane. Kane grabbed for his tumbling body. Missed. Wade banged and bumped, his shaved head and reedy limbs smacking stairs and newels, all the way to the bottom. The large gun clattered across the marble floor. Wade landed with a terrible *crack*. His body was twisted at an odd angle.

Frances screamed, "Oh, my God, is he dead?"

Kane scrambled down the stairs. Wade was still breathing. He opened his eyes. "I didn't kill Angie. I swear." His gaze lifted to where Frances stood in the middle of the open staircase, and horror shone in his eyes. "I'm not the one who brought the kid back from Vegas today. She is."

Kane jerked his gaze upward. Frances held the tiny pistol as she moved toward him. Such hatred emanated from her eyes that it chilled him. "I should have drowned you along with your mother when I had the chance. You've made my life a misery. But you're not going to continue to do so. You will *not* claim *my* grandson as my sister claimed my husband. No one is taking anything else from me."

She thumbed the hammer back and aimed at Kane's chest.

A figure appeared on the landing above, someone who'd approached with the silence of Vaughn Harding. *Carlie.* She hefted the porcelain vase, turned it on its side and lobbed it down the stairs in a direct path toward Frances. The clatter startled the older woman. She started to turn. But the vase cracked the back of her knees, knocking her flat like a bowling ball leveling a lone pin. Frances flopped forward. She landed facedown on the stairs, arms stretched above her head, as the vase steamrolled over her.

The pistol fired. Kane ducked. Too late. The bullet hit him. Warm liquid splashed his cheek. He began to fall.

Sirens sounded outside the door. The police had finally arrived.

The last thing he saw and heard was Carlie, running down the stairs, crying his name.

Chapter Eighteen

The next thing Kane was aware of was that his head ached like hell. Gingerly, he reached to the pain center near his right ear and encountered a large bandage. What had happened? Recall slammed into his brain. He'd been shot. In the head. Should be dead. Had thought he was dying, from the look on Carlie's face. From the blood. Then everything had gone black.

But if he'd died, he damn sure wouldn't hurt like this. He forced his eyes open. "Carlie?"

He was alone. In a hospital room. It was daylight. He swore. How long had he been out? He struggled up. Where was Carlie? Had Frances shot her, too? Dear God, no. But his aunt's vicious threat that no one would ever take Jamie from her replayed with nasty persistence in his mind. She'd killed his mother. Killed Carlie's cousin. Had meant to kill him. Carlie was the last obstacle in her bid for Jamie.

Fear clutched his heart. He ripped out the intravenous line, sat up, swung his legs over the side of the bed and stood. The room swam. The gown he wore gaped. Cold brushed his exposed back. He didn't care.

He rushed to the door. Unsteady on his feet. Determined to find Carlie. Ignoring the weakness in his limbs.

He shoved his door open, and stopped as a startled cop standing just outside jerked around to stare at him. What was going on? Surely *he* wasn't under arrest?

Kane growled, "Where's Carlie Ellison?"

IN THE WAITING ROOM, Carlie paced. It seemed impossible that the horror in the mansion had occurred mere hours ago. The doctor said Kane would be okay. The bullet had grazed his temple and torn off a chunk of skin at the top of his ear. He'd heal with minimal scarring. Carlie didn't care about physical perfection; Kane would always be gorgeous to her. It was his physical and mental well-being that mattered. She'd felt such relief that she'd collapsed in Hugh's arms.

He'd invited Jamie and her home with him. Phyllis had fed them, put them to bed. But the need to come back here and wait for Kane to recover tore through Carlie's restless dreams.

Jamie stirred on the couch where he slept.

She'd intended to leave him with Phyllis, but couldn't stand to be separated from him for even a few minutes, let alone several hours. She supposed the separation anxiety would pass for both of them...eventually.

But for now, togetherness was as essential as breathing.

They'd arrived before noon. Kane had still been unconscious. The doctor insisted they stay in this area until he awoke. That was two hours ago.

"Carlie?"

The voice came from behind her. Kane's voice. She lurched around. Tears filled her eyes. His sun-bleached hair stood on end; two days' worth of ash-blond whiskers decorated his strong jaw; a ludicrously large bandage tented his right ear; and a loose, blue-and-white check-

ered gown barely covered his glorious body. He was
holding the short fabric together at his backside, likely
giving every passerby quite a view. Her heart skidded
sideways.

"Should you be out of bed?"

"I couldn't find you."

Her gaze swept from the tanned length of his legs, up
the skimpy gown that barely hid his very male assets, to
his bright blue eyes so filled with concern for her. How
could this man be both sexy and vulnerable at once? "We
were waiting for you to wake up."

"We?"

She moved and pointed to Jamie. Kane's eyes softened
at the sight of his sleeping son, the look so tender that it
tore at her heart. They had so much lost time to make up
for. So little time left to do it in.

She'd told Hugh and the police about Coral Clayton
this morning, before coming here. It was only a matter
of time until she was arrested. She had to tell Kane. "We
need to talk."

A nurse interrupted. "Mr. Kincaid, you need your robe
and some slippers. You'll be catching pneumonia on top
of everything else."

He accepted the hospital-issue robe and slippers, and
thanked her.

"You can thank me by returning to your room and
letting me reattach that I.V. feed."

"Not yet."

"Make it soon." She spun on her heel and left, grumbling something about stubborn male patients.

He winked at Carlie, shot her a crooked smile so like
Jamie's, shrugged the robe on and tied the belt. It did
nothing to hide his wonderfully proportioned legs. He

sank onto the sofa across from Jamie and gestured for Carlie to join him. "Where's your cousin Richie?"

"Somewhere in this same hospital. The fall snapped his lower spine. He's crippled. Paraplegic. Absurdly, they have him under armed guard, as though he might walk out of here."

"Ran into a cop outside my room a few minutes ago, but he just wanted a statement. I take it Richie's being charged with Wil's and Skip's murders?" he asked.

"Yes. Hugh says a jury might look sympathetically on him, given his physical condition, but not on his crime. He'll be spared the death penalty, but won't get off easy for killing Skip and Wil Ellison or for the attempted murders of the three of us."

"What about the goons who tried running us off the cliff?"

"Just as you thought, the phone can be traced. Hugh swears those ski-masked monsters will be found and arrested."

He reached for her hands, but she pulled back. He had to know everything before making any decisions about the future. "I finally remembered what happened in the cabin with Coral Clayton." She checked to be sure Jamie still slept, then told him haltingly how Coral Clayton had died. She braced herself for his disappointment, his revulsion—the same revulsion she felt every time she envisioned Coral falling away from her, the gaping bullet wound in her back. She'd have to live with that forever.

But would she live without Kane that long?

"Dear God, the woman meant to kill you," he said, obviously aware of the guilt she felt. "Do you know how proud I am of you for fighting for your life? For fighting for our son? It was an accident. At the worst, self-defense."

"He's right, you know." Hugh walked into the waiting area. "People who plan to murder others should be prepared for the consequences of their actions. The Oregon police discovered that Coral Clayton was an alias for a hit woman on the FBI's most wanted list."

He pulled a chair close to them and sat, holding his rain-dotted hat in his hands. His trench coat was also damp. "The investigation has turned up a slew of fingerprints in that seaside cabin. Richie's and Angie's, Skip's, Coral's and yours. The Oregon police will need to talk to you, but you mustn't worry. It's only a formality. They aren't going to press charges. The evidence corroborates your account of what happened. Coral's death will be declared accidental."

Kane snatched Carlie's hand, not giving her a chance to pull away this time. His warmth chased the chill from her flesh and heated her veins, while relief danced through her brain. She wouldn't be separated from her son. Wouldn't be separated from Kane. They would have the time to work on their relationship, to tell each other all the things they'd never said, to figure out how much he wanted to be involved in Jamie's life. In hers.

Kane asked, "What about Frances? Did she kill Angie?"

"Yes. Airline tickets backed up Wade's accusations," replied Hugh. "And that little gun she shot you with proved to be the murder weapon. She's been arrested and charged with Angie's murder, and the attempted murders of Wade Newton—Richie Banks—and Kane."

Kane's head jerked up. "What about *my* mother's murder? She confessed to it."

Hugh shook his head. "I'm sorry, son. But she's denying that now. It's just your word against hers. I'm afraid it will stand as a suicide. The case is just too old. No longer any evidence.''

Kane tipped his head back against the wall and shut his eyes. He knew the hatred he felt for his aunt would fester in his heart if he didn't release it. His mother had been Frances's victim. If he continued to hate Frances, he, too, would be her victim. It was enough, he decided, that he knew the truth. Enough that the people in this room—the only people he cared about—knew.

''Sorry to cut out on you two, but I'm going home to take a nap.'' Hugh stood and stretched. ''I'm getting too old for all this excitement.''

As Hugh walked away, Jamie began to stir. He pried his green eyes open, sought his mother and rubbed his freckled chin. She signaled him in return, then the boy repeated the gesture to Kane. Kane stroked the underside of his own chin, and love filled the spot in his heart that had until minutes ago held hatred. It felt warm and sating and good.

Carlie said, ''Since you and Jamie are both here, would you like to do the DNA test today?''

''No.'' Kane didn't want anyone poking needles into this precious child, hurting him. Jamie had suffered enough these past few days: horror and terror and tragedy and loss. ''I don't need that test to know who his daddy is.''

That he trusted her brought a smile to her eyes. ''I'll tell him soon.''

''No.'' Kane brushed a strand of fiery hair from her pale cheek. ''He's lost the only daddy he's ever known. He needs to grieve without confusion. We have time enough to tell him when he can accept it. When he's accepted me. We'll know when that is.''

"Oh, Kane." She touched his whiskered cheek. "You look beat."

"I am."

She and Jamie walked him back to his room.

Starla was waiting for him. Smudges underscored her cool blue eyes, and she held the oversize man's hankie she'd had at her father's funeral. Kane demanded she sit before she dropped, and he climbed back into bed.

Starla pulled a chair to his side. Her gaze went to Carlie and Jamie. "I'm so sorry for all the pain I caused you. I believed Skip. I should never have listened to him. I won't blame you if you never forgive me."

"I don't have room in my heart at the moment for any ill will." Carlie smiled at her, lifted Jamie and stood to one side.

"Thank you," Starla told her. She turned her attention to Kane then. "I've just come from seeing Mother."

"I really don't care." He laid his aching head against the pillow, realizing he no longer felt anything about his mother's sister. She no longer had the power to wound him. "Nothing Frances could say or do interests me."

Starla wiped the hankie across her face. "I understand, but I thought you might want to know that I confronted her about the DNA test taken four years earlier to identify your father. At first she told me to go to hell, but I threatened that she'd never see my child if she continued to lie. She finally broke down and admitted she'd bribed an unscrupulous doctor, who substituted someone's else's blood for Father's part of the test. To her eternal fury, you are Wil Ellison's son."

"I know."

"But *I* didn't know." She glanced up at him, wringing the hankie into a knot, looking as though the same knot were in her throat. "Kane, I'm glad you're my brother.

I've always felt closer to you than to my own twin. I hope you won't hold the deeds of the other Ellisons against me. I'm appalled at the injustices you've been put through by our father, and the horrors inflicted on you by my mother."

Tears glistened in her eyes, but pride stiffened her spine. It was a pride Kane recognized in himself. She'd suffered her own injustices with Wil. But she'd always been the one with integrity. The one who played by the rules. Kane reached for her hand. She clutched at his as though grasping a lifeline. This was a family connection he'd never expected to have, and the realization that he actually had a half sister who wanted to be a part of his life tied a ribbon of joy around his heart.

Starla smiled at him. "According to Father's will, whichever of his children produces the first grandchild inherits the larger percent of *EL*. Hugh tells me that would be you. You are the new CEO."

Kane laughed out loud. Pain spiraled from around his wound, and he winced but still grinned. "Now that is just too funny. I have no intention of living in Port Luster. I don't know anything about running *EL*. That's your area. I'll tell you what, you can be the new CEO. I'll retain my share in the company for Jamie's sake and the sakes of any other future children, but it will be yours to run as you see fit. "

Starla's newfound happiness froze on her face at his mention of not staying in Port Luster. "Where are you going to live?"

"That depends on Carlie and Jamie."

Carlie frowned at this announcement, and he feared he might be assuming too much. His patience thinned while he waited for Starla to hug him and leave them alone. What if Carlie didn't share his dreams and hopes? His belly pinched. "Close the door, please. I don't want anyone interrupting us."

She did, then spun toward him holding their child, a sight so beautiful he wanted it permanently seared on his brain. Love burgeoned through him. His heart, like his gunshot wound, was healing.

Carlie started to take the chair Starla had vacated, but he patted a spot on the mattress beside him. She settled down with Jamie on her knee. The boy peered at Kane shyly.

She stroked the child's back as though she couldn't believe he was actually in her arms. "What do Jamie and I have to do with where you live?"

Kane touched her denim-clad knee. "Carlie, I don't know how you feel about me. But I love you. I've always loved you. I should have told you four years ago. I don't want to lose you again. I want you to be my wife."

Her eyes widened, and his heart dipped. She'd apparently not been expecting this. He couldn't tell if that was a good thing or bad. His pulse beat at his temples.

"Carlie Kincaid," she said, as though rolling the words around in her luscious mouth, tasting them, testing them. She smiled. "I like the sound of that. Yes, I do. Hmm. It just could be the 'me' I've been seeking my whole life."

Kane gave a whoop of bliss. Jamie startled, then giggled and whooped, too. The joy in the room was contagious.

"I love you, too. I love the way you make me feel. The abandon, the passion, the security." Carlie leaned toward Kane and kissed his lips.

But Jamie pushed against Kane's chest. "Hey, too squishy."

Kane chuckled and touched his son's button nose. He

gazed at Carlie, his expression serious. "I want more like this one. How about you?"

"Yes. As long as you're their daddy."

"A solid, loving family?"

"Oh, yes."

"I can't wait to get started. We'd better be married as soon as the doctor removes this confounded bandage."

Her answer was a huge smile. "Would that be before or after we pick up *Footloose?*"

"Before. How would you feel about a long honeymoon on our own boat?"

"I'd love it."

"Guess I'll have to consider renaming the boat. My footloose days are over."

"Are you already regretting it?"

"Never."

Jamie gazed from one to the other. "Is we gonna be marwied?"

Kane swallowed with an effort. "If it's okay with you, champ."

Jamie pressed his lips together and looked up toward the ceiling in a parody of an adult being thoughtful. "I guess it's okay. But if Mommy is gonna be Carlie Tincaid, can I be Jamie Elwson Tincaid?"

The knot of emotion in Kane's throat grew. "Would you like to be?"

Jamie considered again, his tongue licking out this time. "I guess. Mommy, is Kane gonna be my new daddy?"

"If that's okay with you."

"I miss my daddy." The shadows of pain lit the recesses of his eyes, but his tiny mouth lifted in a smile. "But I like Kane. A lot."

Kane felt his heart swell with happiness. He knew his

son had to grieve, but his heart would one day heal—with their love and guidance. Carlie squeezed his hand and kissed her son's cheek. "Kane can be your daddy always—from now on."

Jamie tilted his head to one side, studying Kane. Then he smiled shyly and rubbed his chin in their secret signal.

Kane realized he and his son shared childhoods with too much loss and too much pain. But his son was found and now, so was he. He touched his own chin, and smiled broadly at his little boy.

What can be stolen, forgotten, hidden,
replaced, imitated—but never lost?

HARLEQUIN®

I N T R I G U E®

brings you the strong, sexy men
and passionate women who are
about to uncover...

**SECRET
IDENTITY**

LITTLE BOY LOST
by Adrianne Lee
August 2000

SAFE BY HIS SIDE
by Debra Webb
September 2000

HER MYSTERIOUS STRANGER
by Debbi Rawlins
October 2000

ALIAS MOMMY
by Linda O. Johnston
November 2000

Available at your favorite retail outlet.

HARLEQUIN®
Makes any time special™

Your Romantic Books—find them at

www.eHarlequin.com

Visit the *Author's Alcove*

➤ Find the most complete information anywhere
  on your favorite author.

➤ Try your hand in the Writing Round Robin—
  contribute a chapter to an online book in the
  making.

Enter the *Reading Room*

➤ Experience an interactive novel—help determine
  the fate of a story being created now by one of
  your favorite authors.

➤ Join one of our reading groups and discuss your
  favorite book.

Drop into *Shop eHarlequin*

➤ Find the latest releases—read an excerpt or write
  a review for this month's Harlequin top sellers.

➤ Try out our amazing search feature—tell us your
  favorite theme, setting or time period and we'll find
  a book that's perfect for you.

All this and more available at

www.eHarlequin.com
on Women.com Networks

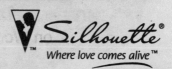

If you enjoyed what you just read,
then we've got an offer you can't resist!

Take 2 bestselling
love stories FREE!
Plus get a FREE surprise gift!

Clip this page and mail it to Harlequin Reader Service®

IN U.S.A.	IN CANADA
3010 Walden Ave.	P.O. Box 609
P.O. Box 1867	Fort Erie, Ontario
Buffalo, N.Y. 14240-1867	L2A 5X3

YES! Please send me 2 free Harlequin Intrigue® novels and my free surprise gift. Then send me 4 brand-new novels every month, which I will receive before they're available in stores. In the U.S.A., bill me at the bargain price of $3.57 plus 25¢ delivery per book and applicable sales tax, if any*. In Canada, bill me at the bargain price of $3.96 plus 25¢ delivery per book and applicable taxes**. That's the complete price and a savings of at least 10% off the cover prices— what a great deal! I understand that accepting the 2 free books and gift places me under no obligation ever to buy any books. I can always return a shipment and cancel at any time. Even if I never buy another book from Harlequin, the 2 free books and gift are mine to keep forever. So why not take us up on our invitation. You'll be glad you did!

181 HEN C22Y
381 HEN C22Z

Name	(PLEASE PRINT)	
Address	Apt.#	
City	State/Prov.	Zip/Postal Code

* Terms and prices subject to change without notice. Sales tax applicable in N.Y.
** Canadian residents will be charged applicable provincial taxes and GST.
  All orders subject to approval. Offer limited to one per household.
  ® are registered trademarks of Harlequin Enterprises Limited.

INT00

HARLEQUIN®

I N T R I G U E®

COMING NEXT MONTH

#581 THE BODYGUARD'S ASSIGNMENT by Amanda Stevens
Texas Confidential
Agent Brady Morgan's specialty was witness protection, and
Grace Drummond was his downfall. The crime she had witnessed
incriminated a dangerous criminal, placing her in serious danger. And the
secret Grace kept was one that Brady needed to uncover if he intended to
keep them safe and rebuild the love they'd once shared.

#582 AMANDA'S CHILD by Ruth Glick writing as Rebecca York
43 Light Street
When a sperm bank pregnancy endangered virgin Amanda Barnwell's
life, Matt Forester appointed himself as her guardian. Caught between
two powerful families, Amanda needed Matt's name to protect her unborn
child and provide her safety. Only by exposing the true source of the
threats could they begin a new life—together.

#583 SAFE BY HIS SIDE by Debra Webb
Secret Identity
"Kate Roberts" didn't remember who she was or how she'd found special-
agent-in-hiding Jack Raine—but now, a killer was after them both. And
though her returning memories hinted she might have been used to betray
Jack, she knew there was nowhere she'd be safer than by his side....

#584 UNDERCOVER PROTECTOR by Cassie Miles
Officer Annie Callahan returned home to simplify her life and instead
found herself faced with Michael Slade—a man she'd once loved deeply.
Now working undercover, Michael knew Annie was in danger from a
stalker and possibly more. Revealing his identity was not an option, so he
became her fiancé. Could Michael keep Annie safe—and perhaps get her
to fall in love with him all over again?

Visit us at www.eHarlequin.com

CNM0800